ESCAPING WALLSTREET

*There is only one way to escape
the presence of WallStreet*

A WallStreet Series Volume I

Brittan Nicholson

Escaping Wallstreet
There is only one way to escape the presence of WallStreet
A WallStreet Series Volume I

Copyright © 2018 by Brittan Nicholson

Edited by: Windy Goodloe, Nzadi Amistad Editing and Writing Services
Photographer: Jay Will of Photo Creations

Library of Congress Control Number: 2018914296

ISBN: 978-1-7322930-0-7

Published by: KRE-A-TIVE MINDZ
PO Box 888 Amityville, NY 11701

www.brittannicholson.com
www.kreativemindzpubllc@gmail.com

Printed in the United States of America

DEDICATION

To all the independent women who made it out of the hood without depending on a man, but by depending on their own independence and God's favor. Keep building your own brand and keep standing on your own two feet.

To all the smart men who used what you got to get ahead and possibly make it out the hood, this is for you also.

To the men and women who are still in the hood, making the best of what you do and making the best with what you have. Never regret any of the steps you've had to take. Just know this is for you also.

To the young generation, know that anything you put your mind to you can do. Just think outside the box and stop thinking about what's inside.

To all the men and women who are currently incarcerated, this is dedicated mostly to you. Just think about how many books you've read while incarcerated; this, too, can be you. You can be the author of your own true story, or you could even make up a story. You may have some time on your hands to spare and figure things out, but just know it doesn't take that long to write a book. All you need is about six weeks and 2500 words per day, so make every day in there count for something. Use this book as an inspiration to explore your mind. Be creative, and always know you can do anything you put your mind to, and don't ever let anyone tell you otherwise.

My prayers are with you, and may God bless you and keep you!

SPECIAL THANKS

To my children, I love you with all my heart. Don't ever
let anyone stop you from pursuing your dreams.
To my mom and grandma, I love you. Thank
you for always praying for me.
To my guardian angels, thank you for watch-
ing over me and for keeping me safe day by day.
To my editor, Windy Goodloe, I couldn't have done this without you.
To my mentors, I am so grateful. I humbly thank you.
Faith, strength, pain, suffering, wisdom, knowl-
edge, and understanding are all KEYS to success!
Thank you, everyone, for your support.

Lord Jesus, I thank you for giving me favor and for allowing me to do
something I never even thought about doing myself. I have encour-
aged others but never myself to be an author, and now look, I can't
seem to stop writing. Lord, I thank you and ask you to continue to
open my mind to new ideas each day and to continue pouring your
blessings upon me and my family.

CONTENTS

Introduction

Today, I woke up feeling like I was on top of the world. Nothing could stop me from feeling the gift of joy that was dancing around inside of me like it was my birthday. The best thing that has ever happened to me, other than him (yes, him, the one that changed my life), was leaving the hood and every bad thing that it stood for behind for good, especially the guns, the murders, and the drugs. Finally, I can say, my past is my past, and my future is my future. Yeah, well, that's what I thought until my past came back to give me a little bit of truth called "no escape."

One day, after I was introduced to my new life on Wall Street, he (my life changer) told me to drive his car and make a few stops for him along the way before my sister and I headed to the office. With excitement and with no hesitation, I said "yes" because driving his car was like riding first class on Delta (real smooooooth). Plus, I felt like a celebrity as I cruised around the city.

Anyway, I was off to do what I was known for doing. I made a quick stop to pick up a few things from the store. After I got what I needed, I headed back to the car. As soon as I opened the trunk to drop the bags in, there it was, staring me dead in the face. It was my past letting me know that there was no escaping it. In an instant, I was shocked at what I was seeing. I wished I was just seeing things, but I knew I wasn't. My present had been so clear this morning before I'd left the house, but now I was at a loss for words. My joy had just gotten sucked in between my past and present and had left me standing here, feeling all sorts of confused. Seeing this, though, kind of confirmed why he'd gone out dressed in all black last night and why he didn't come home till late. I wondered what he would do if he knew that I knew, I thought.

The questions now are: Do I walk away from the present like I did my past? Can I trust him, or should I even be loyal to him now, knowing that he is keeping this secret? Do I face the reality of my past haunting me, or do I ignore it, like it never even existed? Do I get back in the car and explain what I saw to my sister?

This news was a game changer, and I hoped that, somehow, my past, present, and future would not collide because that would be a life and death situation. This could be the death of my past and present because I would damn sure murder them both before they even got a chance to wreak any havoc on my future. Well, only time would tell, and what would happen when he learned about what I'd found in his car? Well, time would tell that, too.

CHAPTER 1

Queens Building Dayz

I t was a hot summer day when my sister Jacelyn and I first moved into the Buildings in Southside Jamaica Queens. It was a neighborhood filled with families, money, drugs, crime, sex, Chinese restaurants, and bodegas on every block. I lived in one of the nicest duplex buildings in a neighborhood called Baisley Park Gardens on 147th Street and Rockaway Boulevard. This was the place where we grew up playing hopscotch, jump rope, skelly, punch ball, handball, and kickball. We did a lot of other stuff, too, but it wasn't your average playing. We did things like playing in the elevators and throwing rocks off the roof, especially during Halloween. Throwing eggs off the roof was a tradition. We used to throw eggs at the carpools and taxis as they drove by. We did a lot of tomboy stuff. We weren't just home playing with dolls and polishing our nails; no, that was the last thing we wanted to do.

My sister Jacelyn and I were just one year apart, so we were very close. We hung out with the same people and went to the same schools. Everyone called us "church girls" because we had grown up in the church. There had been many days when we were in church from sunup to sundown. We may have lived in the hood, but we certainly didn't grow up like we did. We may have been church girls, but we were very popular, and everyone and anyone knew who Bridgette and Jacelyn were for sure.

Our building had three sections that connected the A, B, and C buildings together. There was another building down the block called the D building. I lived in the A building with my moms and my sister Jacelyn in a two-bedroom apartment. As we got older, sharing a room with Jacelyn became difficult, so I was very happy when we moved into a four-bedroom apartment with a living room, dining room, kitchen, and two full bathrooms, but we were still in the A building, just across the grass.

Our building wasn't set up like the projects, with brick walls surrounding every apartment door. When the doors closed, you would hear a loud *slam* that echoed down the hall. Our apartment doors were out in the open. When we stepped out our door, we saw grass, the other apartment doors, and kids playing, not brick walls staring back at us. People really didn't consider where we lived to be the projects. That's why it was always called the "Buildings."

My mom was very strict back then. We were not even allowed to have company until we got older. Nobody even knew what our apartment looked like other than the quick view they got when we opened the front door. My mom always worked hard on her nine to five, and there was one thing that was always for sure—she may have been strict, but she made sure we lived good.

My mom met a guy named Mr. Bill back when me and Jacelyn were little girls. Mr. Bill was handsome. He had medium brown skin and short gray hair. He had a medium build and stood about 5'9", if I had to guess. He always wore dress shirts and dress pants with a baseball cap. He wore dress shoes or dress boots that stopped just above his ankles. I never saw him dress down. He carried himself as a gentleman and businessman at all times. He owned a grocery store around the corner from our old house. He helped my mom take care of us after my father dipped off on us, leaving us with nothing. Mr. Bill became our dad in his own right. His blood didn't make him our dad, but his love and kindness did.

Mr. Bill was also an investment banker, so he had plenty of money to go around. He made sure we had the best of the best. Our apartment was one of the finest in the building. We had big screen TVs and leather furniture. The living room was decorated very nicely. The highlights were a black lacquer wall unit, a black lacquer stereo system from American Express, a mirror that spread across the entire wall of the living room, and plush carpeting.

In the kitchen, we had a range with a built-in microwave and an up-and-down washer and dryer. In the dining room, we had a fish tank that was as long as one wall. It was filled with fish that were as big as my hands. We had a cream lacquer dining table with six cream and mauve suede chairs with a matching glass China cabinet.

My sister's room and my room were nice, but they were nothing compared to my mom's room. My mom had a burgundy lacquer head-board in her bedroom that was so squeaky clean you could see yourself in it. It was like you were looking in a mirror. It was attached to her queen-size waterbed and covered the entire back wall. My mom's room and the living room were the only rooms that had big screen TVs.

That's why, on many days, I would find myself floating on the water-bed, watching *General Hospital*, when I came straight home from school, but I made sure to be out before my moms got home and caught me.

People would always ask, "What do y'all do? What are y'all into?" They wanted to know if we sold drugs or something simply because we had a nice house and wore nice clothes. We always kept it real with everyone, but no one listened. To this very day, I'm still asked if we sold drugs, and I've always said, "No, we are blessed and highly favored."

Imagine looking out your bedroom window at your childhood friend slumped over against the corner store with a bullet in his head. Or imagine running down a dark stairwell and stepping in what you thought might have been water or piss, but it was actually a puddle of blood seeping out of the dead body found lying underneath the stairwell. Or imagine having fun playing in the snow, then, out of nowhere a man's brains were splattered all over the ground, his blood quickly seeping onto the white snow that covered the ground. He didn't have enough money to catch the bus, so he jumped on the back of a fire truck to get a ride. I did not imagine those things. Those things really occurred. I can see it in my head clear as day. Remembering the burgundy rain boots that I had on that day that reminded me of the color of the man's blood that was splatted all on the ground. These are some of the bad memories that would probably never go away.

One day, after this guy had been murdered steps away from our house, my dad said that was enough and promised my mom that he would buy a house for her out on Long Island to get us up out of the hood. The move-in date was not certain, but we knew it was coming up, so until then, we were still the girls from the Building, and we always would be the girls from the Building, no matter where we moved.

We had many friends who were both girls and guys, but we mostly hung out with guys. From the nerds to the drug dealers to your everyday people, we were even cool with the drunks and the crackheads. We never judged anyone; we were cool with everybody. We learned that hanging with the guys meant less drama than hanging out with the girls. Although the guys may have had beef with each other, Jacelyn and I were never involved in any of it. We would just watch from the sidelines while taking cover.

Our favorite thing to do was to go shopping after school, but we mainly did this on the weekends. We would always hit the Coliseum on Jamaica Avenue and 165th Street to buy sneakers and jewelry. We had basically every sneaker out, from Cortez Nikes, Classic Reeboks, Foot Joys, Lottos, Ewings, Adidas cleats, high-top Reeboks, Sauconys…if you could name it, we had it. My mom wouldn't let us shop on Jamaica Avenue for nothing other than sneakers and 14k gold jewelry, even if we begged. She made us shop at the white girl stores like Mandees, Pants Palace, and Strawberries. As long as the clothing store wasn't on Jamaica Avenue, we were able to shop there. Even though we may have wanted a shirt or pants like everyone else from Jamaica Avenue, we couldn't get it because Mom was not having it. As a matter of fact, I do remember that we did have T-shirts and hoodies with our names on them that were made either in the Coliseum or on one of the blocks near the Coliseum. My mom didn't mind those because she claimed they were custom-made. Yeah, right. Custom-made for everyone in the hood.

For Easter, we were allowed to wear whatever we wanted. Taking full of advantage of this option, I remember going shopping at Mr. Lee's on Jamaica Avenue one year. I will never forget that year. I bought a blue and white pin-striped jumper that reminded me of Luigi from *Super Mario Brothers*. It came with a matching hat. Jacelyn bought a jumper that had pockets all over it. At that time, the sweatshirts with the zodiac signs were very popular, so we both bought one of those as well. Despite what we may or may not have felt about how we were raised, I thank my mom for raising us different. It allowed us to have our own identities and not follow everyone else.

Most days, when we weren't in school, on the Avenue, or at the mall, you would probably find us chilling with the guys in front of the A, B, or C Building. Growing up, we also spent a lot of time on Rockaway Boulevard, sitting on this yellow rail that wrapped around a strip mall that had a laundromat, a Chinese restaurant, a dry cleaners, and a pizza place.

Walking was our thing, too. We would walk from 147th Street down to 142nd Avenue to chill with the girls we went to school with and the guys that hung out down there. We would walk across the bridge and chill with the guys from Lincoln and 133rd-135th and Foch Boulevard. We even used to chill in Richmond Hill, which was considered one of the nice sides of Queens. We also hung out in buildings other than our own called the Forty Projects, the Rochedale Village, and the Baisley Projects, which were the more popular buildings. They were not too far from where we lived.

We hung out just about everywhere in Southside Jamaica Queens. We would hit Lincoln Park, Shimer, and Baisley Park. They used to have jams in the park called Baisley Jams. It was the spot to go to and do whatever you wanted. People came out to meet and greet and listen to DJs play all the latest music. We spent a lot of time at the jams, also. It was where all the popular peeps would be, so you know Jacelyn and I were there. Anywhere you might have found a fly guy, we were there.

We hung out on Linden Boulevard a lot, too, not only because my family lived on Linden but because McDonald's was on Linden, and that was always the place to go to get the Big Macs and the fifty-cent cheeseburgers. Besides, some of the best-looking guys hung out on Linden Boulevard. Jacelyn and I mostly hung out with the guys, so we could judge which ones were the cutest, had the most money, and whose sneaker game was on point.

No matter where Jacelyn and I went, everyone always remembered us and never had a bad word to say about us. We didn't smoke or drink or use drugs, and that's what has kept up our appearances to this very day. We used to be all over and met some great people along the way. Oh, but believe me when I say, we met some creeps, too; everybody couldn't be all good now.

One way that we got around town was by cab. There was a cab stand across the street from where we lived, and our favorite driver was this one fine-ass Jamaican. He had pretty eyes, wavy hair, and flawless skin that was Indian smooth. Everyone called him by his cab number, which was Number Twenty-Eight. I will never forget him. No matter where we had to go, he would take us. It could be eleven at night, and if my mom wanted KFC or Popeye's, he would take us. His favorite word was "BLOOOOOD." He drove a brand-new Mercedes Benz back then. Number Twenty-Eight was the man, and he knew it, too. Everyone wanted to ride with him, but Jacelyn and I always had first dibs.

While growing up in the hood, we saw so many people get killed right in our building, across the street, and up and down the block. We would sit in front of our apartment door on chairs or crates and would always be on point if something were to go down. The cops always ran through the building, running right straight past us, knocking over chairs, knocking people down, knocking stuff down, chasing people, and banging on doors, looking for somebody we knew who may have got caught selling drugs or had a gun or something. When the cops weren't chasing them, they were chasing each other. Things were getting crazy, and we knew it was only a matter time before we had to move. Jacelyn and I had both studied criminal justice in high school with the hopes of, one day, helping out with all this violence in the neighborhood. We wanted to bring some positive change to our hood. We both had plans to go to law school together after we graduated high school, but we put those plans on hold to have just a little bit of fun before we dedicated the next few years of our lives to law school. We weren't exactly sure what we wanted to do, but we knew it had to be great and make lots of money to get us up out the hood.

We knew our dad had plans for us to move to Long Island, but we wanted our own place. We weren't about to depend on our moms and pops' money to do it. We also wanted to pay for our own law school tuition, so we had to figure things out quickly because we really didn't know when Mr. Bill would say it was time to go. We knew, once we moved, the Building would never be the same without us, and we would never be the same without Baisley Park Gardens.

CHAPTER 2

Bridgette and Jacelyn Banks

So, of course, you know, by now, that I'm Bridgette. I was always known as "the brown-skinned girl with honey eyes." Most people would say I looked kind of Indian because of my complexion and the richness of my skin. My long, wavy black hair was worn straight most of the time. I often wore it in a ponytail, too, when it was hot, I was being lazy, or in a rush.

Back in the day, I was around 5'6" and weighed about one-hundred-thirty pounds. I had a little-big butt and a small waist. I wore like a 32C, but since big breasts ran in the family, I just knew one day that size would change, even though I didn't ever want it to. People called me "Chocolate." Well, the guys did anyway, and they always complimented me on my beauty. I was and always will be one of a kind.

Jacelyn, my sister, was the light-skinned one. She was about 5'7" and weighed around one-hundred-ten pounds. She wore a 30B and was skinny like a model. I was the quiet, business-type girl, and Jacelyn was the opposite. She was not loud, but she was very outspoken and played around a lot. She didn't really care about business. She was more into shopping. Everyone would always refer to Jacelyn and me as twins, even though we weren't. They would call me her, and her me. We'd gotten so used to it that it didn't matter because we knew who they were referring to. Jacelyn looked a lot like our mom, and I looked a lot like our father, but we had features of them both. Our father was very tall, with smooth, caramel brown skin and pretty black hair. You could say he looked a lot like Leon from *Waiting to Exhale*. Now my mom had pretty brown skin and long auburn hair. She kept it curled up in sponge rollers. She was about 5'6" with very thick thighs. I guess that was where I got mine from. She looked like Ella Joyce from the TV series *Roc*, only she was just a shade darker.

Although I hung out with my sister a lot, some days, I would chill inside the house to do my homework, study, and help my moms around the house. I was always into books and researching to find out ways to make my own money. Yes, I watched *Video Music Box* to catch up on all the hottest new R&B and rap videos, and I played Atari, too, just like everyone else growing up. *Ms. Pac Man, Donkey Kong*, and *Video Pinball* were my favorite games. I loved gospel music, hip-hop, and R&B, even though I was forced, sometimes, by my aunts, to listen to all the oldies but goodies. One thing I hated to do was laundry because we had a lot of clothes, but since I was in the house a lot, I had to do the laundry, all thanks to my mom, who stayed in the store shopping for clothes. We had so much laundry that we couldn't just use the washer in the house; we had to go to the laundromat. We would have every washer and every dryer on one side of the laundromat, and trust me, this wasn't no pile up of dirty clothes. It was one week's worth of clothes every week. I couldn't stand the laundromat, but I loved to go shopping for clothes. I also loved to cook and still do to this day. I actually learned a lot from my mom and my grandma about how to take care of a household. We grew up on all the good soul food, like mac and cheese, collard greens, rice and gravy, yams, fried chicken, chitterlings, pig feet, black-eyed peas, cornbread, and Kool-Aid. I'm sure you get the picture. I knew learning all those skills from them would, someday, land me a great husband, one worthy of Bridgette.

I loved doing hair, too, so I started doing my family's and close friends' hair. That was back in the early nineties when finger waves and the scrunch was popping. I had taken a night course at Wilfred Beauty

Academy for Cosmetology, but I knew it wasn't the career for me mainly because everyone wanted free hairdos, so I got my license and never did hair again because it wasn't making me no money. Plus, my heart was focused on going to law school. I knew I had to figure something else out, though, to make money before starting college because hair just did not cut it for me.

Now Jacelyn, on the other hand, didn't like to cook or do hair, but she loved to eat and get her hair done. Because we had taken a break from school, she wasn't about to be up in the house researching anything. She would rather hang out and shop. I like to shop, too, but I also loved to save my money. She knew that, whatever I found out with my research, it would benefit both of us, so why bother? Overall, we pretty much did and liked the same things.

In the meantime, while I was figuring out what our next steps were going to be, when I needed a break, Jacelyn and I would hang out with the homies. There were many homies to choose from because they were all so cute, and they were always looking good and smelling good with nice haircuts, gold fronts, jewels…I'm talking model-type guys. The crazy thing about us and the guys was we all were homies, and we never looked at each other in that way. Well, I know I didn't anyway. I'm guessing now maybe they were thinking twice about not looking at us like that, but it was meant to be nothing more than a big brother-little sister-type thing. Plus, they were too busy chasing that street money to really even notice us anyway. Besides, we were different since we didn't smoke, get high, drink, or throw ourselves at them. I'm guessing those are a few more of the reasons why we never really hooked up with any of them, and I was cool with that. I was so focused on getting out of the hood that guys didn't really matter to me no way. Jacelyn and I were just around the guys back then to learn, look at them, laugh, have fun, and talk about them later. I'd really learned a lot about the streets, how to protect myself, about guys and their different attitudes, things they liked, disliked, and, most of all, loyalty by hanging with some of the realest and coolest guys in the hood. It was a great advantage for me growing up, and I carried it with me along the way.

As time went on, I started to look around at my surroundings and saw nothing was changing. Everyone was still in the same place, doing the same things, and I just really wanted a change. I wanted more for my life. Every time someone in my family would have an event, they would call me to set everything up for them, such as the food, music, decorations, and the entertainment. It was really something I grew to love, so I decided to do more research on event planning. I went to the library, took out some books on the subject, and went from there.

One day, I sat down with Jacelyn, Mr. Bill, and my mom. We figured out a game plan that would bring in some fast cash and lots of it. My dad said he would handle the business side of everything, while all we had to do was host the events. My dad could easily set up some events for Jacelyn and I because he had connections with some big people in high places that he knew would give us a shot. We didn't have to go to school for it or anything like that. All we had to do was use what we already knew to get what we wanted, which was common knowledge. At that point, I was no longer focused on the homies or what was going on in the hood. I was only focused on minding my own business, literally, since we finally had something to focus on to get us the hell up out the hood and on our own.

CHAPTER 3

Banks Enterprises

Fast forward into spring. It was May, and I had finally reached my twenty-first birthday. Jacelyn was already twenty-two, so she had just been waiting on me to make moves. We had to wait a few months until I was of age to be around and sell liquor to put our company in motion. So, after a few months of research, preparing, and me hitting the big two-one, it was finally happening. We came up with a company name, which was Banks Enterprises. My dad had the connect with this guy in Manhattan who owned two restaurants, a club, and a catering hall, so we were set. It was now time that Jacelyn and I put Banks Enterprises on the map and show the world what it was all about.

Our first event was for a fiftieth anniversary. It wasn't anything too crazy, just a couple that wanted to recreate their wedding day, which wasn't all that hard to do. The only thing we had to do that was really challenging was find the perfect bakery to recreate their wedding cake. They wanted a five-tier cake with steps and a waterfall in the center. It wasn't just any cake. It had so many details. Even the piping work required the expertise of a pro to recreate it. We found the perfect bakery in downtown Brooklyn, and they were able to master the cake. After many hours of hard work and being a little nervous on the day of the event, I am happy to report that our first event went great and that the clients were very satisfied.

The next event was a sweet sixteen celebration. This time, we had to find an event space. We found a loft that was five-thousand square feet. The client wanted for her party to have an eighties hip-hop/R&B theme and for the décor to be red and white. Every guest was asked to dress up as their favorite artist. We got the DJ and his crew to dress up like Run DMC and Jam Master J. We also had a popular recording artist from the eighties come to perform. The client and her best friend dressed as the rappers Salt and Peppa. They wore MCM jumpers with big shell earrings, four finger rings, and they wore their hair in wavy bobs. They were short on one side and long on the other just like the group.

After that party, because it was such a big hit, we started getting nonstop calls, and Banks Enterprises became one of the top event planning companies in Manhattan. We were making so much money that we had saved up enough money to be able to pay for law school and our own apartment in no time. The way things were going, we knew we would only be able to live with my mom when she moved to Long Island for a short period of time. The commute to the city by train from the Building was easy, but it was crazy hectic when we worked late hours and needed to get home, so you know the ride from Long Island into the city and back would be crazy, so we were gonna have to find an apartment closer to the city.

Our schedule was so booked for the next few months from referrals that we had to refer some clients to other companies that we'd worked with in the past. My dad was still handling all the bookkeeping and taxes. He wanted us to have the knowledge to be in control of everything concerning the business, so he set aside time once a week for three weeks to teach us everything and hand over all of our financial records. At this point, we were willing to do whatever it took to get out the hood, so we didn't care. Now Jacelyn and I had officially become Banks Enterprises in our own right, having full control of everything.

One day per week, during our first months of business, we would go to other events to check out our competition since we'd only been in the business for a while, and other companies had years of experience in the business. One day, we were at this event in Harlem where we connected with the manager of this underground, members-only club in Manhattan. Her name was Maryellen. She gave us her card, and she advised us to call her the very next day. Jacelyn and I were speechless when she walked away because we had no clue she was even going to say anything to us. We were there just to check things out, but apparently, we were being checked out instead. We had tried, for months, to figure out who managed that club, and finally we walked right into her presence. She wasn't the owner, but it was just as good because she was in charge of everything. We couldn't wait to see what the next day would be all about, so we just decided to celebrate that night because we knew tomorrow was going to be something big. We had heard rumors about the club but had never come close to finding out the truth, and now look, we were standing right in front of it. Get in good with her, and we in, I thought.

The next day couldn't come fast enough. We just kept watching the clock until around ten in the morning. Since Jacelyn wasn't the one to talk business, I made the call.

After the phone rang a few times, someone picked up, so I said, "Hello. May I please speak to Maryellen?"

"Speaking."

"My name is Bridgette from Banks Enterprises. We met last night at the Forman event."

"Yes, I've been waiting for your call. I would like to set up an appointment with you in hopes of hiring you to be our full-time event planner for the club. Come down on Tuesday at 11:30 am to go over things and to sign a few contracts, but that's only if you decide to accept the offer."

"Thank you, Maryellen, for considering us for the job. We really appreciate the opportunity. I will talk it over with my partner Jacelyn, and we will be there for sure on Tuesday at 11:30 am sharp. We look forward to seeing you then."

She said, "Wait. This Saturday, you're both formally invited to the club. The owners have personally extended this invitation. We are having a black-tie affair. Just show up after seven in the evening. Your names will be on the guest list at the door. I will send you all the details later today."

"Okay. Great. We will be there. Thank you, and have a great day, Maryellen."

She said, "Likewise," and hung up the phone.

Now talk about in. It seemed like we had already made the cut. So Jacelyn and I knew, at that point, we had to hit Queens Center Mall. Since the event was a black-tie affair, you know all the rich and successful corporate cats would be in attendance. We had to represent Banks Enterprises the best way we knew how, and that was to have jaws dropping as soon as we hit the door.

About an hour later, after we'd hung up with Maryellen, there was a knock at the door. Who the hell knocks on the door but the police? Everyone else rings the doorbell fifty-one times like we ain't heard it the first fifty times. I looked out the peep hole, and there was some butler/chauffeur-looking guy. When I opened the door, he said, "I have deliveries for Ms. Bridgette Banks and Ms. Jacelyn Banks."

I said, "Okay. Thank you," and took the packages, then went to grab a tip.

He said, "There will be no tip needed. Enjoy your day, madam," and left.

Who is he, and how did he even know where to find us? Wow! Alfred came to the hood. We busted out laughing so hard because he looked just like the guy from the *B.A.P.S* movie. We opened the packages, and found, to our surprise, everything from bags to dresses to shoes. They were all from Chanel. There were two diamond necklaces, two diamond bracelets, and two pairs of diamond-studded earrings. There was also a card attached that read:

> *You are formally invited to our annual black-tie event on Saturday, January 12th at 9:00 pm sharp. The limo will arrive at 7:00 pm to escort you to the event. Please accept these gifts as tokens of appreciation for gracing us with your presence at our event. There's more to come. Signed, C.M. & M.S.*

Sadly, Jacelyn said, "So much for us going shopping."

"Shut up, Jacelyn. You always want to go shopping and don't buy nothing but sneakers when you do. My question to you is, who are these gifts from? And trust me, they must have been watching us really hard to know where the hell we live at and to figure out our sizes. I might not have the answers right now, but what I do know, J, is that we are bound to find out. One thing I know for sure is that they have very good taste when it comes to picking out ladies' clothing. They've spent thousands on us, and they are sending us a limo. That is a nice touch, but I'm not impressed yet. In the meantime, Jacelyn, we gotta go. We gotta get to this sweet sixteen on the yacht in Manhattan within two hours, so let's go."

We were on our way to catch a cab because we were running late for tonight's event. When we got to the parking lot, why was Alfred, the driver, there and standing outside a limo? We walked over to him and asked if everything was okay. He said, "Yes, Ms. Banks. My name is Stanley, and I will be your personal driver from now on. Anywhere you would like to go, I will take you."

"Hold up. Wait. Who hired you?"

He said, "It's a service provided by your employers at the club."

Wow! Our employers? Hmmm...we hadn't even signed any contacts or even said "yes," for that matter, so how were they our employers already? Whoever they were, they were making sure all Ts were crossed and all Is were dotted. They made sure it was hard for us to pass up this opportunity. That was for sure. I just said, "Okay, thank you. We'll be right back. We're gonna walk across the street to the store."

Stanley said, "Okay, Ms. Banks, but I have to inform you that the limo is fully stocked."

I looked at Jacelyn. She looked at me, and we just took the walk to the store. We both were in shock but excited at the same time. Banks Enterprises had just been taken to a whole new level within twenty-four hours. I said, "Yo, Jacelyn, we're definitely not going to be able to live in the Building much longer. Whoever our new bosses are, they're bringing too much attention to the hood."

After our walk and talk, we got into the limo and found that all our favorite drinks, snacks, candy, and chips were inside, just like he'd said. There was no liquor in sight, which was a nice touch, but right now, my main focus was not on C.M., M.S., or this damn limo, it was on getting to the yacht. Stanley did good. He wasn't Number Twenty-Eight, but we managed to make it there on time. Things went according to plan, and the clients were well pleased. They gave us a three-thousand-dollar tip on top of our service fee.

Later that night, when the yacht docked, Stanley was waiting at the pier for us as promised, and he drove us back home. I guess he was telling the truth about being our personal driver.

For the next three days, we had a busy schedule, but it wasn't nothing we couldn't handle. The days went by so fast. It had to have been because we were so busy, and thank God we had a lot of work to focus on to keep us from focusing on our new mystery employers, C.M. and M.S.

***

On Saturday morning, the day of the event, we got a knock at the door, and once again, it was Stanley. He said, "Good morning, Ms. Banks. I'm here to escort you and your sister to the spa and salon for a day of pampering. You will also be dining there for breakfast and lunch. It has all been accommodated."

I stopped him and said, "Let me guess. Accommodated by who? Our new employers? Hmmm…Is that so, Stanley?"

He answered, "Yes, madam, it is so. I will be waiting for the two of you in the limo. Please gather your things for tonight's event."

As we toasted with ginger ale to another twisted and unexpected turn of events, we arrived at the hotel in Manhattan. Stanley opened the door to let us out and said, "I will be waiting here for your return. Inside you will be greeted by Jasmine. She will be assisting you during your stay. I will have your bags sent up to your room."

Jasmine was a beautiful, tall blonde. After warmly greeting us, she escorted us to breakfast in the dining area of the penthouse facing the patio, where we sat and took in a breathtaking view of the Manhattan skyline. The smell of cinnamon flowed through the air as it rose from the thick stack of French toast that was dripping with warm syrup, and as the fluffy stack of pancakes topped with strawberries and whipped cream slowly slid down my throat, I couldn't help but wonder how the fluffy scrambled eggs topped with melted cheddar cheese would taste. There was a spread of everything, including fresh fruit, waffles, orange juice, and even bubbly champagne. Before she left the room, Jasmine said, "Give me a ring when you're done with breakfast."

***

We waited for about an hour, just sitting around chilling after breakfast, relaxing and enjoying the penthouse. We didn't know what to expect next, but we surely didn't want it to stop. We had been working non-stop and really needed this break.

We got so into chilling and talking that we forgot all about our homegirl Jasmine, but she soon came back and escorted us down the hall to a private spa for penthouse guests only. We got full body massages, manicures, and pedicures. By the time we were finished at the spa, it was time for lunch, so we headed back to the penthouse.

Once again, we walked into a room with a full spread of food. There were cheeses, crackers, mini-sandwiches, salads, and drinks. We were so tired, so we told Jasmine we were going to sleep and to wake us up around four in the afternoon to get our hair and makeup done. Jacelyn and I laid down together on a king-size bed in one of the bedrooms. We talked for a few minutes, and the next thing I knew, Jasmine was calling out, "Ms. Banks, it's four o'clock."

"Okay, Jasmine. Thanks. Give us about thirty minutes to shower, then send in the stylists." Then I turned to my sister and said, "That was some good sleep, Jacelyn. The bed was so soft and comfortable I didn't want to get up."

"Yeah, me either, Bridgette, me either."

It was 6:30 pm, and Stanley was waiting for us downstairs. We were both wearing gold-beaded, knee-length, strapless dresses. They were the same color but different styles. They were accessorized with red heels and red clutches. Our hair was done, nails were done, makeup was flawless, and our jewels were sparkling like disco balls. After we got into the limo, Stanley drove us to this industrial warehouse district in Manhattan.

As he drove, I looked out the window. After what seemed like thirty minutes, the car stopped in front of a non-descript building. There was no name on the building at all. The club was totally unrecognizable. I now understood what they meant by underground and private. After a few moments, these huge gates slid up, and Stanley drove inside. There were so many cars in the building. You name it, Lexuses, BMWs, Mercedes, Bentleys.

Stanley got out, opened the door, and said, "Ladies, you have arrived."

Since everything was such a mystery and I wasn't quite sure what would happen next, I had to ask Stanley if we were going to be okay here. He said, "Why yes, Ms. Banks. You will be just fine."

"Well, Stanley, will we meet the person or persons who arranged all of this?"

He said, "Ms. Banks, I'm not sure about how the events will play out this evening, but I know you both will have a splendid time. Enjoy your evening, ladies."

While thinking, Okay, Alfred, I said, "Thanks, Stanley. We'll see you later."

Jacelyn and I looked at each other and smiled. I looked around at everything and said, "We are a long way from the hood now, J."

Jacelyn said, "We sure are, B. We sure are."

CHAPTER 4

Who's Who

N ow I knew this had to be a glamorous event space, just judging by entryway. We were immediately greeted by a hostess. She greeted us by our names and introduced herself as Maggie. She let us know that she would be at our service for the evening. She handed both of us a gold pendant and told us to press the diamond in the center, if we needed any assistance. She walked us down a few steps, and we entered through huge golden doors. Directly in front of us was a huge sign that was illuminated in lights. It read: *WELCOME TO WHO'S WHO*. It looked like we had stepped onto the set of a Las Vegas movie or something. We continued inside and found a beautiful ballroom full of people of all nationalities. Everything was gold and white. The walls were padded white leather with huge diamond buttons trimmed in gold, which reminded me of an old fashion couch. There were also walls with textured wallpaper. The carpet was gold with tiny white swirls. They also had tall gold cocktail tables for two with white linen all around the room. Each place setting had a gold order of service card which read:

Welcome to the Who's Who Black Tie Affair
The order of events

7:00 pm Cocktail Hour
8:00 pm Casino Royale
9:00 pm Formal Dinner
10:00 pm Party and Dancing
11:00 pm Final Hour
Servers will be walking around the room with
trays of champagne and hors d'oeuvres.
Please enjoy!

Although Jacelyn and I didn't drink, we couldn't help but enjoy the celebration with a little champagne. Slowly glancing around the room, I saw that it was full of ladies dressed in the finest dresses and gents dressed in the best suits, and out of nowhere, Maryellen appeared on stage, dressed in an all-white sequined gown. She said, "Good evening and welcome to Who's Who, where the richest of the rich come to play and unwind. My name is Maryellen, and I will be your hostess for the evening. I would like to introduce you to Bridgette and Jacelyn Banks from Banks Enterprises, our very special guests for the evening. Come up here, ladies, and join me."

Now looking dumbfounded and surprised as hell, Jacelyn and I walked up on stage. Once we got there, Maryellen said, "These two ladies are our new event coordinators. Please make them feel welcome." After the crowd clapped for us, she said, "Thank you, ladies."

We smiled and stepped down.

I had never been so shocked in my life. Mind you, we hadn't even signed any contracts or agreements yet, and we were already hired. Maryellen went on to tell the crowd to be sure to start booking their events with us right away because spaces were limited and time was money. She then said, "Last but not least, stocks are up on Wallstreet," and the crowd started cheering. I guessed it was because they all had invested in stocks and they were cashing in on the big bucks.

After our introductions, Jacelyn and I mingled with the guests, and the players started approaching us, giving us their players' business cards with their photos, phone numbers, and player ID numbers on the front.

On the back of the card, there was a space to write the type of event they wanted to plan, along with the date and time they wanted to book. By the end of the cocktail hour, we had, at least, fifty cards for events to plan. I never thought this night would be about business, but I damn sure would never turn down the opportunity to work and make money.

At eight, we moved over into the next space, which was the casino room. As we entered, Maggie handed us both a rack with $10,000 worth of chips. Our luck just kept getting better by the minute. By the end of the hour together, we both had won over $50,000.

We, then, moved over into the dining hall, which had beautiful chandeliers. The room was also decorated in gold and white. The food was so amazing. Everything had been great up to this point. We moved into the last two hours of the event where we danced and mingled with the members of the club, but still no sign of C.M. or M.S.

When the perfect night came to an end, we met Stanley back at the limo, and he drove us back to the hotel. We entered the penthouse and found more clothes waiting for us. This time, it was casual clothes, sneakers, jeans, T-shirts, sweat suits, underwear, pajamas, and socks. Along with that, there was another card that read:

We hope you ladies enjoyed your evening. We wanted to show our appreciation for your attendance. Please feel free to stay in the penthouse as long as you like, and Stanley will drive you wherever you need to go. Thank you for joining our team at Who's Who, and we look forward to working with you. Good night, ladies.

signed C.M. and M.S.

Now Jacelyn and I were still bugging out, wondering who these two were. I was sure they had been there that night, in the cut somewhere, watching us, but it was cool. They couldn't hide for long. We eventually called home to let my mom and dad know that we were okay and that we were staying at the hotel. All I could say was that it was an eventful weekend and I wouldn't change one thing.

Finally, Tuesday came, and we received another card that read:

Good morning, ladies. Dress comfortably because it's going to be a long day. It would be wise, maybe, to wear sweat suits and sneakers today.

signed C.M. and M.S.

After we got dressed, Stanley drove us to Who's Who. Now we were very excited to, not only, start working, but to maybe meet the mystery men behind all of this. Upon arrival, we were greeted by Maryellen. She took us on a full tour of the club, inside and out. This place was huge. It had four ballrooms, four kitchens, twenty-four bathrooms, a tennis court, a golf course, a basketball court, two spas, four pools, and a club store. This place is massive, I thought. The club was opened from Tuesday to Saturday, and it was closed on Sundays and Mondays. The club members could book events from Tuesday to Friday, while the owners hosted their own events on Saturdays. Club membership was $100,000 per year, and if sponsored in by another member, it was $75,000 per year. There were 580 members so far and 158 employees. Now why someone would pay $100,000 to dance and party was beyond me? Ain't that much partying in the world.

Maryellen started by giving us duplicate ID cards for every member, so we could learn who was who by face and name. We went over and signed a six-month contract. We learned that we would make $15,000 each for the Tuesday through Friday events, and we would make $25,000 on Saturdays because those were the owners' special events, and they required more attention and details. We agreed to everything, as if we hadn't already been hired days ago. Our so-called employers required us to go for a complete physical that same day, so we were to start on Thursday, right after the results of the drug tests came back. We were not worried at all about the results because we didn't use drugs. Meanwhile, we already had our first event setup for the following week, which we had only ten days to pull off. It was a Paris-themed wedding, and since we had planned weddings before, it was cool.

We left the club and headed straight to the doctor. We had a complete exam, along with blood work, and since we were there, we had him check for STDs, STIs, diabetes, and high blood pressure. You name it, we had him for check it. Finally, our physicals were complete, and we had Stanley take us back to the hotel. When we got back, we just ordered room service and got right to work planning the wedding. Everything was on the line, and since this would be our first event at the club, we had to do it up right. For all we knew, the bosses could show up at any given time.

When Thursday came, we got the call from Maryellen saying that the results had come back, and we could start at twelve o'clock that day. Stanley picked us up and took us to the club. Maryellen greeted us at the door and handed us envelopes that contained our test results from the doctor. She said, "Just so you know, the doctor is a private doctor that we use for all our employees. If you ever need him, you're more than welcome to make an appointment with him, and the bills will be covered by the club."

Jacelyn and I quickly looked over our results, and as expected, we both had clean bills of health. We definitely weren't worried about any STDs since we weren't sleeping around. From that point on, everything was smooth sailing. We now had complete control of the club.

The week went by really fast. We had the vendors come in on Wednesday to setup for Friday. Everything was so beautiful, and it turned out to be another successful event. After that, things couldn't get better. We were planning left and right. We loved to see the players play because, the more they played, the larger the tips were for us at the end of every event.

***

We were now four months in working for Who's Who and still hadn't met C.M. and M.S., but by this time, we didn't really care because our main focus was stacking our money and moving to Long Island for a little while, where we would fit in much better now that we had money. Now don't get me wrong, we loved the Buildings where we had grown up, but there was too much attention on us, and that could have possibly put us in danger.

One morning, when we arrived at the club, we got a note from the owners letting us know we had sixty days to coordinate a masquerade ball. They also let us know that we would be celebrating our six-month anniversary working at the club. All I could think was, they're really paying attention. The card also read that we were to choose whatever we wanted for the event as far as entertainment, music, and food, but the guest list would be handled by them. Once again, it read: *Enjoy your day, ladies. signed by C.M. and M.S.*

"These must be some old dudes, Jacelyn, probably old white dudes, at that. Not that it matters at all if they are white or black, but they gotta be old, though. They're moving like some old millionaires, and by the looks of the club, how could they be young?"

Business went on as usual. We were getting paid, having fun doing it, and basically living at the hotel. When we sat down with Maryellen to go over preparations for the masquerade ball, she said, "At the owner's request, dance lessons have been scheduled for the two of you for the next eight weeks, for every Wednesday afternoon for two hours. By the way, the bosses said, 'All work and no play, what's the fun in that?'"

Jacelyn rudely said, "So they call dance lessons fun."

"I guess it depends on what kind of dancing you're doing, but I think it will be fun, J. Something different, other than shopping. Please tell them 'thanks' for us. Wait. Can I please ask you a question, Maryellen?" I said.

"Sure."

"Can you tell me, why would they have this event on a Thursday?"

"Bridgette, your guess is just as good as mine. I've been given just as much information as you have."

"Well, okay, alrighty then, Maryellen. Thursday, it is."

Now Jacelyn and I were already a little overwhelmed with work and all the other events, but we couldn't let it show since we knew they were clearly watching our every move. We had five events planned for just this week alone, including today, and they wanted us to dance on top of that. I couldn't help but wonder, Who do they think we are?

"Look, Jacelyn, after the masquerade ball, this is the plan. If they don't let us know who they are, we're done. For four months, we've been reading them damn cards, and you know they've been following us, even before we started working here."

Jacelyn said, "Yeah, this is crazy, and we need a break, B. I don't mind taking a few months off. Hell! We have more than enough money to take the year off."

"You would say that, Jacelyn, but you're right. We sure do."

Well, another week had passed, and the dancing lessons would be starting tomorrow. I was tired, and I needed to relax, so I went down the hall to the spa. I begged Jacelyn to come, but she was being lazy, so I went alone.

***

When the next morning came, there was a knock at the hotel room door. It was another damn card accompanied by two boxes.

"Jacelyn, please open it because I'm done with these damn notes."

"Okay, B. It says: *We figured y'all would need dancing shoes for the lessons today. Enjoy your day, ladies. Signed C.M. and M.S.*'" Jacelyn looked at me and laughed.

"Ya see, I don't get what's so funny, Jacelyn, but come on. Let's get this day over with."

After Stanley dropped us off at the club, we were greeted in the lobby by Jose and Miguel, the dance instructors. They really weren't wasting no time. They let us know, for the next few weeks, we would learn how to tango, salsa, waltz, and old-school step. Now the old-school stepping, I was with, but the tango and the waltz? They had to be joking.

Both Jose and Miguel were very handsome, very nice, and very married to two beautiful ladies.

The first lesson went pretty well. After we finished up, we changed for the night's event. The evening plans were just a simple candlelight dinner with the Manhattan skyline as the backdrop, a hologram of the ocean, a band, and a full-course meal for two. That had to be the easiest event we'd had in the last four and a half months.

***

Now we were five months in. The lessons were going great. The events were flowing, and we'd made almost $500,000, not including the tips, casino winnings, and perks.

During the week leading up to the masquerade ball, we didn't plan any events since we had to make sure the club was clear for all incoming deliveries concerning the ball. We were so excited when our Venetian full-face masks from China arrived at the club. They were cream and light gold with cream and gold tassels that draped down the right side along the ear and detailed gold and silver flowers that were dipped in glitter on the left side. The masks were on point; they were fit for a queen.

We decorated the space with cream and gold linens. We had soft-colored lighting around the back walls that changed throughout the night. We set up dancers, comedians, singers, and magic acts. There was lots of food, including fresh fruit. There were also fresh flowers and candles throughout the entire club. We had the club's photographers and videographers there to capture everything throughout the night. We had several photo booths around as well, so everyone could capture some crazy moments.

It was finally our last Wednesday to rehearse our dance routine with Jose and Miguel, and I knew, for damn sure, I was not going to miss this when it was over. Hell. My feet hurt from all this working and dancing.

This event was going to be the first masquerade ball that the club hosted. It was called the Roaring Twenties.

***

The day of the event was finally here. Jacelyn and I had breakfast out on the patio and shared stories about how far we had come in the last six months. Thank God for Mr. Bill helping us start up Banks Enterprises, and thank God for blessing us with the opportunity to work at Who's Who. We were so blessed.

We knew that this could be our last night working at Who's Who, so we knew we needed to make the best of it. We still owned Banks Enterprises, so it didn't really matter what happened tonight. Because they were still a mystery, we both wondered, in the back of our minds, who the initials C.M. and M.S. belonged to. Instead of Stanley driving us in the limo that we would normally ride in, he picked us up in an all-white Rolls Royce. As we were riding, Jacelyn looked over at me, grabbed my hand, and said, "This is it, B. The moment of truth."

"I don't know about that, Jacelyn, but I truly have mixed feelings." I was not sure if I even wanted to know who they were anymore since we now had the option to walk away from it all and allow things to be a little normal again. I realized, though, at that moment, that it was just my emotions setting in and that things would never be normal for us ever again.

Pulling up to the warehouse gave me butterflies in my stomach. Stanley opened the car door to a crowd standing along the red carpet. Cameras were flashing everywhere, as if we were the stars of the show. When we walked inside, we saw that there was another red carpet along with a gold backdrop that had Who's Who printed all over it in white letters. It was amazing. Looking around, I noticed that just a few changes had been made to the decorations. It dawned on me that the gold and white must have been someone's favorite colors. All over the club, there were thousands of white roses with the tips dipped in gold shimmer. I swear it felt like someone's wedding, not a masquerade ball. There were so many roses. The cocktails and hors d'oeuvres were on point.

Every club member was in the building. The Who's Who of the corporate world — stock brokers, lawyers, doctors, other professionals, and a few celebrities — were all in attendance. After a quick introduction by Maryellen, the festivities began. Of course, at the end of her introduction, she announced that stocks were up on Wallstreet, and the crowd cheered and went crazy. I just knew somebody was making crazy money. I didn't know why I hadn't invested in stocks by now. I've been here long enough, I thought. I guess that's how they're paying that one-hundred-thousand-dollar membership fee. I don't wanna be in their shoes, but I definitely wouldn't mind having the bank roll they were holding.

We played a cash game of roses. Each table setting had a bouquet of white roses with numbers sprayed on some of them in purple. The prizes ranged from fifty to one-hundred-thousand dollars in Who's Who cash to use for purchases around the club. Jacelyn won the first prize of one-hundred grand, and I won the second prize at seventy-five-grand, but it really didn't matter to me because it wasn't the money I wanted to win. Besides, after tonight, I thought, I may never spend this money because I may never enter this club again.

Just about all the planned events of the night took place. Everyone was walking around, trying to figure out who was who, but because of the masks, it was hard to identify anyone. When it was time for Jacelyn and me to take over the show, we changed into our dancing shoes and short dresses, but we kept our masks on to keep the audience in suspense. Jose and Miguel escorted us to the dance floor. We started off with the tango, and everyone clapped to the beat of the music. Next up was the waltz. It was exciting to know that two girls from the hood were killing it based on the response of the audience. The last dance was a slow dance to "Let's Chill" by the R&B group Guy.

As the introduction to the song pumped through the speakers, the lights shut off, but the music continued to play. It took all of sixty seconds for the spotlights to shine down on Aaron Hall from Guy singing, "Let's chill…Let's chill-ill-ill-ill, baby." My heart dropped. He was live, up close, and personal. Jacelyn and I were standing on the dance floor all alone and in shock from all the excitement. It all seemed so surreal. Then we heard whistles from the audience. We looked back to see two more spotlights, one on each side of the room. We watched as the lights traveled toward the dance floor. At last, there was a masked man standing in front of me dressed in an all-black tailored tux, red shirt, and black tie. His tie clip and the buttons on his jacket had the initials C.M. on them. He was wearing gloves, and it was a little dark, so I really couldn't see much of him, but I saw all that I needed to know that he was real. My heart was racing, and when he pulled me close, my heart skipped a few beats. Once again, I had butterflies in my stomach. That was the feeling I had been waiting for all my life. His cologne smelled so good, it was the type of scent that, when he left the room, it lingered behind. I knew we had an audience, but it was as if we were the only two in the room. I laid my head on his chest as we danced to the music. He never said a word. We just danced.

I took a moment to glance over at Jacelyn and M.S. I knew his initials from the cards they had been sending every day for the past six months. Jacelyn looked so happy. It was like it was her birthday, and he was her present. He was also dressed in an all-black tux, red shirt, and black tie. He looked about as tall as Jacelyn, if not an inch taller, maybe around 5'9". He also wore gloves, so I couldn't really get a glimpse of his complexion. I couldn't wait to talk to Jacelyn later about what was going through her head at this moment, but for now, I quickly shifted my focus back to C.M. as we continued dancing to the music. For a moment, he looked down at me, right into my eyes. Then he grabbed both of my hands, stepped back, and let go. The spotlights went off for a few seconds, then came back on, and when they did, they both were gone. They had disappeared, just like that, into the crowd. Jacelyn and I waved at everyone, as if that was really part of the performance, and walked off the dance floor as the audience applauded.

When the event finally came to a close, everyone headed back to their vehicles. All-in-all, it was a very successful turnout. The night was perfect. We waited for everyone to leave the event. Then we got back into the Rolls Royce and headed back to the hotel. Even though the night had gone great, I had already promised myself that, if I didn't see them tonight, I was done, and that dance didn't count, so when we arrived back at the hotel, I asked Stanley to please wait for us to quickly grab our things from the room and drive us back to Queens. While we were packing our things to head home, I asked Jacelyn what she thought about Mr. M.S. She said, "Girl, I could tell he was fine. He smelled so good, and that suit he had on was tough. He danced really good, too, and he didn't skip one beat. If only I could've seen what he looked like though."

"Yeah, J, who you telling? The only good thing was that we got a chance to dance with them, and that's something I will never forget. But seriously, now that we are finally done playing their game, it's time to let them know what's up. It's time to flip the script. It's time to disappear on them, just like they disappeared on us."

***

We arrived in Queens in no time. It was around two in the morning when we got home. We got out the car and thanked Stanley for everything. "You're a really nice guy, and it's been a real pleasure riding with you. Stay cool, Stanley. Oh, by the way, can you please deliver this envelope to the guys for us?"

He said, "It was an honor to be at your service, and I will be happy to deliver this for you, Ms. Bridgette."

We walked into the building, and he drove off.

Now that Who's Who was over. Jacelyn and I were finally home, and it was time to hit the streets. Time to call #28 to see if he would take us to Jamaica Avenue tomorrow. Since we'd walked around in heels for six months, oh, it was definitely time for us to grab some new sneakers from the Coliseum, even though we already had plenty. We had to hit up Margarita's Pizza on Guy R. Brewer Boulevard and Jamaica Avenue. We, also, had to get some Jamaican beef patties from the Coliseum block while we were up there. I called #28. Even though it was like three o'clock in the morning, as always, he answered. He agreed to take us when we got up, and all we had to do was call him when we were ready. I looked at Jacelyn and said, "Well, we are on our way into the next chapter. Let's see what lies ahead for us now, J."

CHAPTER 5

Game Over

Chase Morgan

"**M**r. Morgan, I'm sorry to call so late, sir, but I have something for you from Ms. Banks. After the event, Ms. Bridgette and Ms. Jacelyn both returned home to Queens. She asked that I deliver this letter to you, sir. I know it's late, but would you like for me to bring it now or deliver it to you in the morning?"

"It's cool, Stanley. You can bring it now, if it's not too much."

"Not at all, sir. I'll bring it right over."

"Okay, I'm at the penthouse. Call me when you're outside, and I'll run down and grab it."

"I'll be there in about thirty minutes, sir."

"Okay. Cool."

Hmm…a letter. I wondered, What does she have to say, and why did she leave the hotel? I didn't know, but all I could do was wait and see. While I was thinking, the phone rang.

"Wassup, Stanley? You outside?"

"Yes, Mr. Morgan."

"Okay. I'll be right down."

As I went to meet Stanley, I thought, This could go one of two ways. It could either be good news or bad news. Either way, I'm about to find out.

When I got outside, the fresh air cleared my head and was just what I needed for a quick second. I hopped in the back of the car, and Stanley handed me the letter. From the start of the letter, she sounded sincere, so I was relieved. I didn't even finish reading it. I decided that I would rather read it upstairs.

"Yo, Stanley. Before you go, did she say anything after she gave this to you?"

"Not anything other than 'goodbye' and 'deliver the letter.' That was it, sir."

"A'ight, Stanley. Thanks."

I rushed back upstairs to read the letter because I really wanted to see what all Bridgette had to say because, not only did she start off nice, she had beautiful handwriting, and she had even sprayed some fruity fragrance on the letter. It was the same scent she had worn at the ball. She had smelled like something I could eat. Once I got back upstairs, I sat facing my window as I read the letter:

Hey, guys!

Thank you for the opportunity to work at Who's Who. It was really a great experience and also great exposure for Banks Enterprises. We really appreciated the royal treatment, even though, at times, it was a bit overwhelming. After six months of playing y'all's little games, it's a wrap; we're done. Game over. Yes, we are highly professional at what we do, but don't get it twisted because y'all know we're from the hood. We are not to be played with in any way whatsoever. We are very independent, and we definitely don't need y'all's money, so let's just get that clear. Not sure why y'all chose to play games anyway and not be upfront with us, but it is what it is. As of tonight, we are done. Our contracts were only for six months, and that expired tonight. We are no longer staying at the hotel; we had Stanley drive us home. It's time for us to spend time with our family and to try to get our lives back to being a little normal. We are very grateful, and we really appreciate everything you guys have done for us. This was an experience that we will never forget. Our lives have changed because of you both, and we wish you all the best.

Love,
B.B. and J.B.

Wow! She was something else. It was that sophisticated, sweet but feisty attitude she had that I loved about her. She was right, though. I had taken way too long to introduce myself, and now she was saying it was over, but nothing was ever over with me. She'd see one day.

CHAPTER 6

Mysteries Unfold

As Jacelyn and I tried to get things back to normal, we woke up to that beautiful smell of home-cooked breakfast. My mom was throwing down in the kitchen. She made scrambled eggs, cheesy grits, sausage, bacon, hash browns, French toast, pancakes, and biscuits. Orange juice was on the side. You could tell she had missed us because she had done it up. It was the best "welcome home" breakfast we could have ever dreamed of.

After breakfast, Jacelyn and I sat and talked a little bit. We talked about the letter and what the guys' reactions might have been. As for me, what was done was done.

Jacelyn said, "See, you should have let me write the letter. You wanna go and be all nice about it. I would have let them have it, B."

We laughed.

"See, J, that's clearly the difference between you and me. You never let someone have it enough to see that they hurt you. Besides, they really didn't do anything but give us the best six months we could have possibly asked for. We just didn't have the privilege of sharing it with them. Plus, we still have a business to run, and you never want to create bad blood, especially when you don't really know who's who. Anyway, that's enough about them. As of right now, we're getting back to what we know best, and that's shopping."

We called #28 to take us to Jamaica Avenue for some sneaker therapy. No matter what was going on, our feet stayed happy. Number Twenty-Eight said he would meet us in the building parking lot in about forty-five minutes, so we quickly got dressed and headed to the parking lot. We wanted to go to the parking lot a few minutes early, just to see who we would bump into. Remember, it had been six months since we'd been home, and we hadn't seen any of the homies in a while.

It was the end of June, almost summer, and it was really nice outside, so everyone was out and about, roaming the streets. We walked through the lobby and out to the parking lot to a great surprise. There were two fine-ass guys standing next to their cars. Jacelyn and I looked at each other like "Nah, it can't be them." They'd waited six months for us to walk out of their lives, for them to walk right back into ours. Hmmm… who would've ever thought this was how things would play out? They both were fresh to death, looking like a million bucks. They both had on white Gucci T-shirts, Gucci jeans, and white Gucci sneakers. They were wearing Gucci down to the socks. They both had diamonds in their ears, a Gucci link chain, and Gucci watches. The only difference was C.M. had a diamond cross on his chain, and M.S. had a lion on his. I could instantly tell who was who buy their height and build. I remembered from the dance with them. They walked toward us. C.M. stopped directly in front of me and introduced himself. With a smile, he said, "Hey, Miss Bridgette. I'm Chase Morgan. It's a pleasure to finally meet you."

My heart stopped, skipped a few beats, and started pumping again. I was so nervous about meeting him for the first time that my stomach had more butterflies than the night at the dance. I was so trying to keep it together.

M.S. introduced himself to Jacelyn as Michael Starks. Then they introduced themselves to us.

Chase said, "I heard y'all wanted to go get some sneakers off the Avenue. Well, let's go."

"Now tell me, Mr. Morgan, why should I go with you? I don't even know you."

"Well, beautiful, I know you, and I know you know of me. I'm not gonna hurt you. Trust me."

"Trust you? Wow! Now you're asking for a bit too much."

"You know what, beautiful? Let me start over by saying, 'I'm sorry.' I didn't mean to hurt you. Please come with me. I would like to make it up to you."

Ignoring him, I tried to step to the side to walk off, but he quickly stopped me in my tracks.

"Beautiful, I know 'sorry' may not be enough to convince you to come with me. Please give me a chance to show you who I really am."

"Chase, I don't need you or anyone else to convince me to do anything. I do what I want, when I want."

"I can see that, so let's go because I know you really want to come with me."

"And how do you know that?"

"I just know, beautiful. I can see it in your eyes and by the smile you have on your face."

"What smile? Do you see me smiling?"

"Yup, on the inside. I can see right into you."

I just shook my head and smiled because I was smiling on the inside. I just didn't want him to see how happy I really was, but I guess that hadn't worked.

"See, there it is. A smile. I told you I could see right into you. Now you can stop acting all tough, so we can go."

Chase opened the passenger door to his white Mercedes Benz coupe with huge BBS gold rims and signaled for me to get in. All you could hear was the clear crisp sound of Jaheim's "Could it Be" in the background. He closed the door behind me after I hopped in.

Jacelyn and Mr. Starks had also exchanged words, but once she saw me give in to Chase, she was ready to see what was next, so she followed suit. Michael opened the door to his white Lexus coupe with BBS gold rims for Jacelyn. After they got in, we all pulled off.

41

As we drove to Jamaica Avenue, both Chase and I were very quiet. I was still in shock, and the butterflies were still flying around in my stomach. I couldn't help but stare at him. He was so fine; his skin was so smooth that he just didn't look real. He had chocolate-brown skin with a goatee that was trimmed to perfection. He had big brown eyes with thick pretty eyelashes. His arms were huge, and you could see his chest and abs right through that white T-shirt. His hands were big enough to cuff both my butt cheeks perfectly. His dark hair was cut in a low Caesar. His lips were so chocolate and juicy-looking. I could have just kissed him right then and right there. He looked like his waist could've been between thirty-four to thirty-six inches. Okay, so his shoe size was maybe like a ten and a half or an eleven, and you know what they say about guys and their feet (smile). I was guessing I'd find out soon enough what the exact measurements really were. He had to be around 5'10" or 5'11". Chase reminded me of Big Daddy Kane without the flattop, and I just loved me some Big Daddy Kane. Michael was a little shorter than Chase, but he wasn't as big. He was fine as hell, too. He reminded me of the rapper AZ. He was light-skinned. His arms and abs were cut up, too. He had a low-cut Caesar, a cute little goatee and light brown eyes with dark thick eyebrows. I could tell he wore between a thirty-two and a thirty-four inch waist. He wasn't your typical light-skinned guy. He wasn't conceited at all; he was actually really cool. There was one thing I definitely knew about that day for sure. It was going to be a good day.

We pulled up on top of the Coliseum roof and parked the cars. Chase said, "This is not where I would've liked to take you shopping, but it's where you wanted to go, and because I want to make you happy, here we are."

I just smiled. I don't think I'd ever smiled like that before in my life. We arrived at the one and only spot inside the Coliseum where we bought our sneakers from. My boy Mikey (he was a Spanish dude) always gave us the discounts. On top of the sneakers, Mikey always threw in T-shirts, socks, and hats. Whatever he had that matched our sneakers, he threw them in. His discounts were always a blessing, and he always looked out for Jacelyn and me. Now that we had even more money, we really didn't care. We just wanted to shop and give Mikey even more business for always looking out for us. Jacelyn and I each got four pairs of sneakers. Chase and Michael got two pairs each. Jacelyn and I didn't pay for anything. Chase paid for mine and his, and Michael paid for Jacelyn's and his. Not paying any attention to the bill since Mikey said he would hook us up, Chase and Michael dropped like seven hundred dollars each and told him to keep the change. I really appreciated Chase for buying my sneakers, even though I had my own money.

As we walked back to the car, with a smile, I said, "Chase, we never come to the Avenue without getting Margarita's Pizza."

He said, "Well, miss, this will be one time you don't get any."

Jacelyn yelled, "I heard that Chase," and we all busted out laughing.

Chase said, "Well, we have something planned for today, something way better than pizza. Y'all will see soon enough," and he winked at me.

These guys were straight hood. They went from a two-piece suit to sneakers and jeans within the blink of an eye. I was so hyped. I couldn't wait to see what events they had planned.

We got back in the car, paid the parking, and headed off the Avenue. Now Chase and I began to really talk for the first time. I started the conversation by saying, "Since you know all about me, Chase, tell me a little about you."

He said, "For one thing, when you're with me, you never have to pay for anything. Never pull out money to pay when you're with me. I always got you, no matter what. And please make no mistakes when it comes to my feelings for you. I want to explain how I felt this morning after reading the letter you gave Stanley.

"For hours, I tried to wrap my head around the thought of losing you. I knew, for a fact that, I couldn't let that happen. I couldn't picture myself living without you. I realized that I'd waited too long to introduce myself, and for that, I'm sorry. After reading your letter over for the third time, I wasn't about to let you go that easy. I knew I had to do whatever it took to get you back and to make things right. I'd waited too long, and I care too much to let you go. You said, 'Game over,' but nothing's ever over with me. You'll see, we're just getting started."

I just sat back and let him explain. That was probably the first time I'd really paid close attention to anyone's words. By really listening, I realized just how he was feeling, and he seemed very sincere. I remember asking Jacelyn what they might've been feeling, but never had I thought he couldn't live without me, had to get me back, or that he had to make things right. I was speechless and in love. I asked myself, Who is this guy? I couldn't wait to find out all about him. It was nice to see that he had actually taken the time to find the perfect words to express the way he was feeling.

We were driving along, listening to music, when we finally reached Queens Center Mall. He said, "We just have to grab a few things out of here really quick before we head out."

We parked the car and headed into the mall. We reached the first store he wanted to go to, which was Victoria's Secret. He said, "You're gonna need a few things from here, like underwear, pajamas, and socks."

Now I knew Michael was telling Jacelyn the same thing because they were right behind us. I grabbed a bra and panty set and attempted to go and get pajamas, but Chase stopped me. He said, "You're gonna need more than one set. Let me help you." It was so nice to watch him walk around the store and pick out underwear for me. He ended up spending about seven-hundred dollars on my underwear. Michael was in there picking up everything he put his hands on. We just couldn't stop laughing. He was a straight fool.

I asked, "Michael, did you get enough?"

He said, "Nope," and laughed.

After we were done, we left that store and went to Macy's. Chase said, "We should be able to get everything else we need from here." He picked out two sweat suits, jeans, two pairs of shorts, and three shirts for himself. I picked out two sweat suits, a pair of jeans, three shirts, two dresses, two cocktail dresses, heels, and flat sandals because we never knew where they were taking us or what we were going to do. We then went to the bedding and bath department and picked up beach towels. Next up was the luggage department. We got a suitcase and a tote bag for both Jacelyn and me. And then we checked out and headed back to the car.

I hadn't paid attention earlier, but he had a suitcase already packed and ready to go in the trunk. I said, "Somebody's packed and ready to go."

He said, "Yup."

At that moment, I just had to beg a little because I really wanted to know where we were going. "Please, Chase, tell me the surprise. Tell me where we're going."

He said, "Chill out. You will see soon enough."

"I hope it involves food because I'm hungry."

He said, "You're disturbing my plans, but we can go grab a bite to eat at that Red Lobster over there."

"Thank you, Chase. I would have been okay with my pizza, but you said no."

"For some reason, beautiful, I knew you were going to mention that pizza again."

We went inside the restaurant, and we all sat at the same table. We ordered drinks, appetizers, and dinner. We started talking about their cars and the color choice. Now we knew for sure why Who's Who's colors were gold and white. Chase said, "My favorite color is white, and Michael's is gold. I can't walk around wearing white clothes every day, so why not have everything else around me white. So let me think…hmmm…what else do y'all need to know? I'm twenty-four years old, and so is Mike. We both grew up in the streets and started off selling drugs for other people. When I first started selling drugs, I didn't really make any money. I made more money on my summer job than on the corner. After working for only one week, I figured out that everybody who started out only made enough money for a pair of Levi's, a sweat shirt, and a pair of sneakers, so I was done with the streets. I definitely wasn't about to be standing out there risking my life for one hundred and fifty dollars a week.

"Mike and I became cool in high school. We hung out together. We even worked on the same side jobs together. One day, we put our money together and started our own hustle. We have never been to jail, and that's because we're smarter than most. After a while, we both decided that we needed to do something bigger and better with our lives to become the man, so fresh out of high school, we decided to go to college to study business management and accounting. It was better for us to learn how to manage our own money than to let someone else do it for us. We met a lot of corporate people while in college by hanging out with the richest of the rich after school and on the weekends. We were able to connect with a stock broker that put us on to the stock exchange on Wall Street. Once we graduated college, we started trading stocks on Wall Street full time. After a year of trading, we'd made half a million dollars each. We used that cash to invest in our own firm, and after that, we opened Who's Who. Long story short, we wanted out of the hood and would do whatever it took to get out and stay out. You know, just like y'all. Y'all some straight hustlers."

They were basically incognito, business suits by day and Timbs and jeans by night. Chase was the more serious one, just like me. Michael was the more playful one, just like Jacelyn. You could tell Michael wasn't the business type at all. They were the male versions of Jacelyn and me. They were so similar to us that it wasn't funny. Looking across the table at Jacelyn and Michael, they seemed to have hit it off and made the perfect couple. Thank God, she has someone to keep her company now, I thought, so she can stay off my damn nerves. Jacelyn and I didn't always see eye to eye on things, especially when it came to the business side of things, so she did tend to get on my nerves from time to time.

Chase and I had this instant love connection. He was very attentive to my needs, always asking if I was okay and if I needed anything. I was curious, so you know I had to be the one to ask the question. "How long have y'all been following us, and why?"

He said, "I will tell you everything, just not here." Then he asked me if I wanted anything else to eat or if I was ready to go. I was ready to go to see what was next, so I quickly said, "No, thank you. I'm ready to go."

The waiter came. Chase paid the bill, and we left.

***

It was now about seven in the evening when we got back in the car, and he turned on the radio. As the music played, the conversation began. He said, "Did you like the performance with Jose and Miguel at the masquerade ball? And did you enjoy dancing with me?"

"I really enjoyed myself, but last night was really crazy. I was very surprised and moved by it all, but the only thing I didn't like was the ending."

"I'm sorry, beautiful. I didn't mean to disappoint you, but that's the reason why it's called a masquerade ball. Everyone wears a mask to remain a mystery."

"I'm not talking about the mask. I'm talking about you disappearing on me like you did."

"Once again, I know I hurt you, and I'm so sorry. You know you're very beautiful, even when you're mad. I'm really enjoying spending this time with you today and finally getting to know you."

"I am, too, Chase, and by the way, I think you're fine as hell."

We both smiled. Now shifting focus on where we were going, I saw we were headed toward the Verrazano Bridge with Michael and Jacelyn right behind us. As he was driving, I looked over at him and thought, How did I get so lucky? Where did he come from?

"Chase?"

"Yes, beautiful?"

"Before I forget, thank you for everything. Thank you because I'm really having a great time with you."

"The night is not over yet, though, so sit tight."

"I need to call home to tell my mom we're okay, so she's not too worried," I said as I picked up my cell phone and called my mom.

When my mom answered, I tried to let her know, but she said she already knew. She said, "I've talked to Chase already, and he told me y'all were going away for a few days and not to worry."

I said, "Wow! He did, Ma?"

She said, "Yes, enjoy your time away and call me tomorrow to let me know y'all are safe. I will be praying for y'all. I love you and tell your sister I love her, too."

"Okay, Ma, I will. I love you, too. Good night."

And we hung up.

"So you thought of everything?" I asked Chase as I put my cell phone up.

"See, I told you not to worry about anything, beautiful. I have everything under control."

All I could do was smile and say "thank you." A moment later, Chase opened the glove compartment and handed an envelope to me. I looked inside to find test results in his name. I asked, "What is this, Chase?"

"It's my physical. I had a complete checkup. I want you to know that I'm free and clean of everything. I have no STDs or STIs, and I take good care of myself. Even if nothing happens between us, I still want you to know that I'm good. I know, for a fact, that you're good as well, Bridgette. I already saw your physical, the one you had to take to work at the club. I was your employer, remember?"

I couldn't help but think, This can't be real. Wow! Who is this guy, seriously?

"Out of curiosity, Chase, I have to ask, did Michael take a physical as well?"

"Well, that's really none of my business, but, yes, he did. He's probably giving his results to your sister right about now."

"Chase, I'm just looking out for my sister. That's all."

"I can understand that, beautiful, and I respect that."

I could really tell he had a lot of respect for me and for my well-being. I was amazed because who does that?

"Chase, I really appreciate you for not only getting the physical but for sharing your results with me as well. Most men wouldn't do that. They don't even like going to the doctor, let alone sharing their results."

"You'll learn, soon enough, that I'm not like most men. Just like you, beautiful, I'm one of a kind."

I smiled, laid back, and listened to the music that he was bumping between Hot 97 and 105.1. I was really enjoying the ride. It was so smooth, even through the crazy Friday night traffic. I looked out the passenger window and thought about everything that had happened so far. While I was daydreaming about Chase, I soon fell asleep.

CHAPTER 7

Spincity

Chase grabbed my hand and said, "Wake up, beautiful. We're here." I stretched and checked to make sure I wasn't drooling. I looked up to see that we were at the Resorts Hotel and Casino in Atlantic City. All the lights were amazing. I had to blink a few times to wake up to really see everything. I asked him, "Chase, where did this blanket and pillow come from?"

He said, "I stopped at Caldors and got them for you while you were sleeping. I had the air-conditioning on, and I didn't want you to be cold."

"Aww, Chase, that was so sweet of you. All I remember was seeing the Verrazano Bridge. I looked over at you, started thinking, and next thing I knew, I was sleeping. I had a dream about you."

He said, "Oh, yeah? Well, you never have to dream about me again because you have the real me right here in the flesh, and I'm about to make all your dreams come true."

I smiled. I couldn't even describe the feeling I had right then. Chase got out the car to get the luggage and the bags from shopping earlier. I quickly checked in the mirror to really make sure I wasn't drooling or anything. I checked my hair and grabbed a piece of gum out my bag before I got out the car. The bellhop put our things on a cart, and we went inside to check in.

Lo and behold, we were on the top floor, in the presidential suite. Oh, my God! The place was so huge, and the bathroom was as big as a bedroom. There were marble floors and counters with a sunken Jacuzzi tub. It had a kitchen, living room, and a bar with a marble countertop. There were two bedrooms. One room had a king-size bed, and the other had a double queen. The view was amazing. The living room had a view of the Atlantic City strip and stores. The bedrooms had a view of the ocean. There were dozens of white roses dipped in gold shimmer all over the entire penthouse. I felt like I was about to play the rose game again and pick my prize.

After we settled in, he took the room with the double queen and gave me the one with the king. I asked him why Jacelyn and Michael weren't staying with us because there was clearly enough room. He said, "I respect you too much to let another man, even me, see you in your comfort zone. That's why I'm choosing to sleep in the room with the double bed."

I just sat there, thinking, Seriously, where did he come from? He picked out one rose from a vase, walked over to me, and kneeled in front of me. He handed the rose to me and asked, "Are you okay, beautiful?"

"Yes, Chase, I'm okay."

He said, "Are you hungry? Can I get you anything?"

"No, I'm okay."

He said, "Do you want to go out somewhere to eat?"

"No, no, thank you."

"So what I'm going to do is order some room service since you don't wanna go out to eat. What do you wanna to do tonight then?"

Mind you, it was about midnight.

"To be honest, Chase, I just wanna sleep."

He said, "Sleep is good. I'll do whatever you want to do. I don't get much sleep, so that will be good for me, too. There's a lot of things I don't get a chance to do, but now that I'm with you, I'll have a chance to do them."

A little while later, there was a knock at the door. It was room service. He had ordered hot wings and fries. He only ate a little bit, and he made me eat a little bit, too. Then we took a shower. I asked him to stay in the room with me, and he agreed. Within minutes of us laying down, I fell asleep in his arms. He didn't make not one move on me. He didn't kiss me or touch me. Well, not that I know of. He just let me sleep. It was the best sleep I'd had in a long time. Jacelyn and I had been working so hard, going from one event to the next without a break in between. Most days, by the time we laid down, it was time to get back up and do it all over again, so good sleep didn't happen too often.

***

When the next morning came, I looked up and saw he was sitting on the side of the bed, watching me sleep. He'd ordered breakfast for me, an omelet and orange juice. The platter had one purple rose dipped in purple shimmer in a skinny glass vase. I knew the rose had a meaning to it, but I wasn't ready to ask. I just enjoyed the moment and decided I'd wait for him to tell me.

"I see you're up very early, Chase."

"Yeah, I had to do my morning workout."

"So did Michael go with you?"

"Yeah, he did. We had to go over a few things and check up on the businesses."

"So does Michael go everywhere with you?"

With a nod, he said, "Yes, Mike and I are joined at the hip during the day, but at night, we go to our separate quarters. We will meet up with him and your sister a little later today, though."

He then excused himself and went to the bathroom. After he'd left, I noticed a scroll letter wrapped around the stem of the rose. I unrolled it and read:

The color purple means royalty, and that's how I'm going to treat you every day because you are royalty to me, beautiful.

Love, C.M.

A tear rolled down my left cheek. I had never had anyone speak about me or to me like this before, especially someone that I didn't even know all that well. He surely knew a lot about me, to make him feel this way.

When he came out of the bathroom, he sat beside me on the bed. He wiped away my tear with the back of his finger and said, "Don't cry."

I said, "But it was so beautiful."

"I know, just like you. And by the way, that's your new name… Beautiful. Now get dressed. I want to show you off to a few people."

"Oh, really?"

"Yup, and wear something comfortable. Today is going to be a relaxed day, full of fun and surprises."

"Comfortable? Then, why are you wearing Gucci from head to toe?"

With a little laugh, he said, "Yeah, you do have a point. I'm gonna change. I'm going to wear that outfit and my white and blue Bo Jacksons that I picked up yesterday."

After about forty minutes, we were both dressed and ready to go.

***

We got on the elevator, and the doorman said, "Good morning, Mr. Morgan."

"I keep telling you to call me Chase, Tommie."

He said, "Yes, Mr. Morgan, I know."

We all busted out laughing.

"Tommie, meet my lady, Beautiful."

"Good morning, Miss Beautiful. It's a pleasure to meet you."

"Likewise, Tommie. Enjoy your day."

"You, as well, Miss Beautiful."

And we got off the elevator. Chase held my hand as we walked through the halls of the hotel. All the staff greeted him as Mr. Morgan, and he said "what's up" playfully to all of them. He knew everyone by name. We went over to the roulette table, and he said, "What's up, Scott?"

"Hey, Chase! I'm good. No complaints here. So I see you brought company, and you never bring anyone with you, so she must be special."

Chase nodded and said, "Special indeed. Meet my lady, Beautiful."

Scott said, "It's a pleasure to meet you, Miss Beautiful," and winked at me.

Now it was about ten o'clock in the morning, and we were the only two at the table, so Chase showed me how to play. He said, "You're my good luck charm today. Even if I don't win, I'm already a winner."

I picked five numbers and put one hundred dollars on each, and red-twenty-one won $200. I put $500 on twenty-one again. Scott spun the wheel, and it landed on twenty-one again. I won $1000. Now I was up to $1200. I put $200 on red-seven. He spun again, and red-seven won. I was now up to $1400, and I couldn't help but ask, "Chase, is this rigged?"

He said, "No, it's not. They have cameras everywhere. You're just lucky."

"Okay, then." It wasn't my money, so I put the entire $1400 on red-twenty-one. Scott spun the wheel and red-twenty-one won, doubling my money. "Okay. Time to go, Chase, because I'm not the one for gambling my winnings back."

We walked out to the gift shop, and he told me to use the money to buy my mom a nice gift. I ended up buying her a dress, along with the shoes and the bag to match. I bought Mr. Bill a blazer jacket, a shirt, a tie, and a handkerchief. What's a gift without a keychain from Atlantic City? So I got two keychains and two coffee mugs for them, and the store manager had everything sent up to the room.

Chase was ready for lunch, so we went and met up with Michael and Jacelyn at an all-you-can-eat buffet in the hotel called Sultan's Feast. Chase was tired of regular food. He said he wanted a variety, and that was exactly what we got. The spread of seafood was so long that it was just too much to choose from. We all sat down to eat at the same table. Chase and Michael were talking about the events for the night. They were speaking in code, so we had no idea what the plans were. Jacelyn and I talked about what she and Mike had done when they went out the night before. She said they went to the club, then got something to eat, and got back to the hotel at about three in the morning.

"So tell me what happened when y'all got back," I said.

"Well, B, it was a night to remember. We got up to the room, and he—"

"And he what, Jacelyn?"

Chase interrupted, saying, "It's time to go, ladies," so we quickly left the restaurant and headed outside to the boardwalk. While we were walking, Jacelyn looked at me, smiled, and whispered, "I'll tell you later." The look on her face let me know she had a good story to tell, and I couldn't wait to hear it.

We were now on the boardwalk at a carnival that was practically in the ocean. So this is what Chase meant by a day of fun, I thought. We went on just about every ride. We went on the bumper cars about three times. We played games and won a few stuffed animals. The best part of the carnival was the Zeppoles. They reminded me of my grandma. I hadn't had this much fun since I was a little girl. Chase, always the gentleman, whispered, "It's getting late, and we have dinner reservations, so let's head back to the room to change."

As we headed back up in the elevator, Chase looked at me and smiled.

"Why are you smiling so hard?" I asked.

He said, "Because you make me smile."

When we got back to the penthouse, I walked into the room and found a dress, shoes, and jewelry to match laid out on the bed.

"Chase, this is so beautiful. You're spoiling me. Thank you so much." I ran over and hugged him.

He said, "We're running late. I'm gonna shower in the other room while you get ready in here."

"Okay, Chase. I won't take long, I promise."

I showered, put on my Victoria's Secret underwear that we'd bought the day before, and a red satin robe to match. I was so exhausted from the long day, and I needed help getting into my dress, so I just waited in the living room until he finished getting dressed. It was now about seven. The sun had gone down, so I opened the curtains to see the view of the Strip and all the lights. He came out into the living room, looking as handsome as ever, in a black suit with a black shirt. The first two buttons of his shirt were open.

"What's wrong, Beautiful? I see you're not dressed yet."

"Yeah, I know. I was waiting for you to help me."

I was still facing toward the window, so he walked over, stood behind me, and wrapped his arms around me. He said, "This is a nice view right here."

'Yeah, I know, right? All the lights are really breath-taking."

"I wasn't talking about the strip view or the lights. I was talking about you."

I turned around to face him to say thank you, but no words came out. He looked into my eyes, moved my hair from my face, and said, "This is a perfect moment."

"Perfect for what, Chase?"

He said, "This."

And he softly kissed my lips.

I did not stop him at all. I put my arms around his neck and kissed him right back. My robe came open, and he gently felt his way around as he continued to kiss me. This was our first kiss, and it was so passionate and well worth the wait. When we finally stopped and came up for some air, he kissed the top of my forehead and said, "Let's get you into this dress before we miss dinner altogether."

I was in relax mode, not wanting to go anywhere anyway, but he was right. We had reservations, and he had planned the entire day just for me, so why spoil it now? I just wanted to go with the flow and enjoy my night with whatever he had planned. Now that we'd had our first kiss, it had kind of broken the ice, and I knew the night wasn't over just yet. After he helped me into my dress, we looked at our reflections in the mirror for the first time and smiled. We both said at the same time, "Damn! We look good," and laughed.

As we headed down to get the car, I thought he was going to drive, so I was anticipating sliding into the passenger's seat, but when we got to where I thought the car would be, I saw that there was a limo waiting. The driver was standing at the door waiting for us. After we got in, Chase poured each of us a glass of champagne and made a toast. "Cheers to us, the perfect couple." Chase had already claimed he was my man and

I was his girl without even asking me. It didn't matter because nothing about him felt wrong. I liked him for the man he was and not for what he had because I had my own money, and I could very well take care of myself. I knew that this was meant to be just by the way we felt for each other. There was definitely something special going on between us. The fact that we started off wanting to know each other and be with each other without being with each other was weird but so true. I was slowly falling in love with Chase, and I knew he was already in love with me.

While riding along the strip in the limo, I was in deep thought about the man sitting next to me. Could he really be this perfect? But if he was not, I didn't even care because he was perfect for me. At this point, I was sure the good in him would outweigh the bad. I just had to wait and see. We pulled up at the same time as Michael and Jacelyn to Caesar's Palace, which was where we had dinner reservations. The dining room was for black card members only. Every table was set with black linen and white candles all around. There were also white rose petals flowing around the candles. The guys had preordered our meals, so as soon as we sat down, we were served. They started us off with glasses of water, champagne, lobster risotto, and a salad. For the entrée, we had honey-glazed salmon with spinach and rice. For dessert, we had strawberry cheesecake and vanilla ice cream topped with fresh strawberries and whipped cream. Everything was so perfect, but I wished we were back at the hotel, eating pizza, watching movies, and relaxing. I loved it all, and I was very grateful, but it was really the simple things that I loved the most. As long as he was willing to do nice things for me, I was not about to stop him, but as soon as he asked me what I wanted to do, it was definitely going to be as simple as pizza and a movie at home. We were always on the go, so a day at home was much needed.

We laughed at Mike's jokes throughout our whole meal. If there was one thing I knew, it was that there was never going to be a dull moment being around the two of them. Mike was joking about how he could use a Big Mac, large fries, and a large milkshake. We fell out as people were looking at us, wondering who we were. I knew they were wondering, Who are those people? They are so loud and crazy. But we were just having fun and enjoying each other's company. Mike finally said, "All right, all right. That's enough joking. This is our last night in Atlantic City, so let's go make the best of it."

We headed back to the limos, and Michael and Jacelyn went their way, while Chase and I headed back to the hotel to change.

***

When we got back to the hotel, Chase got out of the limo first. Because it had gotten cool out, he took off his suit jacket and put it around my shoulders when I got out. He was always such a gentleman. I just wondered how long he would be this nice. Well, for now, I was happy to enjoy him just as he was. The night was still young, so who knew what we'd get into, and it was our last night here, too, so I knew it had to be memorable.

CHAPTER 8

Butta Love

As we headed back to the room, we got on the elevator alone. At this time of the night, there were no attendants controlling things on the elevator, so Chase swiped the card to go up to the penthouse. Then, he looked at me and said, "You look really good tonight, Beautiful."

"Thank you, Chase, so do you." I stepped in front of him, wrapped my arms around him, looked into his eyes, and I thanked him again for a perfect day.

He said, "You're welcome," and kissed me.

The elevator dinged, and the doors opened, but he continued kissing me and let the doors close back, but it didn't move. He stopped kissing me, pushed the button for the doors to reopen, smiled, and said, "Let's go before we start something in here that we can't finish in here."

When we got inside the penthouse, I kicked my shoes off at the door and asked if he could help me with my dress.

"Sure. Just give me a minute." He went into my bathroom for a minute and said, "Come with me. Close your eyes. Please trust me."

One thing he didn't have to worry about was me trusting him because, at that point, I trusted him with my life, so I blindly followed him as he led me, with my eyes closed, into the bathroom. He stood there and looked at me for a minute. Then he took my hair and put it up in a ponytail. It was so cute that he even knew what to do. I just smiled. He kissed my forehead and said, "Open your eyes."

After I did as he said, I saw that I was standing in paradise. A bubble bath had been drawn and white candles were everywhere. I was standing on white rose petals dusted in purple shimmer. There was champagne and strawberries sitting on a gold platter. He'd pulled out all the stops to make me feel loved and appreciated. I threw my arms around his neck and started to kiss him, and that was when he slowly unzipped my dress. I unbuttoned his shirt. Very soon, I was standing in my red Victoria's Secret underwear, and he was down to his black silk Calvin Klein boxers. Oh, my God! His chest and arms were so cut up. I ran my hands all over his chest and arms, feeling every curve and every cut. He stepped into the tub and reached out for my hand to help me in. The water felt and smelled so good. It was so soothing and relaxing. Chase was such a gentleman. He didn't fully undress me or himself, just to keep me from being uncomfortable.

As I sat between his legs with my back resting against his chest, he used a sponge to wash my arms and the top of my breasts. Romance was in the air for sure, and he finally started to really open up to me. He said, "Although you don't know a lot about me, I've been getting to know you for a year now. I've even been making sure you made it home safe every day. I had #28 looking out for you for the first six months until I was able to have you work at the club and stay at the hotel. I know most of the things you like and dislike. I know your favorite color is white. You love strawberries. Your favorite food is seafood, but you really love pizza, too. You don't like crowds, but you tolerate them because of work. I love everything about you, Beautiful. You're smart, loving, funny, ambitious, classy, professional, very independent, and a little hood at the right times." He laughed. "I knew you were mine on the day I saw you at an event you hosted at the water club. I went to every event you hosted after that, and I grew to like you more and more each time I got to see you. I loved to see you in work mode, doing your thang. You never let any guy talk to you at any event. You kept it classy and professional, and you always kept it moving."

"So why is it you never said anything to me, Chase?"

"Seeing how you always kept it moving, I knew I had to come correct. I had to grow into the guy you needed me to be. You deserve even more than I can offer you."

"I don't know why you would think that, Chase, because you're perfect for me, even without all the money and flashy lifestyle."

"Yeah, I know, but I was afraid of you running away because of my flashy lifestyle. I'm a good, quiet dude, but I'm far from perfect, Beautiful."

"Well, from what I see, Chase, you're not bad at all."

He said, "It's not what you see; it's what you don't see that might be a problem. I love spending time with you, though, Beautiful. You keep me grounded. You help me enjoy life more and focus on what's important. What's the point in having so much when you have nobody to share it with? Now I can share everything since I've found my one and only true love."

At that moment, he opened the clasp of my bra and slowly slid it down my arms. Then, he threw it onto the floor. I turned to face him and put my arms around him. Next, he slid down my underwear, and then he removed his. I wrapped my legs around his waist, and I gave him a nice, passionate, juicy, and unforgettable kiss. The water was still warm, but our body temperatures were rising by the minute. He took the sponge and washed my body as I washed his in return. After about ten more minutes of sitting in the tub, he said, "Let's get out now before we get all wrinkled."

As he slowly got out the tub, I got to see every inch of his body as the water rolled down his chocolate frame. He looked like a model in a hot beach commercial. He wrapped a towel around his waist, then opened one for me. As I stood up, he wrapped the towel around me, then took my hand to helped me out the tub. Next, he led me to the room.

To my surprise, the room had white roses all over the bed and candles all around the room. I didn't get a chance to see all of this before our bath because he had made me close my eyes when we walked through the room to the bathroom. He put on a track by the group Next called

"Butta Love," hit replay, and poured us some champagne. As I reached toward a chair to grab my robe, he said, "You're definitely not gonna need that." Standing tall, next to the bed and holding a bottle of lotion, he motioned for me to come lay down. He said, "Come. Let me rub some of this citrus lotion on you." He kneeled down at the end of the bed and slid me down near him. He started with my feet, then moved up to my calves, and by the time he had massaged his way up to my thighs, my legs were shaking. He didn't say one word. He just continued. He rolled me over and slowly massaged my cheeks, then moved up to my back. This was the best massage I'd ever had. I was so relaxed, and I had never felt as comfortable around anyone as I did this man at this moment. His touch was so gentle, so soft, and so smooth. He whispered, "Your skin is so soft and beautiful, like a baby's."

"Yeah, I know, Chase." I smiled. I rolled back over, and he massaged the front of my legs, then slowly moved up to my inner thighs. I took a few deep breaths in and slowly whispered his name when I exhaled. "Chaaase." Then another deep breath. "Chaaase." I was having an orgasm just from the touch of his hands massaging my inner thighs. I grabbed the pillow that was next to me and squeezed it tight. Then, he grabbed the pillow and tossed it to the side. He said, "What are you doing? Don't cover your face. I need to see every expression you make. I need to see that I'm pleasing you in every way." He then squeezed lotion all over my breasts and my stomach, then gently massaged it in nice and slow. I just laid there and enjoyed every minute. When he was done, I said, "Now it's your turn."

He said, "No, that was all for you, Beautiful. I wanted to make you feel like royalty, and that was my gift." He laid next to me, moved my hair off my face, and said, "I love you, Beautiful, and deep down, I know you love me, too. I want to be your first love, and I want for you to be my last. Watch. I'm going to make you my wife soon enough."

"Chase, I've had guys look at me and want to be with me, just because I'm pretty, for the things I have, or what they think I may have, but never for the person I am inside. I now know what true love feels like.

To have someone I can love, that truly loves me back for who I am, is an amazing feeling."

I didn't say "I love you" back, but deep down, I wanted to.

As we laid naked, starring eye to eye, we kissed each other very slowly, very passionately. We did not stop for air for one moment. He quickly flipped me, so I was on my back, and that was when the magic began. Everything he did was slow and passionate. He made sure I enjoyed every minute with him. In my mind, I was thinking that it was too soon to be sleeping with him, but my body couldn't resist him. He had me on cloud nine, and I was willing to stay on that cloud with him for as long as I possibly could. He did things to me that I never imagined could or would be done to me. The pleasure of love, the love of pleasure, and the pain of them both were all worth waiting six months to embrace. After a while, we stopped for a water break. Then we went back at it again till the crack of dawn. By then, we were exhausted, and I finally fell asleep in his arms.

***

We were awakened around ten in the morning by a knock at the door. It was room service. Chase had pre-ordered breakfast the day before.

"Good morning, handsome."

"Good morning, Beautiful."

"Breakfast is here. Are you hungry?"

"Yes, ma'am, I'm starving."

I rolled the cart into the room, then went to use the bathroom to wash my face and brush my teeth. He came right behind me to do the same. Now it was daylight, and the lights were on. I got to see it all as he stood naked at the toilet and aimed. Umm...he was a sight I didn't mind seeing first thing in the morning. For one, he was very blessed. His body was like a chocolate statue. He had to be packing, at least, nine inches. Lord, have mercy on me. I had to take my eyes off him in order to finish brushing my teeth. We both washed up and got back in bed to eat breakfast. He asked if I'd enjoyed myself last night, and of course, my answer was yes. "I didn't want the night to end."

He said, "It was okay for the night to end because we'll get to spend plenty more nights together, maybe not here but somewhere."

"You know you missed the gym this morning."

"No, I didn't. I had my work out all night till the break of dawn."

"Ugh, I really hate that the trip is over, Chase."

He said, "It's not over until we check out."

"Oh, really now, is that right?"

"Yeah, that's right, so let's make it count."

We were so exhausted that we just laid there and laughed.

He said, "Okay. Let's just sleep for a few more hours. I'm tired as hell, and you wore my ass out." Just the thought of his comment made me tired, so I laid on his chest, and we both fell right back to sleep.

***

We woke up around one o'clock in the afternoon. He kissed me on my forehead and said, "We have to get going." We got up and headed to the shower.

I said, "I will never forget the smell of this citrus body wash. It smells so good."

He said, "Don't worry. I'll get you some when we check out."

We stepped into the shower, and I washed him down from head to toe. I started with his head, neck, stomach, and back. As soon as I got down to his nine inches and legs, it hit me; I had to give him a name. I smiled up at him and said, "I just named him."

"Oh, really, Beautiful? And what's that?"

"Royal. That's what." I laughed as Royal started to grow from my touch, but I tried to ignore it as I continued washing Chase's legs. I stood up and said, "That's for my massage last night and for my royal treatment."

As the water showered down on both of us, he kissed me and said, "Thank you." He turned me, so my back was facing him, put my hands above my head, and placed them against the shower wall like he was about to search me. He, then, washed down my neck and my back. Lastly, he washed my butt cheeks in a playful circular motion. The shower glass fogged up, probably from my body temperature rising. He turned me around and put soap suds on my nose from the sponge and smiled, then wiped them off. He washed the front of my neck, shoulders, and breasts. As he kneeled down and continued to wash my stomach, he came face-to-face with my goodies, and as he moved down to my inner thighs, he laughed. He said, "Now I just named her."

"You're funny, Chase, so what's her name?"

"Royalty."

"Hmmm…I like that."

He finished washing down my legs and both of my feet. Then, he stood up and kissed me. One thing I did know was that he loved to kiss me, and I wasn't at all complaining because I loved to kiss him, too. He picked me up, wrapped my legs around him, and pressed my back against the shower wall. While kissing me, he smiled hard and said, "I think it's about time Royal met Royalty," and at that moment, the two slowly met to celebrate their new names. In minutes, we found ourselves lying on the shower floor with the water showering down on our naked bodies. He said, "I've waited a year for this, and I will remember every moment with you for the rest of my life. I love you, Beautiful, with everything in me."

"I love you, too, Chase, with everything you've put in me."

We both busted out laughing.

"This is why I love being around you, Beautiful. You always make me laugh. Let's really wash now. We gotta get out of here to try and beat the traffic."

We showered, got dressed, packed up, called the bellboy, and went down to check out. Chase gave the bellboy a hefty tip and told him he would see him on the next visit. He told the lady at the front desk he wanted a few bottles of the citrus lotion and body wash to go. She said, "Sure, Mr. Morgan." She called up to the spa and had them bring some down. In about ten minutes, they brought down two big bottles of each inside spa bags. She handed him the bags and said, "They are on the house, Mr. Morgan." She gave him the checkout receipt, and we left the hotel. His car was already waiting with our luggage inside. He had called Michael before we left the room to let him know it was time to check out, but Michael and Jacelyn were already waiting outside when we got there.

As Chase started to drive, I looked over and said, "Thanks again for a great *royal* weekend."

He looked over at me, smiled, and said, "So I see you like Royal."

"No, I don't like Royal. Royalty loves Royal."

That was when the laughing and joking began, and we were only twenty minutes into the ride. The next two hours were filled with jokes about our weekend. With all the laughter between us, I knew this was going to be a ride to remember. We were now headed for the New Jersey turnpike/Interstate-95 North, home sweet home. New York, here we come.

CHAPTER 9

Something New

Michael Starks

Being with someone like Jacelyn was definitely new for me. I'd always been with chicks that wanted my money and the fame that went along with it, but Jacelyn wasn't like them. Since I'd officially introduced myself to her, she hadn't asked me for anything. I knew she had her own money and could do for herself. That made her so much more interesting. She didn't need me, and that was a definite fact. She seemed to like riding for ya boi, though, because she had genuinely showed she cared, and I wanted to do nothing more than ride for her, too. Now that we'd made it to Atlantic City, I wasn't really sure what to do for the night because Chase and I had planned a day for the ladies for the next day. I figured, why not just go gamble a little? But we could always do that. Since I was always the one to clown around and joke a lot, I knew I had to show her another side of me, so I took her for a walk along the boardwalk and down on the sand near the water. I wanted to get to know who Jacelyn really was and for her to get to know the serious side of me. We walked and talked for about two hours. While we were walking, she gave me this look, and I just couldn't help it anymore. I had to kiss her. She smiled and kissed me right back. It was getting late, and we damn sure was tired of walking, so we headed back to the limo. On our way back, we spotted a snack truck, so we grabbed a few bags of chips for the ride. Once we got in the limo, I couldn't help but touch her. She was bad. She had this fire inside her that I couldn't explain. I just knew I wanted a little touch. We kissed and played around, but that was as far as it went. I didn't want her to think that all I wanted was to hit it, so I just chilled out and showed her the respect she deserved. We headed back to the room around three in the morning. We both were so tired that we fell asleep on the couch with our clothes on. For once in my life, I could say I had been a total gentleman.

***

The next day was cool. By the time we woke up and got dressed, it was time to meet Chase and Bridgette for lunch. After lunch, Chase and I took Jacelyn and Bridgette out for some fun at the carnival. We sat and ate a nice little dinner. Then it was time to leave. I was happy to leave after that nasty-ass dinner. I mean, it was definitely food for the birds. The lobster risotto was supposed to be like some kind of lobster and rice, but the shit was more like lobster oatmeal, and the salad was like any other salad from Red Lobsters. The honey-glazed salmon was dry as hell and the rest of the food…I don't even remember the shit. It was still pretty early, so going to sleep or chilling back in the room wasn't an option. I wanted to party with Jacelyn and show her a good time in Atlantic City, so I took her to a club not too far from the hotel. We had a few laughs, a few drinks, and danced a bit. She was cool with it all. She didn't complain at all like most dumb-ass females would have been, saying "I'm tired," "My feet hurt," or "Are you ready to go?" Nope, not her. She enjoyed herself all night. I ain't gonna lie, though. At first, I was a little scared to be around her because she was one tough cookie. She was intimidating, but she was sweet as well. After being around her for these few days, I got to see the real Jacelyn, so it was only right to show her the real me and see if she would be willing to rock with me or not.

So far, so good. We both may have had a few too many drinks because that night we ended up having sex in the back of the limo. I may have been a little drunk, but I remembered everything that happened. She was everything and then some. I described her as hood sexy, professional, independent, funny, and classy, and she had the goody goods, so she was definitely a keeper. I was not sure what love felt like because I was not into all of that, and I'd never been in a situation where I had to really love someone other than myself, but I really thought Jacelyn would be the one to change all that. She could really teach me a few things about love. I knew, for a fact, that I liked her a lot, and I didn't see either of us going anywhere anytime soon. I could honestly say I'd had a lot of fun with her on this trip. I was sad the weekend was over. I knew Chase would be calling soon, reminding us about our checkout time.

***

Later that morning, me and Jacelyn were both starving because we'd drunk more than we'd actually eaten the night before. I called room service and ordered practically everything I could off the breakfast menu. We shared our first breakfast in bed, which was cool. I could really get used to this other side of me. I just had to stop playing around so much and really get serious if I wanted to keep her, though.

In the meantime, it was time to go. Time to check out and hit the parkway. As Chase and Bridgette headed to the car, all I could do was say to myself, I hope they'd had as much fun on this trip as me and Jacelyn had. I was going back to New York a happy man, looking forward to whatever came next, including love, which was something new for me.

CHAPTER 10

Back to the NYC Grind

Back home to reality.

"I hate being back here, Chase, after the weekend we just had."

"I know, but I'm going to go take care of some things to fix all your feelings right now, Beautiful."

Not really paying him any attention, I just said, "Okay."

He came around to the passenger side of the car, opened my door, and grabbed my bags from the trunk. Then, he kissed me and said, "I'll call you later."

As Jacelyn and I walked inside the building, people stared at us, trying to figure out who Chase and Mike were. They would never figure it out because they surely were not from around here. Thank God. When we got in the house, my mom said, "You're just in time for dinner but very late for church. Don't miss next Sunday."

She had made collard greens with smoked turkey wings, five cheese mac and cheese, crispy fried chicken, oh, and the yams were dripping with vanilla, brown sugar and cinnamon. You could smell them as soon as you hit the door. She'd also made cornbread that was so moist and fluffy. It was like a super moist cake. The different smells of all the foods filled the air, making it feel like Thanksgiving. It felt so good to eat my mom's cooking after a weekend of store-bought and restaurant food.

It was only around seven o'clock, so it was way too early in my hood to be going to sleep, so Jacelyn and I took a walk to the store. We sat on the yellow pole for a while and talked to our homeboys Cam and Dennis. The first thing they asked was, "Who are those two dues y'all be rolling with now? We see y'all. Don't think we don't be watching y'all."

"Guys we work with. Why?"

Dennis said, "Work with?"

Cam said, "Y'all work with them?"

"Yeah," I said.

"Like we're supposed to believe that?" Cam asked.

"Wow! What kind of work do they do?" Dennis said.

"Why, Dennis? Nothing you would be interested in," Jacelyn said.

"Well, I'm gonna tell y'all both like this. I better not see them around these streets no more or else," Cam threatened.

"Or else what, Cam?" I asked.

"Or else they gonna have to answer to me as to why they really coming around. Y'all know the rules around here."

"The rules? Last time I checked, the hood don't pay my bills, so I'm free to do whatever I damn well please."

Jacelyn jumped in and said, "Don't get yourself hurt, Cam. You don't have a clue who these guys are, and you ready to start a war."

Cam said, "Sleep on me if y'all want to, but y'all know what it is."

So I said, "Okay, whatever. It's been real, but we gotta go."

I didn't want to give them another chance to get slick at the mouth. We just walked off and left them standing there, looking stupid. See in our hood, and I'm guessing in every other hood, guys were very territorial. If you lived in the hood, you had to date someone from the hood. The guys felt, if you dated someone outside the hood, they had a motive other than just dating. They didn't want some outside cats coming in and taking over their street corners or their chicks. If this had been a few years back, before Chase and Mike went legit and I told them what Cam had said, there would've been a hostile takeover for sure, leaving Cam on the streets working for them.

As Jacelyn and I walked back home, we laughed because we were not bothered at all by what Cam and Dennis had said. It was funny because they hadn't the slightest clue who Chase and Mike were or what they were about. All I could say was, "I can't wait until we move, Jacelyn, because people are watching everything we do. I'm so glad Mr. Bill brought the house in Long Island for Mommy, so we can finally get the hell up out of here. Thank God, the closing on the house is really soon. We have to let Chase and Mike know what is up, though, so they will know to be on point when they come around. Anyway, on another note, Jacelyn, tell me what happened that first night in Atlantic City with you and Mike."

"Oh, yeah, I forgot to tell you, didn't I? After dinner, we walked along the Boardwalk and talked till about three in the morning. When we got back to the hotel, we played around a little bit, talked a little bit, and then we fell asleep on the couch. Yo, B, he is fine as hell, and I think he's the one."

"Well, Jacelyn, I'm happy for the both of you, and I pray everything works out. Chase and I had an amazing weekend full of fireworks and lots of laughs."

In my mind, I was saying to myself, A good girl never kisses and tells. Plus, I didn't want to compare the two guys. Whatever Chase did for me was for me, and whatever Michael did for Jacelyn was for her. As long as he made her feel special, that was all that counted.

***

At about nine pm, the phone rang, and it was Chase telling us to get dressed, put on some jeans, T-shirts, some Timberland boots, and come out to the parking lot. Without asking any questions, we got dressed quickly and went outside to find the two of them standing out there next to two motorcycles. Chase had a white and red bike with black designs going through it, and Mike had a yellow bike with black designs going through it. They took their helmets off and smiled at us. Chase said, "Come here, Beautiful. I missed you just that quick, so I had to come back and check you. Come on. I wanna take you for a ride."

I said, "Oh, hell no, Chase, not on that thing."

"Don't worry. I got you. It's Sunday night, so there's no traffic. You'll be just fine. We're going to take a quick ride to the city to shoot some pool and get something to eat."

"Quick? See, Chase. I'm not feeling no quick ride."

"Look, scary. Come on. Let's go."

"I'm not scared, Chase. I'm just cautious."

He totally disregarded what I was saying as he put a helmet on my head and a cute leather riding jacket on my back. He showed me how to step up and hold onto him, and trust me, I was gonna hold on for dear life. After we all got on, Mike and Chase both started up their bikes and rode off. It was my first-time riding on the back of a motorcycle, so I was a little scared, but knowing Chase was controlling things made my nerves calm down a bit. I knew he would never do anything to hurt me or himself, so I was definitely in good hands.

It took all of forty minutes to get through the Midtown tunnel. We pulled up to a spot called the Dice Lounge and Billiards. After we went inside, Chase said, "Come on. I'm going to teach you how to play. The first game is on me, and the second…well, we can bet a little wager on that one."

Mike made the same bet with Jacelyn. They won the first game. The wager for the second game was whatever the winner wanted. They should've never said that because Jacelyn and I had been highly trained by our uncle Bishop, who was my grandma's brother. Growing up, we spent weekends at his house, learning how to shoot pool on his state-of-the-art pool table. I said, "This is going to be a very interesting game, fellas."

Now, Jacelyn and I got serious because whatever we wanted was on the line. I took my first shot and hit four solid balls into the corner pockets. I kept going, knocking in all my balls, while Chase stood there, looking at me with his eyes wide open. He was smiling.

"Last shot, Chase, the black ball," I predicted.

He said, "You're not making that shot. I didn't even take a shot yet."

"Well, guess what, Chase, you're not going to either."

I shot the black ball into the side corner pocket. Boom. And I said, "Hmmm…I already know what I want." I was now laughing really hard.

"Okay, Jacelyn, let's go. Why are you giving him a chance to shoot?"

She said, "I got this, B. Trust me. He won't shoot again, meaning game over." She made a shot that cleared five balls.

Mike said, "Y'all cheating, man."

I said, "No, we learned from the best. Plus, y'all both said that y'all were going to teach us how to play, but y'all never even once asked if we already knew how to play."

Jacelyn hit the black ball in the corner pocket, and the game was surely over. She gave me a high-five. We laughed so hard that we were in tears. I walked over to Chase, kissed him, and said, "Don't be sad, baby," and laughed.

He said, "You got jokes. Now what do you want since you won?"

"I want you to take me to the Bahamas."

He said, "That's about twenty grand right there, but you've earned it, so I can't say no. Do you have a passport, Beautiful?"

"No, neither one of us do."

"Okay. Y'all can go tomorrow and apply for one. It takes just a few weeks to come in. As soon as it gets here, then we will go."

Jacelyn looked at Mike and said, "Well, you heard them. That's the prize."

He said, "It's cool, Miss J. No problem. We can go."

We left that spot and walked down the block to get something to eat. We ordered slices of pizza and some sodas. While we were sitting down eating, Jacelyn and I let them know about the conversation that had taken place earlier with Cam and Dennis. Chase said, "It's cool. I'm not worried about them clown-ass niggas around there. Plus, I stay strapped, and trust me, they don't want it. The good thing is, unlike them clowns, I'm licensed to carry my piece wherever I go."

"Wow, Chase. You're licensed to carry a firearm?"

"Yeah, we took an armed security guard training and bodyguard course and became licensed a few years ago. We, somehow, always manage to find legit ways around things to protect ourselves and our investments. Now, back to what I was saying, the only worries those dudes would ever have from me is if they messed with my money, which they could never do, or if they did something to y'all, and that's never gonna happen, so there's no beef. Niggas just wanna have something to talk about, and it just so happens the talk was about us. That's all."

Now Mike, on the other hand, had a different approach to the situation and was ready to step to them. He said, "When we get back, y'all gonna take me straight to those clown-ass niggas. We'll see if they be talking all that shit when I'm all up in their faces."

Chase said, "Mike, haven't you learned, by now, that we're not those same street cats we used to be?"

They knew exactly what they were doing by telling them that.

Mike said, "Chase, man, you're getting soft."

"Soft? What, Mike? Ain't shit soft about me. My dick stays hard and so do my stacks of cash. Never forget that, Mike. Those niggas are soft for even telling them some pussy shit like that. If they had any balls, they would have just walked up to us and asked us any questions they wanted to because that's how we handle shit. That's the difference between boys and men. We handle shit different. Damn! I always gotta school you, Mike. You're gonna have to start paying me for these lessons. Now come on, y'all. Let's get out of here."

We walked back down the block, hopped back on the bikes, and headed back home. We got back to the building in no time, hopped off the bikes, and took the helmets off.

"Chase, you're a man of many surprises," I said.

With a confident smile, he said, "Yeah, I know. I just want you to get to know everything about me, like I know about you. You surprised me, too, though because I never knew you could play pool like that. I have to be more careful about my next wager, or maybe I'll take you golfing or something."

We both laughed.

"Okay, Beautiful, let me get outta here. We have work in the morning."

"Well, since Jacelyn and I quit Who's Who, we have to find something to do. Banks Enterprises is running smoothly with the team we've put together, so they really don't need our help right now."

He said, "Beautiful, you never have to work another day in your life, if you don't want to."

"That's sweet and all, Chase, but I was born to hustle. For me, not working is not an option."

"Okay, we'll figure something out for you to do then, but no worries and no rush."

"Chase, this has been the best weekend of my life."

"Well, Beautiful, let me know when you get to the greatest weekend of your life because I only want to give you the greatest of all things this lifetime has to offer." He pulled me close, kissed me, and said, "I love you, Beautiful."

"In time, I will love you, too, Chase, but just know that I'm really feeling you."

"Please. I know you already love me, Beautiful, and that's why I'm the happiest man alive right now. Good night, Beautiful. Sweet dreams."

He put his helmet on, started up his bike, signaled for Mike, and they pulled off.

Jacelyn and I went inside, and we started talking about our next move.

"Look how much things have changed for us in one short weekend. J, I never thought, in a million years, that my weekend would turn out the way it did. But on a serious note though, we have to work, so we gotta get on it first thing in the morning, and if that means back to event planning with the team, then so be it. Also, we have to go to the post office for our passports, so we can take that Bahamas trip because I need longer than a weekend vacation right about now."

"Wait. What, Bridgette? Didn't they say we didn't have to work, though? Why not take them up on their offer?"

"Jacelyn, you know we were raised to be independent. We were not raised to be dependent on a man's money, and we ain't about to start now. Plus, it's way too soon in the game to start depending on them anyway."

"Okay, I guess you're right, B, but don't front. It was a great offer."

"Whatever, Jacelyn. Stop being so damn lazy. No matter how good the offer is, it ain't happening."

CHAPTER 11

Wall St.

Nothing but business as usual for Chase and Michael. They were not your average stock brokers on Wall Street; they were both hood-made. They were business smart and street smart, which put them ahead of most. They knew what it was like to not have money and live in the hood, so they had made a smart investment in themselves and had made it out. They ran their own firm called the Morgan and Starks Investment Firm. The office was on the top floor of a forty-story corporate building on Wall Street in Manhattan, New York. Their main thing was staying on the top of everything. They were usually in the office from six am to six pm, bringing in the bread.

Since we had been back from Atlantic City, we hadn't been apart. Every night, Stanley would drive us to Manhattan by seven in the evening to have dinner with the guys. I always looked forward to seeing Chase walk through the restaurant doors every night, not only because he was fine as hell, but because I never knew how he would be dressed, since he was both corporate and hood.

Meanwhile, back at the house, Jacelyn and I were trying to figure things out and pack at the same time. My mom was set to move to Long Island the following month, so we had no choice but to pack as well, since we hadn't found our own spot yet. Thank God Mr. Bill was buying all new furniture, so all we had to do was pack up our clothes and personal items. I loved Mr. Bill so much, just as if he was my real dad. He always looked out for us and made sure we had the very best.

Jacelyn and I took a break from packing to have lunch with our mom. We decided on Chinese, but since they didn't deliver to the buildings, we walked over to get it. We made it back within about twenty minutes with the food. As we began to eat our honey barbecue wings and fries covered with honey barbecue sauce, the phone rang. To my surprise, it was Chase. He sounded a bit uneasy, as if something was wrong. I asked him, "What's up?"

He said he needed my help. He asked me to come to his office. He said, "Be ready in thirty minutes. Stanley will be there to get you and bring Jacelyn with you."

I said "okay" and quickly hung up. We both rushed to get ready. I threw on a pink satin blouse, a black skirt, and some black heels. I always wanted to look the part of a businesswoman when I headed to Wall Street. I peeped outside and saw Stanley was parked near the lobby, waiting, so we kissed Moms and headed out the door.

When we got to the office about forty-five minutes later, the security was so tight that you would have thought we were entering the White House. We showed our IDs and signed into a log book, along with giving up our thumb prints.

We finally made it past security and headed upstairs. When we entered the office, my eyes lit up. It was beautiful. Everything in the office was white and gold. White walls, white desk, white leather chairs, and gold carpet. There were even gold computer monitors. You could tell everything was custom-made, including the paintings on the wall. The ceilings had that industrial look, like a warehouse. The beams were all painted gold. There were about twenty employees working hard. Chase's office covered the entire left side of the office. There were wall-to-wall and ceiling-to-ceiling mirrors all along the outside of Chase's office. Michael's office was on the right side and was designed the same way. There was a desk right outside both of their offices that was not occupied by anyone. By the looks of things, they ran a tight ship because everyone was minding their own business and managing their work.

I stepped inside Chase's office, and he greeted me with a kiss and a long hug. He said, "Although I want to keep it professional, I've had a stressful morning, and I really needed that hug and kiss. I know I'm going to need a lot more hugs and kisses by the time this day is all said and done."

"No worries, Chase. I got you."

"I hope you do. We will see just how much, when later gets here."

"So, Chase," I asked, "what exactly do you guys do here?"

"Well, first off, *we* don't do anything. I do almost everything while Michael plays video games and spends money."

"Wow! That sounds a lot like Jacelyn, minus the video games."

"Yeah, he's always playing and joking, but that's all about to change today."

"Chase, y'all's security is tight."

"I know. That's the way it has to be for my clients' privacy and protection. I like keeping my clients satisfied, reassured, and happy. They are always happy to know that they're making money but are even happier knowing their investments are safe and secure. You see these eight monitors right here? They control cameras throughout the office, even in the kitchen and break room. We have two more, but those are for what goes on behind these mirrored walls. We only turn them on when we're out of the office. Now, Beautiful, let's get to why I called you here. Come with me."

He used the intercom to call Michael. He told him to meet us in the large conference room and to bring Jacelyn. As we were walking through, Chase advised all the staff to cut their calls short and to head to the meeting. Once everyone arrived, Chase said, "Good afternoon, everyone. I know it's been a long day, but this won't take long. I want to introduce you to Bridgette and Jacelyn Banks. They are our new assistants. As you can see, Natalie is no longer here. She had to be let go this morning. Just so you all can understand exactly why she was let go, here is a copy of your contract agreement. Please refer to page 2, section B, which states 'no unauthorized person or persons that are not employed with Morgan and Starks shall be permitted in the office due to our clients' privacy and protection.' There are no exceptions, not even for the courier or Chinese food delivery man.

"Natalie took it upon herself to escort her boyfriend up to the office this morning to meet everyone, which cost her her job. In this business, there's a lot of information floating in the air, and I will not be sued for anyone's slip ups. Natalie was cool, but she slipped up. Now to make sure that does not happen again, I'm using Natalie as an example of what not to do, if you want to keep your job. If anyone violates their contract, they will be terminated immediately. Does anyone have any questions?"

"Well, yes, I do," said a young man.

"What is it, Jeff?"

"Why does Michael need an assistant since we all know he only plays video games all day?"

We all laughed.

After the laughter died down, Chase said, "On a serious note, Jeff, he'll be needing one now. We have some serious new clientele coming through real soon, and I need everybody to be on their A game. Can everyone please sign their contracts right now, below their original signatures, date it, then pass them forward when you're done? Also, from now on, there will be tighter security when you enter the building. We will require you to use your ID badges and thumb prints, along with signing in, just until the new system is put in place. This is just to verify who is coming and going. You are dismissed. The phones are ringing, so let's go make some money. Bridgette, Jacelyn, and Michael, please stay. We have work to go over. Bridgette, your desk will be outside my office, and, Jacelyn, yours will be outside Michael's office."

Jacelyn said, "Chase, please let me know what I will be doing since everyone is saying Michael doesn't do anything?"

"Sure, Jacelyn, and to answer your question, as of today, Michael will be taking over eight clients."

Michael complained, "Eight? Yo, you trying to kill me?"

"Not at all, I'm trying to remind you why we started this business in the first place. Keyword, Mike, 'we.'"

I laughed to myself because Jacelyn and Michael were so much alike. They both were very playful and likable, but when it came to work, it was like "what work?"

Chase said, "Mike, since it's late, I will have Jeff go over things with y'all in the morning. Oh, and don't worry, Mike. They are small clients. I wouldn't want to put any of our big clients in your hands just yet."

Michael laughed, but for some reason, Chase didn't laugh with him. Instead, he said, "Show Jacelyn around the office and let her get comfortable at her new desk. Bridgette, come with me."

Chase showed me around the office and to the desk where I would be sitting right outside his office. After that, he led me into his office and closed the door. His office was like a mini-bachelor's pad. It had a mini-kitchenette to the left with a table and four chairs. His desk was in the center of the office, and to the right was a living room area with a sixty-inch TV built into the wall with a book shelf surrounding it. He had two video games, but by the looks of things, they hadn't been touched in a long time. He said, "I have a lot to go over with you. Thank you so much for helping me. I really love you for doing this, Bridgette."

I said, "Well, Chase, you didn't really give me much choice. Besides, I needed something to do."

"Trust me. It's all for your benefit that you get to know the business. It may be yours someday."

"It all sounds good, Chase, but it's definitely not my dream."

"Yeah, I know your dream is to be a lawyer and that you will be as well, Beautiful, soon enough, and that's a promise."

"Well, until my dream comes true, Chase, I will have fun learning something about your dreams. Besides, how could I turn down learning from one of the best?"

Chase was sitting in his high back chair, looking so good. I couldn't resist. I had to walk over to him. I sat on the desk directly in front of him and kicked off my shoes. He quietly sat there, waiting for my next move. I grabbed his tie, pulled him close to me, and kissed him just to tease him a little. "Chase, you looked so sexy in there, taking charge and giving orders. I've never seen this side of you, and it's making me love you more and more."

He said, "Really? Now you love me? Well, I'm ordering you to kiss me some more then."

"Yes, sir, whatever you like. Remember I'm here to assist you."

He playfully said, "All I want is a kiss. Now Royal, on the other hand, wants a little bit of Royalty."

"Really, Chase? Right here, right now? There are people in the office."

He said, "No, there are not. It's 5:56 pm. Turn around. Everyone has left for the day. Besides, even if they were here, my office is sound proof, and that's a two-way mirror. Nobody can see inside. Only we can see out. I designed it that way."

"Okay. Understood, Chase, but that doesn't keep them from guessing."

"Let them guess because you're in charge now, Beautiful. You're the first female to enter my office, besides the cleaning service. My assistant Natalie never stepped foot in my office. We always met on the other side of that wall, in the open, or in the conference room. I didn't want her to get any ideas, thinking I liked her in any other way than professionally. Plus, I would never let any female get the opportunity to sue me over some bullshit lies. I've made it too far away from the hood to let anyone send me back. You got it, though, Beautiful. I'm gonna behave since this is your first day on the job, but the next time you jump on my desk in front of me, take your shoes off, and seduce me, you better be ready to finish what you start, Miss Banks."

He got up, put on some music, and poured a glass of champagne for each of us. He put on Jaheim's "You Can Have Anything" and asked me to dance. As we were dancing, he sang in my ear. Ugh! He always knows what to do to get me in the mood, I thought. He was looking so sexy and so fine. He was as smooth as a Hershey's chocolate bar, and he had me right where he wanted me. As the song was going off, our clothes were coming off. Just then, the intercom buzzed. It was Michael. He said, "Yo. Let's go. Did you forget we have dinner reservations at Black Spice?"

Chase said, "Saved by the bell, but we will pick this up later. Did you, at least, enjoy you first day at work, Beautiful?"

"Yes, Chase, I did, but if work is going to be champagne, music, and dancing every day, we won't get any real work done at all."

He said, "It's after hours. Besides, all work and no play won't be good for either of us. Come on, Beautiful. Let's get out of here. I will see you tomorrow morning at eight sharp, ready to work."

"Yes, sir, I will be here bright and early."

He opened his office door, and we walked out. Michael and Jacelyn were both standing there, laughing. Michael said, "What were y'all doing?"

Being smart, I said, "Apparently not what y'all were doing. Y'all always clowning. Get a life."

Jacelyn said, "We have a life, and we are enjoying every minute of it. That's why we're laughing."

Chase said, "Okay, y'all. Let's go." He set the alarm, and we left.

We made it to the Black Spice restaurant in Harlem and went inside. It was a nice spot. It was a Caribbean restaurant. Chase said he wanted to switch it up a bit. Chase and I both had a dish called Shrimp Rasta Pasta. Jacelyn had oxtails with rice, and Michael had jerk chicken with rice. The food was very good, better than I expected. It was a place that I would love to come back to any day. Chase leaned over and whispered, "I want you to stay with me tonight."

"Chase, I have work in the morning. Plus, I don't have any clothes with me."

He said, "No worries, Beautiful. I have everything covered. I promise I will have you to work on time, and you will have something to wear. Just trust me."

"Well, Chase, since you put it that way, if I say no, that means I don't trust you, which I do. Plus, you're so cute. I can't say no."

After we finished eating, he paid the check, and we walked to get the car.

As we are walking, he put his arm around my shoulder and said, "I'm so in love with you."

"What makes you so in love with me, Chase?"

He said, "I love you because you're a beautiful person inside and out."

He opened the door to the car and closed it behind me. After driving for a while, we ended up in Times Square. The city was so pretty at night. NY was the place where no one rested, even when the sun went down, because the lights kept going and going.

"So where are we going, Chase?"

"To my house?"

We pulled up to his high-rise apartment building. It had a parking garage inside. It was really nice; the entire building was made of glass. "I'm so glad that you love the finer things in life, Chase."

"I sure do, and you're one of the finest."

"So what floor do you live on?"

"There's no place better than the top, baby."

The building was twenty stories high, and he just so happened to live in the penthouse. We stepped out the elevator and straight into his apartment.

While Chase went to the bathroom, I went on a self-guided tour. I had never seen any apartment, well, penthouse this nice before. The windows extended from the floor to the ceiling, just like in his office, except the windows at his office were a light blue. These were a light gray. The place was custom-built and made for sure with white carpet, white leather living room furniture with gold pillows, white marble counters in the kitchen. It had two bedrooms and three bathrooms, one bathroom in each bedroom and one in the hall for guests. The ceilings were so high, not even Chase could change the lightbulb. Each bathroom had the same décor, white and gold wallpaper with white linens trimmed in gold. The master bathroom had a fireplace and a Jacuzzi tub. The tub was so big we could actually swim in it. The house had so much white and gold that it was crazy. There was a den that had red leather furniture and black carpeting. It was really nice. It was different, so it stood out from all the white throughout the house. That was basically the chill-out spot. The guest room was purple. It was as big as the master, if not bigger.

He came looking for me in the purple room. He said, "I see you have showed yourself around. This room used to be empty, but I recently had it designed for you."

"For me?"

"Yes, for you. When I first saw you, I knew you would be mine, and I knew I would have to live somewhere fit for a king and give you a space fit for a queen."

"Thank you, Chase. It's definitely fit for a queen, but I would change just a few things."

He said, "Well, do whatever you want. It's yours."

"Right now, all I want to do is sit in the bath and relax."

He said, "Well, that's good because it's already ready for you."

We went back to his room where the bath water was running. Candles were lit, and slow jams were playing in the background. "Wow, this is nice. I can see all that hotel living has rubbed off on you, Chase."

He said, "Not really. I don't always need people to do things for me. Besides, I wanted to show you I really love you by doing it myself."

His phone chimed. It was a text from Michael telling us that he and Jacelyn were together and that they were across the hall.

"I thought this was the only apartment up here."

"No, it's not. Michael has the other one. It's just not as big."

"Y'all really are inseparable. I'm just glad we get to spend time alone."

He said, "Me, too. That's why he has Jacelyn over there, to keep him company. Now back to this bath, and this time, everything is coming off. I was just being a gentleman by trying to make you comfortable before, but we both know we are way past that now."

We both stepped in the tub. First, he sat down. Then I sat down and laid back, against his chest, right into his arms. "Chase, this is exactly what I needed...a relaxing moment with you. I could fall asleep right here in your arms."

He said, "Go ahead. I will wash you up, then carry you to bed."

I laughed and asked him, "Is there anything you wouldn't do for me?"

He said, "Nope. I really enjoy our talks in the bathtub. It's where we really get to know each other better. I'm looking forward to tomorrow's bath already, Beautiful. Before you know it, we will be old and wrinkled from all these damn baths."

He added some hot water, and we bathed each other. No sex. Just pure love and affection. As we finished, Chase stood up, grabbed a towel, and wrapped it around himself. Then he held one open for me as usual. He was just the perfect gentleman.

The bed had never felt more comfortable than it did at that moment. I crawled into his arms and laid my head on his chest. In less than ten minutes, we had both fallen asleep.

***

The next morning, the alarm sounded. Chase got up and went to shower. He said, "Stay in bed. You don't have to get up right now."

After he showered, he headed straight for the kitchen.

"Once I'm up, I'm up," I said, so I showered and went into the kitchen as well.

He made us vegetable omelets with a glass of orange juice on the side. He kissed me on my forehead and said, "Good morning, Beautiful. Did you sleep well?"

"I sure did, Chase, so well I almost forgot where I was again."

"Well, I'm glad you slept well. That makes two of us. I have to get to the office by six, so you can just chill until it's time for you to go to work."

"Okay, Chase, but you're forgetting about one thing."

"And what's that, Beautiful?"

"What am I supposed to wear?"

He said, "You didn't see all the clothes in your closet?"

"No, I was being nosy but not that nosy."

"Well, everything you need is in there." He kissed me again and went to get dressed.

He came back into the kitchen a few minutes later wearing this gray suit with a white shirt. I noticed his tie, which was different shades of gray, wasn't tied. I quickly jumped up, stepped in front of him, and tied it for him. He said, "Okay. So you know how to tie a tie, Miss Lady?"

"Yes, sir, Mr. Bill taught me very well." As I finished tying the tie, my towel dropped.

He put his arms around me and grabbed my cheeks. He said, "Damn, girl. You're gonna make me late for work."

"Oh, no, you got to go."

He laughed and said, "I love you, and I'll see you at the office. I will have Stanley pick you and Jacelyn up around 8:20, so you can come in today at nine. I left the keys on the table by the door for you to lockup when you leave." He kissed me again and said, "Damn, Royal is on the rise."

"Well, you can tell Royal that Royalty is still sleeping." We both laughed as he walked out the door.

I went in the room, looked in the closet, and found all kinds of clothes and shoes, all with tags on them. I decided, since he was such a gentleman at the office and at home last night, I was going to pick out the sexiest dress in the closet. I would be sure to keep his mind off work today. I chose a sexy red dress that showed off all my curves and complimented my long legs. It was cut low in the front, so the little bit of cleavage that showed would get his eyes popping. I paired the dress with a pair of leopard stilettos. I curled my hair, put on my jewelry, my lip gloss, sprayed on some Peace body spray, smiled, and said to myself, "I'll be sure to turn heads my first day at work for sure, but the only head I'm interested in turning is Chase's."

***

Stanley arrived at 8:20 as promised, so I grabbed my bag and the keys, set the alarm, locked up, and met Jacelyn downstairs. Jacelyn had on a black two-piece pantsuit. She said, "Well, damn! You trying to get fired?"

I said, "Nope. Fired never. A raise is what I call it, J."

We both laughed. As we got into the limo, Stanley said, "Good morning, ladies."

"Good morning, Stanley," we said in unison.

It was always a pleasure to see Stanley. I wondered if he had a family since he was always at our doorstep. I thought, One day, I will ask him, but not today because I have other things on my mind. One being Chase. Damn! The ride was so quick. I really didn't have time to think about anything. The office was literally twenty minutes away from the house.

Once we reached the building, Stanley got out, opened the door, and let us out. In an instant, all eyes were on me, even the ladies. It felt good because my plan was working, and Chase hadn't even seen me yet. We showed our IDs, signed in, gave our fingerprints, then went upstairs. When Jacelyn and I entered the office, not only the guys', but the ladies', mouths and eyes were all open wide. Talk about jaws dropping. Hmmm…Now I was laughing on the inside because, if their reaction was like that, I could just imagine what Mr. Morgan's reaction was going to be when he saw me.

Everyone said "good morning" while wiping the drool from their mouths. Mr. Starks came out of his office with his eyes wide open and said, "Damn! Good morning, ladies. Welcome to your first day at the firm. I can see it's going to be a lovely day around here." As usual, he was cracking up, laughing at his own comments. Jacelyn and I laughed at his dumb butt.

Then I said, "Move. You play too much, Mr. Starks."

Chase came out of his office and said "damn" loud enough for the entire office to hear. He said, "Excuse me. Good morning, ladies."

I said, "Good morning, Mr. Morgan," and winked at him.

He said, "Michael, take Jacelyn and help her get familiar with things. Mrs. Morgan, you can come with me, so I can go over what you will be doing today."

I said, "Okay, I can get used to being called Mrs. Morgan."

We went into his office. He closed the door, and it automatically locked behind us. He shook his head, pointed at his two-way mirror, and said, "Look what you did." I turned and looked through the tinted glasses to see everyone looking our way, pointing and talking. He said, "I called you 'Mrs. Morgan,' so if any of the guys had any thoughts or ideas of saying a word to you, they will think twice about it now. I really don't know what you are trying to prove, Bridgette, by coming in here dressed like that, but you damn well proved your point. One thing I must tell you, though, is you can't dress like that because nobody in here will be able to focus on work. I know I won't."

"Well, you bought the dress, Chase. I didn't."

"Bridgette, you know damn well there was plenty more clothes in the closet, but you chose to go and put on this come-fuck-me dress. Plus, I didn't know you would look this damn good in it. Shit." He started clearing things off his desk. Then he walked over to me and said, "I've wanted to do this since you walked through the door. I never imagined loving anyone the way I love you. I am one lucky man."

He picked me up and sat me on the desk. He looked me over and said, "I never want to have sex with you. I always imagine making love to you. I can't imagine quick moments with you. Every moment must be long and memorable. I will never have any quickies with you in this office either with everyone around. My respect level for you is greater than you know. Besides, a quickie would not please you or me. Shit! I really can't control myself or think straight right now with you sitting here on my desk with this come-fuck-me dress on."

"Well, Chase, would it be better if I just took the dress off, so you can come fuck me?"

"Nah, you can keep it on, but I can tell you what we are taking off, and that's the day. Oh, and I'm definitely picking out your clothes from now on."

We laughed as he grabbed his jacket, and we headed out of the office.

He told one of his employees, "Hold my calls. For the first time in a long time, I'm taking the day off. I'm taking my work and my laptop, and I have my phone. If anyone should need me, just call."

Chase told Michael and Jacelyn that we were leaving and for him to have Jeff go over the accounts with them. "I expect a full report on Bridgette's desk in the morning, Mike. No BS."

I walked over to Jacelyn and whispered, "It looks like my plan worked. See ya later."

We both smiled.

We headed downstairs and got into his car. "I'm sorry, Chase. I didn't mean to make you leave work. I just wanted to see exactly what you would do if other eyes were on me, and it worked."

"Never do that again please. You almost gave me and some of the other guys heart attacks, especially old Bernie." We laughed. "Plus, I have seen you up close and personal before, when other eyes were on you, but it didn't have the same effect then, as it did today." He held my hand, then rubbed my leg, and said, "I can't wait to get you home." He loosened his tie and unbuttoned his top two buttons. From the looks of things, he was very heated and ready to bust, and little did he know, I had been ready since last night. This day will be a day off to remember, for sure, I thought.

From the moment we hit the door, it was on. Our clothes were off within seconds. He whispered in my ear, "I'm thirsty for some Royalty juice." He took a quick feel around to see just how juicy Royalty was, and she was just as he expected…dripping. He was so eager to dip his Royal crown into Royalty's juices that he quickly said, "Fuck the room. I can't hold out no longer. You got my head spinning right now." With my back pressed against the entry wall, he quickly picked me up, wrapped my legs around his waist, and slowly dipped his Royal crown inside Royalty's juices. I moaned softly from all the pain and pleasure that I was feeling inside. Oh, my God, it felt so good to be back on cloud nine once again with Chase. Within in a few minutes, we both started sweating and breathing out of control, holding and grabbing on to each other tightly. He kissed my neck and my chest, while softly holding my cheeks in the palms of his hands. He really couldn't move the way he wanted to while standing up, but I damn sure felt every inch of Royal inside me. I was "right and tight," and he was "large and taking charge." He whispered, "I want you to feel every *royal* inch," as if I wasn't already feeling every inch. Seriously, how much deeper could he go? He said, "Hold on tight." As he attempted to carry me to the room, I couldn't stop kissing him and moving around, so we only made it as far as the entry floor onto this big furry white area rug, but this time, we switched it up a bit. I was in control now. Royalty slowly slid down on Royal very, very slow, up and down, making sure Royal choked on Royalty's juices.

Taking Mr. Morgan by surprise, all he could say was "Oh, shit. Please don't stop, Beautiful. I've waited so long for this moment." I just smiled and continued bouncing a little faster but still slow enough for us both to enjoy every bounce, after bounce, after bounce. Things started to heat up pretty quickly. Within about twenty minutes, my breathing got shorter. I was panting and panting. My moans got louder as Royalty released her milkshake down on Royal, and not a minute after, Royal added some extra cream of his own to Royalty's milkshake. Chase took a few deep breaths and said, "If it wasn't for birth control, you would be having my baby."

I didn't say a word. I just laid there as my legs shook from the after-shock of the Royal-quake that had just erupted inside of my inner walls and now the mixture of creams started slowly seeping its way down my inner thighs. I had never felt that way before. It was a first for me, but I knew, for a fact, it wouldn't be the last.

We laid motionless on the floor for a few more minutes to catch our breaths. Then we went into the bedroom to take a shower, but we never made it. We made it as far as the bed before we were going at it again. After the second round, I said, "Hold up, Chase. You do know that sometime today we might want to do some kind of work, right?"

"This is work. Remember this is part of your training as my assistant. We really should get to know what we both like in our coffee, so why not start with the creams that our bodies produce? It's called Anatomy 101, a study of the structure or internal workings of something. I'm definitely studying your structure and your internal works. Well, let's just say Royal is putting that work all up in ya. Besides, I took the day off just so we can play and make love all day. We can work tomorrow."

We laughed.

"Well, in that case, Mr. Morgan, since I did show up to work this morning, I'm expecting to be paid and with a bonus."

He said, "Just know, you will be paid, and by the way, I am your bonus. Never forget that." He tapped the tip of my nose and smiled.

I grabbed his hand and said, "Come on, Chase. Let's take a shower." I pulled him off the bed and into the bathroom because we really needed to cool down for a bit.

The magic between us was unstoppable. I was truly in love with this man, and I didn't think I'd ever be able shake this feeling. I couldn't figure out which were the best moments — taking a bath, taking a shower, or lying in bed in his arms. They were all just so relaxing. Sometimes, being with him felt like a dream. I worried that, one day, I would wake up, and my life would go back to where it was six months ago, or I would wake up with him not being such a perfect guy. Well, for now, I would continue to live in this fantasy life that he had created for me.

The shower was so refreshing and so needed. When we got out the shower, I threw on one of his business shirts, and he put on some shorts. I said, "Seriously, Chase, enough playing around. Let's get to work, but first, I'm gonna need you to put on a T-shirt because your abs are such a distraction."

He laughed, put on a T-shirt, and climbed in bed with some files and his laptop in hand. Now we could get down to work. He taught me everything I needed to know about investments and strategies on how to make my money work for me. He gave me updates on each client that I would be working with and showed me how to run client reports. Some clients wanted weekly reports, some monthly, and some quarterly. My job was to keep track of their stocks and whether they rose, fell, sank, or swam. I had to also keep track of potential clients, active clients, and clients that wanted to trade or wanted to cash out. Oh, and most of all, I had to be at Mr. Morgan's beck and call, but from the looks of things, he would always be at mine.

"Chase, I don't mind being your assistant at the firm, but you know I still want to host events at the club on Saturdays, right?"

He said, "Okay, cool, but most Saturdays, we won't even be in town because we're gonna definitely need time away from the firm, the club, and all the noise and chaos that comes with it. What you see, Beautiful, is not all that it is; there's much more that you don't see. Behind every door, there's crazy shit that goes on. Trust me."

After his little lecture and training, he began to teach me how to invest my own money. He said, "Pick something, anything, and we will buy one-thousand dollars in stocks."

I picked Sony stocks.

He said, "Now, we invest, and we will watch it over the next month and see what it does."

Thank God, I'm a good and fast learner, and I had the perfect teacher. I knew this job was going to be a piece a cake, that I could have and eat, too.

***

It was now three weeks later, and things were going great at the firm. I was enjoying being Chase's assistant. Jacelyn was working hard and running all the reports for Michael's clients. I had to train her on what Chase had taught me because Michael was in training himself, so he couldn't do it. As it turned out, Jacelyn and I now both had a regular nine-to-five on Wall Street. We started going back to the club on a regular after work and on the weekends. Chase wanted us to get to know the members of the club now that we weren't really working there and had time to mingle. We still hadn't hosted an event there yet, but Chase promised me that he would be having some big event soon that Jacelyn and I would be putting together.

It really felt great to walk into the club with the guys now, not having to guess who they were. As usual, every night, Maryellen opened every event and started the night off by saying that "stocks are up on Wallstreet." The all-too-familiar crowd cheered as I said to myself, "I hope my one-thousand-dollar stocks went up some more, too, because I want to cheer just like them, but it ain't happening yet with only one-thousand dollars in my stock account."

Life was great for Jacelyn and me right now, and things couldn't get any better. We both had the men of our dreams and great careers on Wall Street. Not to mention, we still had Banks Enterprises. We both had lots of our own cash, and we were set to move to Long Island next week. Who would have thought any of this would have been possible seven months ago? We were truly blessed, and none of this would have been possible without God. Going to church was a big part of our relationship with the guys. As long as we were in town on Sundays, we made our way to church. Church was a way to keep us covered from all the haters and devils floating around. Plus, the more money, the more problems, that only God knew how to keep in check.

I could already see that this was going to be one hot summer to remember, and well, the rest of the year, no telling what it held for the four of us. I just knew that things could only get better with time.

CHAPTER 12

Moving on Up

Oh, my God! The day was finally here, moving day. We had so much to do because we hadn't been home in about a month. Stanley dropped us off at the Building in a Lincoln Town Car this time, but at this point, I really didn't care if it was in the limo because we were finally moving out of the building. It felt good to be moving, but thinking of all the people we grew up with that we were leaving behind made me a little sad. I prayed that they made it out one day, just as we had. I was really going to miss everyone, even Cam and Dennis. Just because they had said something stupid didn't mean we didn't have love for them, just as we did for everyone else.

As we were walking inside, Jacelyn and I were reminiscing about growing up in the hood. We walked inside the house and greeted my mom, Mr. Bill, and the movers. Since they were here doing everything else, Jacelyn and I had the honor of cleaning the apartment. We went upstairs to gather our things, but when we got up there, our things were already gone. Mostly everything upstairs had already been moved to the new house, given away, or put in the trash. We started out vacuuming the floors and cleaning the upstairs bathroom which only took about thirty minutes.

Once the house was completely empty, Jacelyn and I stayed behind to vacuum the downstairs. We called Stanley to come back and get us since we were almost done and there was no need to stick around any longer than we needed to. We took out the garbage and then called the building management to inspect and lock up. After one last walk-through, it was all behind us. We walked around to say goodbye to everyone in the A building, while we waited for Stanley. It was so bittersweet.

***

Stanley finally arrived an hour later. He opened the door, we got in, and he drove off. For some reason, he always knew where we were going. He had our schedule all mapped out. I guess that was all part of being a good driver. He said, "Ladies, we'll be there within an hour."

Out of nowhere, Jacelyn started reminiscing again about the years we spent in the building, the people we grew up with, and how things would never be the same. I changed the subject because we had already talked about our past earlier, and I wanted nothing more than to focus on our future with the guys.

Changing the subject, I asked Jacelyn, "How are things going with you and Mike?"

"Mike is great. He keeps me laughing. Well, we keep each other laughing. We are so much alike till it's not funny."

"Yeah, I know. Chase and I are, too. He's definitely my soulmate. I can tell you this. They are nothing like the guys we grew up with, Jacelyn. That's for sure."

Out of nowhere, Stanley said, "Ladies, we have arrived."

It hadn't even taken the full hour to get there.

We pulled up to this huge house in Glen Cove, Long Island. This house had curb appeal. The lawn was beautiful. The grass was so green I could sit out on it and have a picnic with Chase. The house was different shades of brown brick and taupe siding. It had a two-car garage. The backyard had a patio for barbecuing and chilling. It also had a huge swimming pool. There was a large foyer, den, dining room, living room, and a large kitchen with the family room attached. The second floor had five bedrooms and three full bathrooms. The basement was a full apartment with a pool table, theater room, kitchen, laundry, two bedrooms, and three bathrooms. There was a full bathroom in each bedroom. Mr. Bill had had the entire house nicely furnished.

While Jacelyn and I both looked around excitedly, we noticed none of our things were there. We saw boxes all over, but none of them were ours, so we headed back upstairs to ask our mom about it. I said, "Ma, where's our stuff?"

She said, "Well, I don't know. You would have to ask them." She pointed to the backyard. Jacelyn and I quickly went out back to find Chase and Mike, drinking bottled water, laying on the patio lounge chairs. I walked up to them and asked them, "Where is all our stuff?"

Chase took off his shades and said, "Wait. I don't get a hello? No kiss? No love? This is not like you, Beautiful." He started laughing.

"I'm sorry, Chase, but what's so funny?"

As he stood up, I gave him a hug and a kiss, but still he gave me no answer to my question. "Chase, I thought you had to work today?"

"I did, but I'm done now."

Mike was still sitting there, laughing.

I said, "What's so funny, Mike? What are y'all up to 'cause Mike is laughing way too hard?"

Chase said, "Damn, Mike. You gotta keep it together. You're way too happy right now."

"Look, y'all still ain't saying anything about where our stuff is."

Chase said, "Come with me, Beautiful. We're going to take a ride somewhere really quick."

He grabbed my arm and walked me back through the house to where my mom and Mr. Bill were. He said, "Ms. Banks, you have a beautiful home, and I will definitely be back for dinner and the barbecue."

My mom said, "Okay, Chase, you're welcome here anytime."

He went over to Mr. Bill, shook his hand, and said, "You're a great man, Mr. Bill, a great man. You've made so much possible for me, and I'm so grateful."

Mr. Bill said, "All I ask, Chase, is for you to take care of my baby girl. Chase, don't let me have to get my shotgun out," and they both laughed at the comment that every father makes at one time or another.

"So, wait, Chase, you know my dad? Dad, you know Chase?"

"I told you, baby girl. I know lots of big people in high places, and he's definitely one of them." In my mind, I thought, BIG. Who you tellin', Pops?

"So now it's all starting to add up. Now I know how you know so much about me, Chase."

"That's not true. Mr. Bill put me on that his daughters ran Banks Enterprises. He showed me some pictures of y'all, and I wanted to know more, so I did my own investigation. He just put me on to when and where you were gonna be at certain places, but the rest was up to me."

I wasn't even mad at my dad for keeping the secret because the best thing about it all was that I had his approval. For him to approve of me being with Chase meant the world to me. I knew my dad wouldn't just let me be with anyone, especially without the third degree, so this was perfect. I kissed my mom and dad, told them I loved them, and that I would be back soon. My dad said, "You're in good hands, baby girl. He's a good man."

I just smiled and said, "Thanks, Dad."

Now after all the conversation, Mike and Jacelyn came in the house from out back, playing around. Jacelyn said, "Mom, we're leaving."

Mike said, "We will definitely be back, Mrs. Banks. Your house is really nice, so nice that I'm going to have to invest in my own backyard real soon. Thanks again, Mrs. Banks, for having us. Mr. Bill, I will check you soon."

After our goodbyes, we headed to the cars, got in, and drove off.

***

We made it back to the city within an hour, and as we got a few blocks from their apartments, Chase handed me a small white box with a purple ribbon. He said, "Hold on to that for a second." He handed me an eye mask to cover my eyes and said, "Put this on and no peeking."

I said, "Chase, are you serious?"

"Yes, I'm serious, Beautiful. Put this on."

I took the mask and put it on without asking anymore questions. He drove about five minutes more, so I knew we had to be close to the apartment. He parked, shut the car off, got out, and opened my door. I waited patiently, standing still, blindfolded. Chase said, "Yo, Mike, come on. You're so slow."

We got on the elevator, and it went up so fast that I knew we had to be going to the top. It got quiet for a second. Then all I heard was punching on the keypad and the click of a key opening the door. Out of nowhere, Chase picked me up into his arms and carried me through the door. He put me down and took off the blindfold. Then he said, "Welcome home, Beautiful."

After I opened my eyes, I saw my boxes from the building over in the corner and some of his things from his apartment. I just started to cry. He said, "Stop crying and open the box." I took the ribbon off the box and opened it. It was a gold key. There were two codes inside — 2126, which was the code to the alarm and another code, 528, which was the door code.

I walked over to the window, and he followed me. He held me in his arms with my back against his chest while we took a moment to look at the view of Manhattan. He said, "My apartment was cool, but it wasn't ours. I heard what you said about the guest room in my apartment, about how you would have changed a few things and decorated it a little different. Now we have this brand-new penthouse to decorate however we choose. We are the first two families to make a purchase here in the building."

"Wow, Chase, I don't know what to say because you're so full of surprises. I never know what you're going to do next. Thank you so much, Chase. I love you. So my mom and Mr. Bill knew the entire time that we wouldn't be living in Long Island?"

"Yeah, they knew, but don't be mad at them because I told him to keep it a secret. I wanted it to be a surprise."

"Don't worry. We're still gonna go out there whenever you want but only to visit. This is home now."

"Come with me, Beautiful. I want you to see the bathroom. I know how much you love taking baths, so I had to make sure the tub was perfect."

When we got to the bathroom, I was overwhelmed. I said, "This tub is way bigger than the one at the other house."

"It sure is, and it's all ours. Come. I have something else to show you. Let's go over to Mike's and Jacelyn's apartment."

They had the penthouse across the hall. It wasn't quite the same, the layout was a little different, but their spot was nice, too. Jacelyn ran up and hugged me and said, "Bridgette, do you see this? Do you see what they did for us?"

"Yeah, J, it's beautiful."

Chase said, "We wanted y'all to be happy and comfortable living with us, and y'all needed to be closer to the firm and Who's Who, and now y'all are."

Mike said, "I'm gonna need y'all to come with me for a minute, though."

"With you, Mike? Now why would we want to do that?" I asked with a smile.

"Look, Bridgette, just come on. You'll see."

We got on the elevator and went down to the garage on the lower level. As we stepped off the elevator, our mouths dropped because directly in front of us were two white cars with big bows on them. One had a purple bow, and the other had a red bow sitting on the hood of the car.

Just by looking at the purple bow, I already knew which one mine was. It was a white Mercedes Benz coupe with purple leather interior and the piping on the seats were trimmed in white. The license plate read BEAUTIFUL. Jacelyn's car was a white Acura Legend coupe with red leather interior and white piping trim on her seats. Her license plate read JACELYN. This was a great moment. We got the guys, the houses, and the cars. It all was a lot to take in, and I just needed to sit down.

Chase said, "Let's go back inside. The delivery guy will be here with the bed soon. Since you loved my last bed so much, I thought I would just go ahead and get an even better one. I didn't want you to have to sleep on the floor our first night here. After the delivery guy leaves, we will go grab some stuff from the store. Are you hungry, Beautiful, because I know I am?"

"Yup, I sure am. I'm starving."

"Well, we can order takeout really quick or wait to eat when we leave."

"Well, Chase, what I really want to do is stay at the other house tonight and wake up early to go shopping for the new house. At least, we can get takeout, take a bath, and relax. It's just been such a long day, and all I want to do is sleep."

Chase said, "You do have a point."

The doorman called up to let us know that the delivery guy was on his way up. He came right up and set up the bed. It was huge, bigger than a king-size bed. It was custom-made for sure. Chase said, "I made sure it was big enough for the both of us."

"Big enough, Chase? This bed is big enough for a few of us, not just us."

After the guy finished assembling the headboard and connected the bed, he was done. The guy said, "Give me a minute to bring up all your custom linens."

They were custom Ralph Lauren sheets, blankets, and pillows. Wow, we actually had linens for the bed. "We could stay here, but there is so much more we need, Chase, so I'd rather wait."

We headed back to the old apartment with Mike and Jacelyn behind us. We grabbed takeout and chilled at Mike's house, eating, drinking, and playing video games for a while. Chase was very eager to leave. He said, "It's eleven-thirty, and we have a long day ahead of us, so let's go get ready for tomorrow, Beautiful."

We left, got home, showered, and fell right to sleep.

***

The next morning, I woke up around four-thirty, showered, and made breakfast. Chase finally woke up to the smell of breakfast around five-thirty. He said, "Good morning, Beautiful."

"Good morning, handsome. Did you sleep good?"

He said, "I sure did. You're making breakfast for me? Just for that, I have a surprise for you later."

"Chase, that's so sweet, but wait. Now you have to slow down and give me a chance to surprise you."

"Well, Beautiful, that will probably never happen because it's my duty to please that booty." He slapped my cheeks. "Nah, seriously, I love surprising you. I just love seeing that smile on your face."

"Chase, that's cute and all, but can you give me a hint? Please?"

He said, "Nope," and walked away eating a piece of sausage and drinking orange juice. "And don't be late for work."

I smiled and said, "I won't, boss."

He said seriously, "I'm not your boss. We're partners now."

"Well, in that case, I'm definitely going to need an office."

We both laughed as he went in the bathroom to take a shower.

I was sitting at my vanity table in relax mode, wearing one of his dress shirts that I'd thrown on when I got out the shower. While I was sitting there, I was instantly distracted as he walked out the bathroom with a towel wrapped around his waist, showing off his incredibly beautiful body and sexy abs.

I kept my eyes on him, watching his every move through the mirror. I closed my eyes for a second, just imagining what I would do with all that right now. I could feel him getting closer without even opening my eyes and looking in the mirror. Umm…he was so damn fine and making me want just a little piece of his chocolate before work.

He walked up behind me and put his arms around me and said, "You gotta stop putting on my shirts. They make you look so sexy, and it drives me and Royal crazy, especially early in the morning. You be making me want to skip work every day, but today is a special day, so I have to go. In my mind, I'm saying, 'Damn! If only today were yesterday or tomorrow, we'd be skipping work.' I have some new clients coming in today that I have to sign. You have my permission to look sexy today but not sexy enough to send my clients to the emergency room, Bridgette, and I'm not playing."

Now I knew he wasn't playing because he'd called me Bridgette, and he never called me Bridgette.

"Okay, Chase, but I don't know how to be sexy without being sexy. That's just who I am, and this is how I look, no matter what I put on."

He said, "Yeah, okay," and laughed. After he got dressed and I tied his tie as usual, he said, "You're gonna love being my wife."

"Well, what about you? Are you gonna love being my husband?"

"I'm already your husband. You just haven't realized it yet. I'm just loving the fact that it's going to be official one day. That's all, Beautiful. Then while you're tying my tie every day, I'll get to see that big rock I put on your finger." He grabbed his laptop, kissed me on the forehead, and walked out the door.

***

By the time, Jacelyn and I got to work, the guys were already in the conference room with the new clients. We walked in and all their heads turned. There were two black guys and one white guy. They all had on cowboy hats and had cigars in their hands. Chase said, "Please let me introduce you to my partners, Bridgette and Jacelyn Banks."

They all smiled. The white guy said, "Damn. The meeting is over. Where do we sign? If they're in charge, we know our investments are definitely in good hands."

They looked like straight-up oil tycoons or something. They seriously signed the paperwork and shook everyone's hands, and one of the black guys said, "We'll be in touch."

The other black guy, who was real big and dark-skinned, said, "Enjoy the ride, ladies. Fellas take care of these beautiful ladies and always keep them happy."

Then they left.

Mike said, "Damn. Y'all gotta walk in every meeting looking like that from now on. Y'all don't know how much cash they just dropped." He opened the briefcase to show us half a million dollars. It was three-hundred-and-fifty-thousand dollars to invest and one-hundred-and-fifty-thousand dollars in profit for the firm.

Chase said, "We are taking y'all to lunch for all the hard work we put in."

"What hard work, Chase? All we did was walk in." Jacelyn and I laughed. "It must have been y'all's hard work because looking this fine has never been hard for us at all. This is what we do daily."

Chase said, "We are going to lunch, and just for looking so good, we're going shopping, too."

"Good, Chase. Are we going shopping for the new apartment?"

"No, Beautiful, for ourselves. The house can wait. Plus, we still have my penthouse, so like you said before, there's no rush. Now grab your bags and let's go."

We got in the cars and drove to Queens Center Mall. The guys bought shades, watches, and gold bracelets. Everything that they bought, they bought the match to it for Jacelyn and me. These two really made shopping fun and easy. We had to have spent, at least, one-hundred-thousand dollars just buying stuff. We went to the Gucci store, and they spent twelve-thousand dollars on luggage. I said, "Chase, we just got luggage when we went to Atlantic City."

"Yeah, I know, but it wasn't matching sets. Not to mention, it came from Macy's. Shopping's over. Now let's go."

We left the mall and got on Grand Central Parkway, headed toward Interstate 495- Eastern Long Island. I was quiet, asking no questions at all, just wondering where we were going. As I looked at each exit sign, I saw we were passing towns that I had never even heard of before. For a minute, I thought we were going to my mom's house for a visit, but we passed right by her exit. When we got to an exit called Ronkonkoma Veterans Memorial Highway, Chase got off there, and that was when I saw the sign that read AIRPORT KEEP RIGHT. I was still trying to figure out where we could be going, but I kept quiet because obviously it was a surprise, or he would've told me.

When we got closer, we made a left turn into the airport with Mike and Jacelyn right behind us, as usual. We pulled into this private air yard. The guy opened the gate and said, "Mr. Morgan, we've been expecting you."

Chase said, "We had to do a little last-minute shopping. Sorry for the delay."

He said, "No problem, Mr. Morgan. No one is considered late when you have access to drive through the gate and fly on your own time, sir." He instructed Chase to pull the car around the building and pull into the garage. When Chase pulled around, the gates opened and inside sat this huge private jet. The guy said, "Complements of your new clients."

Chase got out, opened my door, and said, "Let's go." He grabbed my hand and helped me out of the car. He put his hands on my waist, kissed me, and said, "This is all for you. This is why I work so hard, just to put a smile on your face."

"Thank you, Chase. I'm just so in love with you. I don't know what to do. Sometimes, I don't even know what to say."

"You don't have to say anything else, you've already said 'thank you.' Now let's just enjoy the ride."

I looked over at Jacelyn and smiled. I had to keep calm and act like it wasn't my first time on a private jet. The steps were already down, so he helped me onto the jet and said, "Sit tight. Let me get our bags."

When Jacelyn got on, we both smiled at each other. We both knew we wanted to scream, dance, and act like five-year-olds. We had to keep it cute and quiet, but for sure, when we landed and were alone, we were gonna act like straight-up kids. Chase and Mike came back with all the bags and luggage. Chase said, "So we have some packing to do really quick before takeoff, so they can secure the bags. The pilot let us know the flight was only going to be around two and a half hours."

Still not knowing where we were going, we were excited to get there already, so we packed really quickly. The bags were now secure, and we were ready for takeoff. Chase said, "Beautiful, I just want you to enjoy this trip. Don't think about work, the house, moving, packing, unpacking or nothing, just enjoy yourself. We will figure all that out when we get back."

"Yes, sir, not a problem at all."

Mike was sitting across from us, laughing. He couldn't hold water, but all he said was, "We about to have some fun," and continued laughing. We fastened our seat belts for takeoff, and within minutes, we were like twenty-thousand feet in the air. The views were amazing, looking out over the ocean, the houses, and the roads were all just beautiful. We went up above the clouds, and — oh, my God! — it was heaven, so peaceful and unbelievably beautiful.

As Chase sat directly facing me, he poured both of us a glass of champagne. Mike and Jacelyn had their own bottle which Mike shook up and popped open, making a mess and a lot of noise. Chase made a toast. "Here's to the good life, a peaceful trip with lots of love, lovemaking, eating, and dancing, but we ain't tanning 'cause we already black enough. We gonna leave that to the…I almost slipped, but I didn't. I forgot who was flying us for a second."

We laughed.

"But here's to a great trip with you, lovely ladies."

We all raised our glasses, and that was when the party began. The pilot put on Jay-Z and Jermaine Dupree's "Money Ain't a Thang." We were up there partying hard. It was the best two hours in the air I'd ever had.

***

About an hour later, the pilot lowered the music and said, "Please fasten your seatbelts. We will be landing in approximately thirty minutes."

Chase said, "Mike, close the window over there. They can't see anything until our feet touch soil."

***

Once we landed, customs came aboard and cleared our exit. Chase handed them our passports. They stamped them and then gave them back. One of the customs agents said, "Welcome and enjoy your stay." We exited the jet, and we all got straight into a limo. They had us cover our eyes with masks. They didn't want to reveal where we were until we got there. The driver said, "We have about a forty-five-minute ride."

Chase said, "Thanks, man. There's no rush. Take your time. We just want to sit back and enjoy the ride to our unknown destination."

CHAPTER 13

Fantasy Island

C hase started talking with the driver. He said, "Driver, as you're pulling up to the location, I would like you to pull over, so we can see the view of everything from a short distance."

With his Caribbean accent, the driver said, "Not a problem, sir."

Butterflies fluttered in my stomach as the car pulled over and stopped. Chase asked the driver if he could please take our pictures when we got out. He said, "Sure."

Chase told him to try and capture everything and to take about one hundred pictures. "I really want to capture the looks on their faces when we take off their masks."

He said, "Not a problem, sir. I will do just that."

They helped us out of the car, walked us around to the front, and took our masks off. Jacelyn and I both started yelling and acting like two fools. I jumped into Chase's arms, and he spun me around. I started tearing up and said, "Thank you, Chase. Thank you so much."

He said, "Don't thank me. You won the bet, and a bet is a bet. I'm just glad I was able to keep my promise, Beautiful."

Michael and Jacelyn were standing on the side of the limo laughing, joking, and playing while the driver continued snapping pictures. The driver did a good job while taking our pictures. He managed to capture so many good photos. It was definitely a moment to remember.

When we got back into the car, Mike said, "Yeah, yeah, yeah, it's on now."

All we could do was laugh at him.

I said, "Chase, how did you get our passports?"

He said, "They came in the mail the other day at the Building, so Mr. Bill dropped them off to me. Good, old Mr. Bill. I love that guy. He sure can keep a secret."

"I'm going to get my dad."

"Nah, Beautiful, he's happy for y'all, and he really knows y'all needed this trip."

"Okay, if you say so, Chase."

We pulled into the resort, and the bellboy took our luggage. We were immediately greeted by the hotel management. The lady said, "Hello and welcome to Atlantis in the Bahamas. My name is Lucille, and I will be at your service throughout your stay. Mr. Morgan, I received a call from a Mr. Henderson back in the States. He has taken care of your entire stay and has arranged all your accommodations. He said it was a pleasure doing businesses with you. He says 'treat these ladies like royalty while they are here and give them whatever they want on him.'"

Chase said, "Royalty. Hmmm...Beautiful, you're going to get so much of a *royal* treatment that you're gonna be moaning 'royal' in your sleep."

We both smiled as he put his arm around my shoulder and quickly kissed me on the cheek. Only the two of us knew what Royal and Royalty meant because they were our love names for each other. Now I knew Mr. Henderson had no idea about the names, but we sure did. Now Royalty was getting all excited, so I couldn't wait to see what the tub looked like. Lucille said, "Come with me. He has arranged a private villa in the water for each couple tonight. The villa has its own private Jacuzzi and pool surrounded by the island waters. Tonight, you will each have a private intimate dinner on the patio with your own chef and butler. Tomorrow, you will dine for breakfast on the island just a pathway away from the villa. You may choose to stay another night in the villa, or you may choose to stay in the honeymoon penthouse suite that we have arranged for you."

"Hmmm...Mr. Henderson is very impressive. He's pulling out all the stops on this one," I said.

That was when Chase said, "I have to put a call in to Mr. H."

Lucille said, "One more thing, Mr. Morgan. He would like for you to call him tomorrow after you have enjoyed your lovely evening with the Mrs. He said to call him when you all arrive at breakfast."

Chase said, "Okay. That's cool. No problem."

Lucille said, "Last but not least, Mr. Morgan. He said not to worry about a thing. There are no strings attached. He saw how the two of you talked so much about how much you loved your ladies, and when he saw them, he knew every word was true. Not to mention, the ladies blew his socks off. He said, 'Any man would be lucky to have ladies as lovely as yours,' and he felt all of you deserved a vacation fit for kings and queens."

Mike said, "Okay, Mr. H. That's what I'm talking about. *Coming to America* in the Bahamas."

We just shook our heads all at the same time as I said, "You are a damn fool, Mike."

Mike said, "Chase, you're Akeem, the prince of Zamunda, and I am Semmi. Mr. H is James Earl Jones, the king, and we are at the damn Waldorf Astoria. We have found our queens. Come now. Let's go, Akeem."

Jacelyn said, "This fool done lost his damn mind. Can't take him nowhere."

Now with the four of us on this island, we were bound to have a ball. We all kind of completed each other. I guess that was why Chase and Michael were always together, and Jacelyn and I were always together. Now nothing could stop or separate the four of us. We were bonded for life.

Lucille led us down to the villas and advised that guest services would bring our bags. The walk down was breathtaking. The clear water and pink sands were amazing. Chase held my hand as we walked along the romantic path that led to the villas. Lucille showed each of us to our separate villas that were surrounded by the tropical sea. The roofs were made out of straw. The pool and Jacuzzi were totally private. If we wanted to get in naked, nobody would see us. There was a chef inside, ready to prepare a romantic dinner for two. There was an oversized king bed, and the entire villa was filled with purple and white roses. They were in every room, even out by the pool. If there was one thing I knew, it was that the roses traveled with us everywhere we went. There were buckets of champagne all around. The table was set for two with white linen, silver dinnerware, and white candles. The chef had made sirloin steaks, red potatoes, and asparagus. Chase and I held hands and said a prayer right before the food hit the dinner table. The steak was so good and tender it melted in our mouths. I said, "You know, Chase, I could get used to this kind of living."

He said, "Everything is about to get better, Beautiful. Just wait and see. We can basically live wherever we want, do whatever we want, go wherever we want, whenever we want."

He always talked about things getting better, but what could be better than the way we lived now? From where I was standing, our lives had the perfect view and didn't need any fixing.

After we finished dinner, the chef cleared the table, cleaned up, and left. Chase opened a bottle of Moet and walked out to the patio with two glasses in hand. He truly set the mood when he put on some slow Caribbean music, which was perfect since we were on this Bahamian island. He handed me a glass and said, "I'm about to give you the best *royal* treatment of your life. We're about to make the best of all Mr. Henderson's accommodations."

He danced with me a little bit, then took the glass from my hand, and sat it down on the table. He started slowly kissing and undressing me. Our clothes came off very quickly, but we managed to stay in tune, moving in a slow Caribbean motion. His kisses were juicier than usual, but his touch was the same, soft and smooth. He led me into the bubbly Jacuzzi where the stars shined down on us. It was the most beautiful sight I had ever seen, besides Chase's chocolate naked body. It was like another dream I didn't want to wake up from.

We slow danced around in the bubbles for a bit, until Chase decided to take a seat while slowly taking me down along with him. He took me down so slow, slow enough for Royalty to slide right down on Royal.

As we moved to the rhythm of the Caribbean drum, things really began to get heated. The feeling of Royal so deep inside my inner walls had me deeply inhaling and exhaling slowly to each slow wind. Chase gently ran his fingers through my hair, then held it up to expose the back of my neck. Licking his way up the side of my neck, he reached my earlobe and softly nibbled on my ear. I closed my eyes for a moment to inhale the feeling of ecstasy, then exhaled. I couldn't help but sigh. He knew that, as soon as his tongue hit my earlobe, it would get me to wind even faster. Now that he'd managed to hit both spots at the same time, winding to the music was a wrap for me, and I started bouncing to the beat of Royalty's heartbeat thumping inside. Bu-bump, bu-bump, bu-bump, bu-bump. Trying so hard not to lose his grip, he moved his hands from under my arms and cupped my breasts, putting one in each hand and gently massaging them to the beat of music, all while still trying to keep a grip. He then gently massaged Royalty while keeping Royal inside, locked, loaded, and ready to shoot.

Things really heated up at that point, from a mixture of our body temperatures and the warm Jacuzzi water that flowed around us. When he turned my body around to face him, I smiled and playfully slow winded in front of him to the beat of the Caribbean music that flowed in the air through the speakers. The motion of my body turned him on so much that he wanted more. We were in the Jacuzzi for all of thirty minutes before he picked me up and carried me over to the candlelit cabana. He laid me down on a bed of roses and made love to me until the sun came up. There was something about this slow Caribbean music, the palm trees, the warm breeze, the surrounding waters, and the outdoor lovemaking that made the night extra special, relaxing, and so romantic, that I fell asleep between his legs with my head resting in the center of his chest.

That was the best sleep we'd had in a while.

***

We woke up to a cool breeze bouncing off the water as we laid naked in the cabana with a white towel thrown across my cheeks. He kissed my forehead and said, "Good morning, Beautiful."

"Good morning, handsome."

Just the thought of having Royal right under me had Royalty wanting more of him for breakfast. We both jumped up and went straight to the bathroom, came back, jumped on the bed, and had a few quick rounds before breakfast. That was the best lovemaking we'd ever had, and we'd had plenty. If I could've stayed in bed all day getting the Royal treatment with the fresh air blowing through the villa, I would have, but I knew it was almost time for our big breakfast on the island. Once we stopped playing around, we managed to shower and get ready for breakfast.

Fresh purple and white roses, fruit, and orange juice were delivered to the villa just before we were ready to leave.

There was another knock at the door. It was Mike and Jacelyn. After they came in, Chase and Mike pulled out their laptops and got right to work. The guys checked the surveillance cameras at the firm and Who's Who every morning and every night. I could hear them talking, going over things. Chase said, "It's time to check in to see how Wallstreet is dancing around in Who's Who while we're out of town and make sure nobody's sleeping at the firm."

Mike said, "Now, we both know we're only about two and a half hours away by plane if need be. Now I'm trying to pay them no attention and trying to enjoy this lovely fruit with Jacelyn."

For the sake of everyone back home, I pray to God everything is good at the firm and Who's Who because I wouldn't want to underestimate these two right now, especially when it comes to their cash and their ladies, I thought. They had that look, and if and when they gave you that look, you already knew what was up. They were smooth but still hood. Mike was the type to shoot someone first and ask questions later. Chase would give you a chance to plead your case because he was all about protecting his livelihood and investments, but don't cross him, though, because he would get you before you got him, and you wouldn't even see him coming. They were both so loving and sweet, but their other sides were unknown to many. Nobody knew how they would react to certain situations. Everything they did was private and in closed quarters. Hell, we didn't even know they owned Who's Who or who they were for six months, so I'm sure you get my point.

When they finally finished checking up on home, it was time to head up to breakfast on the island. Breakfast was under a gazebo on the beach. As we approached, there were two people already sitting at the table. As we got closer, we realized it was my mom and my dad. Jacelyn and I went crazy. We were filled with excitement and joy. "Chase, you knew they were going to be here and didn't say a word?"

My dad said, "We arrived at the same time as you all did, just on another private jet."

I was so happy to see them because we hadn't seen them since the move. I was so excited that my mom had finally been able to go on a trip alone with my dad, and not to mention, it was on this beautiful island. The servers started bringing breakfast out, which was a spread of vegetable omelets, sausage links, bacon, all varieties of fruit, croissants served with champagne, orange juice, coffee, and tea. Lucille walked over with two boxes on a platter. One had a purple ribbon, and the other had a red ribbon. Chase placed the box with the purple ribbon in front of me, and Mike placed the box with the red ribbon in front of Jacelyn. The boxes were long, like they could've had necklaces inside. Chase also had a big yellow envelope. He opened it up and took some papers out. He said, "Beautiful, you are the beauty of my perfect world, and I can't see myself doing anything in this world without you."

Mike said, "I really don't have a lot to say, Jacelyn, except I love you and I need you with me at all times."

Chase handed Mike and Jacelyn a piece of paper, gave me one, and he kept one for himself. The letter said:

- — — — — — — — — — — — — — — —

MORGAN AND STARKS ENTERPRISES
XXX WALL STREET
NEW YORK, NY 100XX
212-999-9999
#1 investment firm on Wall Street

CC: Joshua Infinity, ESQ.

Subject: MORGAN AND STARKS ENTERPRISES
INVESTMENT FIRM

ATTN: Shareholders

MORGAN AND STARKS ENTERPRISES, which became a 50/50 shareholding company from 1998-2001, now duly notes the following changes to be entered into agreement and filed with the **state of New York:**

Upon signatures, the firm name change, effective immediately, from **MORGAN AND STARKS ENTERPRISES** to **MORGAN, STARKS AND BANKS INVESTMENT CORPORATION**

The shares are now as follows:

Chase Morgan, CEO, 25 percent controlling stocks

Bridgette Banks, CEO, 25 percent controlling stocks

Michael Starks, COO, 25 percent controlling stocks

Jacelyn Banks, COO, 25 percent controlling stocks

If all parties enter into this agreement, please sign below to accept changes of Corporate Name, Shares and Ranking. This agreement will be legally binding until one's death or sale of the company; there in which, share-holding stocks would be divided and disbursed accordingly.

By signing this document, all parties agree that this is a true and legally binding contract. All statements that are false are punishable by law in the state of New York.

X_____ x_____

Chase Morgan   Witness 1

X_____ x_____

Bridgette Banks   Witness 2

X_____ x_____

Michael Starks   Joshua Infinity

X_____ x_____

Jacelyn Banks   Notary Public

Date: _____

— — — — — — — — — — — — — —

I jumped up and kissed Chase after reading that he had officially made me a partner, changing the name, making me CEO, and giving me 25 percent in controlling shares.

"Chase, I love you. I love you so much, and I've never thought I could be so happy with someone. You mean the world to me, Chase, and for you to give me part of your company shows me that I mean the world to you, too."

Chase said, "I love you, too, Bridgette Banks, with all my heart, and me giving you the world has just begun, Beautiful."

Jacelyn and Mike were sitting across the table. Mike was laughing, asking Jacelyn why was she crying. Jacelyn said she was crying because she was so happy. She had never felt that way in her life, and no one had ever done anything like that for her before. She said, "Michael, I love you, and I will never forget what you've done for me."

"Jacelyn, it was nothing to give you that, and I'm nowhere near done yet. I love you, too, J."

My dad said, "Congratulations. That's why we came, to celebrate, and for me to notarize these documents and make them official."

Next, Chase said, "Open the boxes." So we did.

We both had door plates inside with our names and titles on them. It was so special that it had my mom in tears. She was so happy that she just sat there and cried. She said, "My girls are no longer babies. You have grown into such beautiful, successful young women, and I love you both very much."

My dad said, "Those are my girls. We taught them well."

Wow, now this breakfast was a blast and full of surprises. I was still in shock but in a good way. Jacelyn and I never knew what was coming next with these two.

Chase said, "Give me a second. I have to make a call." He dialed the number.

Ring.

"May I speak to Mr. Henderson?"

He answered with a deep southern accent. "Hey there, Mr. Morgan. How's everything going? I hope you and the ladies are enjoying yourselves."

"Yes, sir, Mr. Henderson, we are, and you can call me 'Chase' please. That's why we are calling, to say 'thank you' for your generous hospitality. We greatly appreciate it. The private jet was a great touch."

Mr. Henderson said, "Anytime. It's the least I can do, knowing that you guys are about to make me even richer."

They laughed.

Mr. Henderson said, "I'm gonna let you guys go now, Mr. Chase. Don't keep those fine young ladies waiting."

"We won't, Mr. Henderson. I will call you when we arrive back in the States," and they hung up.

Lucille came over to the table to give us a rundown of events for the week, which included spa treatments, live concerts, horseback riding, casino gambling, jet skiing, a yacht tour around the island, and much more. First off, the guys wanted to hit the casino to play at the craps table. We stayed there until around lunchtime. Once we arrived at the restaurant, we were seated on this beautiful patio that overlooked the beach. Everything on the menu was on point. We ordered fried plantains, coconut shrimp, onion rings, spicy Jamaican wings, and some conch fritters. Lunch actually turned out to be pretty good. After lunch, we went up to the resort to shower and change for dinner and dancing. I was so excited because I loved dancing with Chase, especially after our dance lessons. I knew everyone would be watching and cheering for us. I put on a white fringe dress that moved when I moved. Chase put on an all-white linen suit and Gucci sandals.

Chase was standing by the window when I walked out the room dressed and ready to go. He said, "Oh, wow, you look beautiful, but there's something missing." I watched as he removed a white rose from a vase, broke off the long stem, and stuck it into my hair, just above my ear. He said, "Perfect. Now we're ready," and led me to the door. We met up with everyone downstairs. To my surprise, we all were wearing white, even my mom and dad. You know what they say. Great minds think alike. We dined outside under a gazebo while watching a fire show, then went inside to a club where we danced, danced, and then danced some more. The four of us danced like we were at the masquerade ball. Everyone circled around us, cheered, and clapped as if we were professionals. For some reason, wherever we went, we always stood out as the center of attention. The night was going great, and we were having a ball. When the show was over, we all went our separate ways for the night. Chase and I were so tired from all the festivities that we ended up falling asleep on the couch.

***

The days had started to go by pretty fast. It was now the morning of day five. Mike and Jacelyn had come to our room before breakfast, as was their usual routine. Every morning, like clockwork, Chase and Mike would check the surveillance footage from the firm and Who's Who. They were very protective of their investment, especially Chase. For some reason, it seemed like Chase had more to lose than Mike, but I could have been wrong. Chase was just more serious when it came to the business than Mike. I think Mike knew Chase would always take care of everything, and if something went down, Mike would be ready to go to war for Chase.

After breakfast, my mom and dad were going back home, so Jacelyn and I couldn't wait to go downstairs to spend their last breakfast on the island with them. Once again, breakfast was amazing. I loved the spread of fresh fruits, eggs, croissants, sausages, grits, and hash browns. Today, there was more of an assortment of food on the table than any other day. When breakfast was over, it was time to say goodbye, so we walked them out to their car. We said our "I love yous" and gave our hugs and kisses. My mom said, "See you guys in a few days," and waved at us as the car pulled off.

Off to some fun in the sun, Chase, Jacelyn, Mike, and I all went jet-skiing. I always felt safe with Chase, no matter what, but with all this water surrounding us, I had to be on the safe side. I put on a life jacket and placed extra float pads around my arms and legs. Jacelyn wasn't playing either. She geared up so tight that, if she fell off, she would float back home. Mike asked, "Jacelyn, you don't trust me?"

She answered, "Hell no! This is different."

We all laughed and hopped on the jet skis for a little ride around the Bahaman waters. It was like being a kid again, just having good, old fun, not worrying about anything. The instructor took us across the island, where we got off and had lunch. They served us a variety of hors d'oeuvres, and to wash it down, we had drinks mixed with vodka and exotic fruits. Chase said, "Before we drink too much and can't get back across the island, let's go."

We hopped back on the jet skis and went back to the resort.

When we got back to the room, Chase looked at the numbers to see how the stock market was doing. He watched the surveillance cameras at the firm and Who's Who just to see what was going on. He had to have seen something crazy because he called Mike, and he didn't sound happy. Mike picked up, and Chase said, "Yo. You gotta see this shit, man. Come over here now."

Chase wasn't one to get angry or curse around me, so I knew it had to be something crazy. Mike came right over, and Jacelyn came with him. She asked me, "What's up?"

I said, "I don't know, and knowing these two, we probably won't find out."

Chase said, "I have some good news and bad news, Mike. The good news is that stocks are up and are as high as they should be. We're cashing out on Wallstreet like crazy, and the profits are way up. Unfortunately, the bad news is, it's not for us; it's for him. Y'all come and take a look."

He was now showing all of us the footage at the firm. It was Jeff. He was trying to gain access to Chase's office. He had waited around until everyone had left for the day to do it. Chase asked, "What is this dude looking for?"

We watched as Jeff tried to enter the code once, and when it didn't work, he walked away and looked in my desk outside Chase's office only to find absolutely nothing because it was empty. He walked back and tried the code again. It still didn't work. He put his hands on his head, then started banging on the desk. He then grabbed his stuff off his desk and left. Mike went crazy. He was ready to go home at that moment. He said, "Call and have them fuel up the jet. I'm about to go check ya boi. He's done."

Chase was calm. He said, "Chill out, Mike. We gotta play this cool. We have these ladies to think about now. We are definitely going to check him, though, but there's no need to rush back right now. Plus, we're leaving tomorrow anyway."

Mike was pacing back and forth, saying, "Chase, I don't know how you're this calm right now because I'm ready to go end this dude for real."

Chase said, "This is exactly why I'm CEO because I think logically. I have a plan that he will never see coming."

Mike said, "Well, tell me what the plan is because, the way I see it, he's a snake sneaking and slithering his way around our office. His head needs to be cut off. He needs to be dealt with."

Chase said, "Sometimes, snakes get caught in traps before they can even make their next move. Ladies, I'm sorry for all of this, and you haven't even gotten through your first day as partners yet. This just shows y'all the type of people y'all are gonna be up against, and always know, nobody is to be trusted in this game."

Jacelyn and I both understood what was going on and also understood both Chase's and Mike's approach to handling the situation. We, also, both agreed that Chase was being more levelheaded than Mike when it came to this situation, though. This was where we got to see the other side of the guys. I wasn't sure if I wanted to even know the details of the plan. As long as we were safe, it didn't matter what they came up with. I knew they would make him some sort of example, and if they did use him as an example, they couldn't kill him because people would know right where to look for the suspects. I knew Chase's plan wasn't to kill anyone which was good, but Mike...I wasn't too sure of.

Chase walked over to me. I was at the bar, making cocktails. He said, "No worries, Beautiful. Everything is cool." He kissed me, took a sip of his drink, slapped me on my butt cheek, and said, "Yo! This is pretty good. One thing we're not going to do is spoil our last night here. I want this night to be special and memorable. We are going to celebrate all of us being here together. We are not going to plot to kill someone. Let's stay focused. Y'all go do whatever it is y'all were gonna do, and we're gonna do what we were about to do before y'all got here. Meeting adjourned."

Now I was looking at Chase like he was crazy because I had no idea what we were about to do before they came over besides take a shower.

Chase took me by the hand and said, "Let's go. We're late."

"Late for what?"

He said, "Well, I have plans for us since you need to know." He hurried and walked quickly out to the beach, dragging me along. He stood behind me with his arms wrapped around me and said, "This is the moment we couldn't miss. The Bahama sunset. When you watch the sunset with the one you love, it's a sign of a lifetime of sunrises and sunsets together."

He always gave me these hints of being together forever but never a ring or a proposal. I was sure it would happen one day though, maybe even today. You just never knew with Chase. I just watched the sunset with him and smiled.

He said, "Now for a night to remember."

"What's that, Chase?"

"You will see, Beautiful. Come on."

"Chase, we still have on our swimsuits from earlier. What can we possibly be doing dressed like that this?"

"You'll see. Don't worry about clothes. Plus, you're spoiling it by asking me so many questions."

I stopped walking and said, "I'm sorry, Chase. I know whatever we do is going to be perfect as long as I'm with you."

I hugged him, grabbed his hand, and we continued our walk along the beach while the sun continued to fall, and the moonlight shone along the waves of the night waters. We ended up back where we started the first night at the private villa. This time, we were alone. No chef, no butler. A candlelit dinner was prepared. White roses were everywhere. They trailed all throughout the villa. In every place you could sit, stand, or walk, there were roses. The sound of Guy's "Let's Chill" could be heard in the background. It took me back to the day Chase first danced with me and held me close, and the smell of his cologne that was left behind when he vanished into thin air also replayed in my mind. We sat down. He took my hand and said, "I love you. Everything I do is for you. If you're not happy, I'm not happy. I want you to know that I will never leave you or vanish on you the way I did that night. I want you to remember this song because it won't be the last time you hear it." He said, "Listen," and started to sing the words to me: "Let's chill, let's settle down, that's what I wanna do, just me and you…"

I smiled, and at that moment, he made my heart skip a beat. "Chase, I live for these moments. It's these moments with you that take my breath away and give me new life. Each time, I start to breathe again. Just a small amount of music can make someone's life feel a whole lot better. Chase, you're my melody. You're my song, and you fill my heart with love, over and over and over again."

When the song went off, we blessed our food and ate dinner. I just knew he was going to propose after that song, but he didn't. The night was still young, though. After dinner, he said, "This is why we didn't need clothes." He led me to the bath, where the water was already drawn. He put on Luther Vandross, and our clothes hit the floor. This was the most intimate bath Royal and Royalty had ever taken. The feeling of us both letting go at the same time while Royal was still inside of Royalty was the best feeling in the world. He held me so gently but oh so tight, making sure Royalty got every ounce of liquid pleasure Royal was shooting out. At this point, Royalty was in love mode and so juiced up; she couldn't resist. She wanted more, and Royal was determined to fulfill her every need.

The water was getting cold, and we were getting wrinkled, so we took a break and got out the tub. Chase poured us some drinks, and we went out to the cabana. It wasn't even ten minutes later before his kisses, his touch, and the liquor heated things back up again. Juices flowed, and those towels dropped. Just looking at Chase and his Royal package… umm…he was very blessed, and I was ready and willing to accept every blessing he had in store for me and Royalty that night. His tall, dark chocolate, handsome, and fit body was all that I needed at that moment. He looked so good. He could model naked and make millions. Luckily for me, though, he couldn't be bought by anyone because he was already mine. The night was perfect. We laid in the gazebo and made love until the sun started to rise.

***

We slept till about ten in the morning. After waking up, we showered, put on white robes and headed back to the resort to pack and check out. We met up with Mike and Jacelyn downstairs in the lobby. Lucille greeted us and told us what a pleasure it was to have us stay at the resort and for us to come back soon. She had packed our breakfast to go since we were running late to the airport. We thanked her, got in the limo, and drove off.

Now we were back on the private jet, air bound for the States, and all Mike could talk about was beating the bricks off Jeff. Chase said, "Patience, my brother, patience. Watch and wait. It's all being handled."

After we were at our cruising altitude, the pilot announced that our arrival time would be in about forty-five minutes. We fastened our seat belts and prepared ourselves for our return to U.S. soil.

CHAPTER 14

The Real Wallstreet

It felt so good to be home, but so much was ahead with the new partnership, moving, and dealing with Jeff. Since it was Sunday, we had a day to figure things out. Chase had his plan in motion but did not say a word to any of us about what it was. We were in relax mode, so Chase and I were taking it easy for the night by sitting on the couch, watching episodes of *Martin*. I told him, since things were about to get really busy, I wanted to hire an interior decorator for the new penthouse.

"Yeah, that's a good idea because we will be really busy. Tomorrow, Mike and I are going to announce your partnership to the firm. Can you pick up a few things around ten in the morning for the celebration?"

"Sure, Chase."

"I'm going to ride with Mike, so you and Jacelyn can drive my car."

"Okay. No problem, but what's the point in me having my own car if I'm always in yours?"

"I know, Beautiful, I guess one day you will be able to drive it, but tomorrow I need you to drive mine."

"Well, that's all right with me because your car rides so smooth and it makes me feel like a celebrity when I'm in it."

"I'm about to run out with Mike really quick to check on the club and grab something for dinner."

"Okay, Chase, it doesn't matter what you get for dinner as long as you bring me back an orange soda and some barbecue chips."

He threw on a black tee, a black hoodie, some black sweats, and some all black Bo Jacksons. This was the first time I saw him dress this down, but I wasn't about to question him about anything. No matter what he put on, he still looked like a model, so I had no complaints.

Mike and Jacelyn came across the hall. When the guys left, we sat and talked. Jacelyn said, "I'm so excited to announce our partnership tomorrow."

"Speaking of that Jacelyn, Chase wants us to pick up some stuff to celebrate on our way in to work tomorrow. I'm guessing it'll give them time to address the Jeff situation. So, Jacelyn, how was the Bahamas with Mike?"

Jacelyn went on to tell me this lengthy story about how crazy Mike was and all the things they did. They seemed to have actually had a lot of fun on the trip. She said, "Girl, the sex was everything, and he is packing. He broke down so many walls I lost count. Just know there wasn't ever a dull moment. We had sex all over the resort. The bathroom, the pool, the beach, and we were even fooling around on a golf cart until we got caught. Mike is very adventurous. It was the trip of a lifetime that I will never forget."

"Yeah, me either, J. I will never forget it."

There was one thing I would never do, even though Jacelyn was my sister, and that was discuss anything about my Royal treatments with her. I just felt like all my intimate moments should be kept between Chase and me. One thing I could say was that Chase and I never had sex. He always made love to me, but I would never say that to her. Whatever we did behind closed doors or in public, for that matter, would remain between him and me. I would never give any woman information about Royal and Chase, to make them curious as to what he had. No, sir, not me, even though I knew he only had eyes for me. Plus, I never wanted Chase and Mike to be compared because they both were really good men in their own right and had very different but lovable personalities. I just knew we were all made for each other. Yes, I knew I'd asked her what happened, and she had every right to tell me it was none of my business, but she didn't.

***

The guys were finally back with gyros, orange sodas, and lots of snacks. They had been gone for a good three hours. They seemed okay, but something was a little off. Their moods had shifted, but I didn't say a word. I left it alone.

After we ate, Mike and Jacelyn went home, and Chase and I fell asleep on the couch. It was about two in the morning when Chase woke me up and carried me to bed. He laid me down, kissed my forehead, and held me in his arms. What he didn't know was that I wasn't sleeping. I was laying there with my eyes closed. He kissed my forehead again and whispered, "You have nothing to worry about. Everything will all be over soon enough. I promise. Everything I do is for you, Beautiful, and nobody can ever change my mind."

Then he fell asleep. What he said was all so puzzling to me. I knew, for a fact, now that something was wrong when he came home. I was sure I'd figure out what was wrong since he had just given three pieces of a puzzle that I now had to piece together, which was me, him, and what he'd just whispered. I was pretty sure the rest of the puzzle would take no time at all to piece together because he was always giving me clues. I just had to pay close attention to his words. This was something I was not even gonna share with Jacelyn. I was gonna consider this pillow talk. What was said on the pillow stayed on the pillow and would never leave this room.

***

Early the next morning, the alarms sounded, and he said, "Stay in bed. I will grab breakfast on my way to the office. I'll see you when you get there."

After he had showered and put on his suit, I jumped up to tie his tie. It was just something I had gotten used to doing. I loved seeing him in his suit, all bossed up and ready to go. He left around five am and let me know his car keys were on the counter. I couldn't go back to sleep, especially when I thought about what he had whispered. What could possibly happen to Jeff today, and how would everyone accept this partnership? It really didn't matter because I was now a 25-percent shareholder, and nobody could change that, not even if they tried.

I showered, did my hair, and put on some lip gloss. Then I found a little two-piece dress suit hanging in the closet that Chase had picked out a few weeks ago. I called the bakery for some sweets and called the florist to deliver some fresh purple, white, and red roses. I called Jacelyn to see if she was ready. She said yes and came right over.

To my surprise, we both were wearing the exact same suit, just in different colors. We laughed, and I said, "Oh, well, we ain't changing because it's time to go."

I grabbed Chase's keys off the counter, set the alarm, locked up, and we left. First stop was to pick up some plates, cups, and utensils. We got what we needed and headed back to the car. Jacelyn got in, and I went to put the stuff in the trunk. As I did, I spotted a tiny little clear red Ziploc bag that had the words WALLSTREET written across it in bold black letters. I picked it up to get a closer look, but it was just an empty bag. Now I knew, from watching TV and from my neighborhood, that that type of bag was only used for one thing, and that was drugs. I looked around the trunk before placing the bags inside, but I didn't find anything else. The trunk was spotless. At that moment, it hit me. I had just been given another piece of the puzzle. I just didn't know where it fit. I put the bags in and closed the trunk. I got back in the car but didn't say a word to Jacelyn about what I had found.

Jacelyn and Mike had kind of the same personality. They could both be loud and unreasonable at times, so news like this would have Jacelyn running right to Mike, getting him all worked up, and I would never be able to figure out the rest of the puzzle with ease. My grandma always said, "You see this puzzle of trees, Bridgette? They may be beautiful, but the roads and the paths between them tell a story about a journey one has traveled. Both the good and the bad."

She said, "Always look closely at the pieces that you find and figure out how they fit together."

Chase wouldn't even know that I knew this information right away. I had to wait until the right time to say something or see if he would tell me before I asked him. One thing that was for sure, I knew today was going to be a long day. We picked up the champagne and the sweets from the bakery. Now I was driving, headed to the office, with all sorts of thoughts in my head. I knew Chase and Mike had to have said something to Jeff by now, and I couldn't wait to see what happened.

After all the shopping, we finally arrived at the office, and it was full of purple and red balloons, a cake, champagne, and a CONGRATULATIONS banner. My mom, my dad, and even Mr. Henderson and the guys were there. I was surprised to see Jeff was still there, but I guessed Chase wanted to wait. Jacelyn and I were all excited, smiling and nothing but happy. Mike surprisingly made a toast, saying, "To the most beautiful partners in the world, welcome to Morgan, Starks and Banks Investment Corporation."

Everyone cheered, whistled, and clapped. They were just as moved as we were with his speech. We both hugged and thanked Chase and Mike for making it all possible. The phones were ringing nonstop, so I said, "Although I love a great celebration, we have money to make. Thank you all for your warm welcome but please answer the phones."

Chase said, "Now that's what I'm talking about…money in the making. She has the best interest of the company at hand. Before anyone moves, though, we have one more surprise."

To the left of Chase's office used to be a large conference room, which they took a portion of that and a portion of Chase's office and converted into a private office for me. Of course, there was an adjoining door inside that led to Chase's office. Chase said, "You needed a door to put your name plate on, so now you have one."

Everything was nicely setup. I never expected to walk in and find that I had an office. Jacelyn also had a similar office to the right of Mike's office. She started crying when they opened the door. She was always crying, just like a little baby. I, on the other hand, was very much enjoying everything, but I just needed a minute alone with Chase. I said, "Mr. Morgan, can I see you in my office for a minute?" Everyone laughed, but I was serious. He came in and closed the door. I asked, "Is my glass a two-way mirror like yours is, where nobody can see in?"

He said, "Yes."

I couldn't help but grab him, rest my head on his chest, and just hold him while he held me.

Full of concern, he asked, "What's wrong, Beautiful?"

I said, "Nothing. I just wanted to thank you for everything. I love you so much. You have done so much for me in a very short period of time, and I want you to know that I'm really grateful, and I appreciate you."

He said, "I love you, too, Beautiful."

I didn't want to give him any hints that I was overwhelmed with thoughts, so I just went on as if nothing happened. I hated to do that because I knew he trusted me and he would tell me anything if I asked, but he didn't tell me what the hell Wallstreet was when we met, and I had just decided to keep this quiet. Maybe it didn't belong to him, but he was not the one to carry anyone else's baggage but his own. I knew, without a doubt, that Wallstreet was some sort of drug. I had to wonder, though, if Wallstreet had anything to do with the firm, since it was located on Wall Street. Maybe he hadn't said anything for my own protection.

After our brief conversation, we went back into the office with everyone else and dismissed the celebration. Chase and Mike wanted to take us to lunch. Before we left, I said, "Well, Chase, tell me something."

"Sure. Anything, Beautiful."

"When do we actually work?"

"Lunch is work. Now let's go."

Mr. Henderson, the guys, and my mom and my dad headed out as well.

We headed to the café right downstairs from the office. It was nice but not a place the guys would take us for lunch. Chase said, "Like I said, this is work. Watch and learn." He took out his laptop, plugged it in, and set it up. We were seated in the back of the café where nobody could see us or what we were doing. Chase turned on the surveillance to the office and made a call to Jeff. He said, "Jeff, I need you to go into my office. I have a file on my desk that's worth a lot a cash, and I need the client's contact info."

Jeff said, "Okay, sure. I'm going to need your code. Thanks, boss, for trusting me to do this. I know nobody has the code to your office but you."

Chase said, "It's all good. I trust you, Jeff." Chase gave him the code.

Jeff walked inside to the desk and got the folder but not before glancing around the room. He quickly gave Chase the client's info. You could tell by his tone he was overjoyed, like he'd just hit the number or something. He said, "Okay, boss, do you need anything else?"

Chase said, "No, that's it," and hung up.

I asked, "Now what?"

Chase said, "Now we really go to lunch and come back around 5:45, right before everyone leaves for the day. Do you really think I gave him my code to get info for me? Nah, it was for his stupid ass to go back in there and show me what he so badly needed to get out of there the other day. Like I said before, plant the trap, and the snake will get caught. Now once I find out what he needed, I'm going to beat the dog shit out of him, just for invading my privacy."

Mike was nothing but excited because he wanted in on the action.

All I could say was, "Please be careful, guys, because we have a lot to lose."

Chase said, "Who are you telling? And then some."

My puzzle radar immediately went up because what more did we have to lose other than the firm? Oh, and there was Who's Who, but the firm didn't even know they owned that. Such a mystery, but it would all come to the light soon.

We sat down to a nice lunch at an Asian spot a few blocks away. Chase said, "We need to be as close as possible to the office."

We ate and talked about the trip, trying not to think about the upcoming events of the day. It was now 5:15 pm, time to walk back to the café. We got back to the café within ten minutes, set up the laptop, and watched the surveillance until everyone left, everyone except Jeff.

He played right into the snake trap. He sat there, acting like he was still working, not realizing this would be his last day at work. He got up and went to Chase's office, just as Chase knew he would. We watched as Jeff entered the code, and that was when Mike said, "That's it. I can't watch this. I'm about to go light his snake-ass up."

Chase said, "Mike, we about to go up there right now, and if you strapped, do not pull your piece out on camera."

They told me and Jacelyn to stay put and watch the footage while they went upstairs. So now Jeff was in the office. He was checking behind the pictures, I'm guessing, to see if there was a safe behind them. Then he checked the desk drawer and found ten-thousand dollars in cash. He quickly put the cash in his pocket, closed the drawer back, and wiped his fingerprints off the desk with a tissue.

Mike and Chase quickly got upstairs, into the office, and walked toward Chase's office. The door was still open, and Jeff was still in there. Jeff heard them and tried to hurry out the office, but Mike put his hands up, pushing Jeff's chest, and saying, "Whoa, whoa, whoa! What's the hurry, Jeff? You got somewhere you need to be?"

Jeff said, "Yeah, as a matter of fact, I do."

Mike said, "Well, there's just been a change in plans, and you're not gonna make it to wherever you needed to go."

Chase looked at Jeff and said, "What's so important in my office that you had to get in here so badly?"

Jeff said, "Nothing."

Chase said, "I find nothing hard to believe. I'm gonna give you sixty seconds to come clean before I beat the dog shit outta you, and I'm saying that in a nice way, Jeff."

He said, "Okay, Mr. Morgan, I'm sorry, I'm sorry, I'm sorry."

"Sorry for what, Jeff?"

"I needed some cash."

"Cash for what, Jeff, and why steal it from me? You couldn't have just asked me for it."

Jeff said, "I owe some people some money, and if I don't pay them, they are going to kill me."

"How much do you owe, and what do you owe them for? Stop playing and beating around the bush. You're still gonna get the dog shit beat out of you, so let's move this along."

You could tell Chase was mad by his facial expressions.

Jeff said, "I got some coke from my doctor. It's some really good shit and worth the money. It's called Wallstreet. I just didn't have the cash, so I told him I would pay him Friday, but I didn't have it on Friday, so I tried to get in your office then, but I couldn't crack the code, and when you gave me the code today, I said, 'Let me just try my luck.'"

Chase asked, "How much do you owe?"

Jeff said, "Twenty-thousand dollars."

"For some coke? Damn! It must be some good shit for twenty grand. Here's what I'm gonna do. Today is your lucky day, Jeff. I'm going to pay off your debt. What did you say his name was again?"

Jeff said, "Dr. Blockerick over on Park."

"Okay, me and Mike will pay him a visit. Meanwhile, take my fucking cash out your pocket and put it back where the fuck you found it."

Jeff put the money back, and that was when Chase bitch-slapped him. Chase said, "You wanna steal and use drugs like a bitch, so now you will be treated like one. I'm not sure what I'm going to do with you just yet because you've become a liability here at the office. You can no longer work here, but you will be working off this debt you owe. If you have to clean my car for the next twenty years, you're gonna work this shit off. Now get the fuck out my office, and leave your badge on the desk, along with that doctor's address. Oh, and if I were you, I would lay low until I go pay him. It would be a shame for him to pop a cap in your ass now that you found a way to pay him. Tomorrow morning, bright and early, go check yourself into rehab, you fucking junkie. Rule number one: Don't sniff dope if you can't afford to."

Mike just looked at him and said, "You owe this man your life. You wouldn't be so fucking lucky if you had tried to get into my office. We wouldn't even be having this conversation. You'd be dead already." Mike snuffed him and said, "Bye, you fucking snake bitch."

Chase said, "Now we got to go pay Dr. Fuckboy a visit and teach him a valuable lesson about rule number two. Look, Mike, chill out. You know the rules. We said, if anyone we knew ever got hooked on this shit, we would help them get clean. We're not out here to destroy people, man. That's why we only sell it privately in the club to people who can afford it and have something to lose, not everyday people."

"Yeah, I know, Chase. I feel you. He's lucky we have rules, though, because, if we didn't, he'd be floating in the river somewhere by now."

Now me and Jacelyn were still watching, but we couldn't hear anything because it recorded images, not voices. I so wished I was a fly on the wall to hear what was actually being said, but I trusted the guys had made the right decision. Jacelyn said, "It couldn't have been that bad since Mike let him live."

"Please, Jacelyn, they knew we were still watching, and they would've shut the cameras off if they were going to kill him."

"True, but I thought for sure they would, at least, beat the blood out of him…well, Mike anyway. Chase is not getting his pretty hands dirty."

"And what's that supposed to mean, Jacelyn?"

She said nothing.

I was already not in the mood with everything I was trying to piece together. Then she went and said something stupid.

"First of all, Jacelyn, if Chase wasn't so sane and civilized, there probably wouldn't be a company. Mike would be the one to run everything into the ground because he acts on impulse. Just think about that. Maybe you should try telling Mike to be more business-minded or even try to act like it now that we're partners. I wouldn't want things to start crashing down because he can't leave the hood in the hood."

Jacelyn said, "You know what? You think you know everything, B."

"I don't know everything, but I know enough not to argue my way back to the hood with you. I'm definitely staying on Wall Street for whatever it's worth to you."

Jacelyn said, "Yeah, because you never really fit in the hood anyway."

"Neither did you, Jacelyn, but you're just too stupid to see it."

Now the guys came back and heard us in the middle of our little disagreement. Chase said, "Yo, we leave y'all for a few minutes, and this is what we come back to? Y'all bugging like we don't already have enough to deal with. Everything is cool with Jeff. He won't be doing that again, and I fired him."

"That's good, Chase. I'm glad you handled it. Well, I'm glad y'all handled it. Now can we please just go?" I said.

Chase packed up his laptop, and we headed to the cars.

***

It had been a long day, so when we got home, we showered and just laid in bed. I said, "Chase, do you really love me the way you say you do?"

"What kind of question is that? Don't I show you every day that I love you? You never have to question my love or loyalty when it comes to you, Beautiful." Then he softly kissed my lips a few times, then paused, and said, "What were you and Jacelyn arguing about?"

"Nothing. It was petty and stupid. She was just being my sister, and I love her no matter what we argue about."

"Okay, I'm just making sure y'all are good."

"Yeah, we good. No worries."

We both were so exhausted that, within minutes after finishing that conversation, we both fell asleep in each other's arms.

CHAPTER 15

Pay Up Or Shut Up

It had been about a week since we'd been back from our Bahamas trip. The firm was doing very well, and we had landed a few new clients. Now it was time to really pull in the clients, and Jacelyn and I knew exactly how to do that. We mingled throughout Who's Who, looking stunning from head to toe, on a mission to recruit potential clients. Chase and Mike had a business meeting with a Dr. B, who was already a club member, to go over some contract agreement. I was guessing it was time to renew his membership.

As we walked through the club, Maryellen introduced us to the new event planner for Saturday nights. His name was Robert. His work was very pleasing to the eye. I said, "It's nice to meet you, Robert. You've outdone yourself tonight. Everything looks lovely."

While Chase and Mike quickly excused themselves in order to go to their meeting, we continued to mingle. We basically knew who everyone was and who had the big bucks to invest. So our first target was Mr. Blackman. He was a millionaire real estate investor. After a bunch of smooth talk, we reeled him right in. He set an appointment for Tuesday evening to go over everything. Before we walked away, I said, "Oh, and by the way, Mr. Blackman, don't forget to bring cash and lots of it."

He said, "I don't roll any other way, miss."

Jacelyn and I were sure to bring up our clientele that night and add a pretty penny to this partnership of ours. "Hey, Jacelyn, I'm not sure if Chase and Mike will approve, but we may need an office here at the club to sign all of our new clients."

"That's really a good idea, B. All we have to do is ask them whenever they decide to come out of their meeting, but for now, we will just keep working the room."

THE BACK OFFICE

Chase and Mike were in the office, waiting for Dr. B. When he knocked on the door, Mike opened it. Chase immediately told him to come in and have a seat. Chase said, "What's up, Dr. B? How's the club been treating you?"

Dr. B said, "All is good, and as a matter of fact, things couldn't be better."

Mike moved to close the door. When the door closed, it automatically locked, and the alarm chirped to let them know it was locked. Nobody could leave, and nobody could come in without the code.

Chase said, "Is that so, Dr. B? It's good to hear things couldn't be better with you."

"It's funny how, when things are going great, things can go wrong in a split second, ya know?" Mike said.

Dr. B said, "I don't quite understand what you're saying."

Mike said, "Well, you're about to find out. Keep quiet."

Chase looked at Mike with a look to keep him calm. Then he said, "So I hear you have a new profession."

Dr. B said, "Oh, really? What's that?"

Chase said, "I'll be asking the questions. You just need to be ready to answer them. So, I hear, Dr. B, you're in the wholesale business now."

Dr. B said, "No, no, I'm not. You're mistaken."

"Mistaken? Hmm…you've been distributing Wallstreet outside of the club, and it just so happens that we know your client very well.

What's rule number one in the Who's Who handbook? I'm sure you've read it many times since it was part of your membership requirement to memorize it."

Dr. B said, "Rule number one...umm...'Who's Who is for members only.'"

"Okay. Now, Dr. B, what's rule number two?"

"Umm...'What's behind these walls remains behind these walls.'"

"Good, Dr. B. Now we're getting somewhere."

"What's rule number six, Dr. B?"

"Umm...umm...'Wallstreet is part of the club and never to be taken beyond the walls.'"

"Now for the last one, what's rule number ten?"

"Umm...umm..."

Chase said, "Really, doc? Now you're playing with my intelligence by saying 'ummm' because I know you're not stupid, and you know exactly what rule number ten is."

"No, I'm sorry."

"It says: 'If you break any of the rules, your life will come to an end.'"

That was when Chase pulled out a 9mm from his top drawer, cocked it back, aimed it at Dr. B, and asked, "Are you ready to die now?"

Dr. B started shaking and crying.

Mike said, "Oh, he's acting like a little bitch now."

Chase said, "Well, you have to be ready, Dr. B, because you know the rules. You broke them, and now you have to pay the price. Isn't that exactly what you told your boi when he didn't pay you that twenty grand for product that wasn't even yours to begin with? So I hear, if he doesn't pay by tomorrow, he's dead. Well, too bad you won't be around to collect that twenty grand."

Dr. B said, "Wait, but I don't need it. He can keep the money."

"Now, wait. Let me get this straight. You distributed my product at wholesale, and you don't want the money? I'm a businessman, Dr. B, and I collect any and everything that is due to me, and considering you work for me now, I want my money, and not from him, but from you. Better yet, I'm just gonna follow the rules, and let you go. Goodbye, Dr. B."

BOOM!

Chase pulled the trigger point blank to his head, but luckily for Dr. B, the gun wasn't loaded. Mike yelled, "Yeah! Now that's how it's done!" When he saw nothing happened, he said, "Yo, Chase, finish this cat. He doesn't need to be around any longer."

Dr. B then pissed on himself. He was shaking and crying as he said, "I am begging you. Please. I'll do anything you want. I will pay you your money."

Chase said, "Shut the fuck up while I figure this out. I want one-hundred grand by Monday morning, or your little medical practice will be long gone by Monday night. Plus, you're going to set an example for all the club members." Chase then proceeded to pistol-whip him and beat him until he begged for his life. After he finished, Chase said, "Do we have an agreement, Dr. B?"

Dr. B said, "Yes, yes, Mr. Morgan. I will bring your money by Monday morning."

"I will be watching your every move, Dr. B, and if you cross me, you're dead."

MEETING ADJOURNED

Chase and Mike walked Dr. B out where everyone could see them. They grabbed the mic and walked on stage. This was the first time we'd seen this side of them, besides the Jeff situation. I was sure, though, it was another piece of the puzzle. Chase said, "Can I have your attention for a moment? Good evening, everyone. We would like to thank you all for coming out tonight. We would like to give a special thanks to Dr. B for giving the club a generous donation of two-hundred grand toward any charity of your choice. Dr. B is now the face and spokesman of Wallstreet throughout the club. He has become quite the entrepreneur when it comes to bringing in clients and introducing them to Who's Who and Wallstreet. Take a close look at Dr. B., ladies and gentlemen. Look very closely. When you get too comfortable and decide to ignore the rules of the rulebook, this is the result. The only reason why Dr. B is standing here before you right now is because he's now an example for you all of what not to do at Who's Who. Remember, we take membership here very seriously. That is why we have a rulebook. If the rules are broken, you will pay the consequences with rule number ten. Dr. B will be the only exception because he's now the example that will be stuck in your heads as a reminder not to cross us. On that note, let's get back to the party. Enjoy your evening." Chase then whispered to Dr. B., "Yeah, the price went up, and you still have till Monday to bring me that two-hundred grand in cash or consider yourself dismembered."

Mike said, "Please don't bring it, Dr. B. Please don't because I want the pleasure of dismembering your body. He might let your sorry ass live, but I have no sympathy or need for you. So please don't bring it, and by the way, you can run, but you can't hide."

Chase said, "Always remember, Dr. B. I have the power to make you disappear just like that. If I wanted you dead, you would be. Now get the fuck out my face, asshole, and go tell everyone how bad you fucked shit up for them. Don't leave either. Be sure to stay the entire night to answer everyone's questions, just as any other employee would since you work for me now."

Chase called Maryellen over to let her know what happened. He said, "As of tonight, I'm putting a temporary cap on Wallstreet. There will be a maximum of two bags per night, and each bag will be collected and accounted for at the end of every night."

Mike said, "You bugging. Slow down, Chase. The way you're making moves right now ain't the way, man. Getting rid of snake motherfuckers like Jeff and Dr. B, now that's the way."

Chase said, "Look, Maryellen. We will put it to three, but that's it because who the hell needs more coke than that in one fucking night anyway? We're taking nightly inventory, so whatever number of bags we give out, they all better come back at the end of the night or shit's gonna get crazy around here. No telling who else has been selling our product on the other side of these walls. Just know Wallstreet stocks won't go down until I say they go down. Until then, they're still up, but these motherfuckers just won't get as high off the shit as usual."

Now I was thinking to myself, Wow, there are way more pieces added to the puzzle than I expected. Nobody even knew that I knew Wallstreet even existed, and I now knew that it was definitely not another piece of stock. Chase and Mike walked over to Jacelyn and me, and Chase asked, "Y'all enjoying yourselves?"

We both said, "Yes."

I asked, "Is everything okay?"

He said, "It is now. There's nothing you have to worry your beautiful self about. It's just club business. That's all."

"Chase, I wanted to ask you if Jacelyn and I could have an office here at the club to recruit clients for the firm."

"I'm sorry, Beautiful, but that's not going to happen. I don't want you or Jacelyn having any dealings with the club business anymore. This is why y'all don't plan events here anymore. We put y'all at the firm where, we figured, it would be more of a challenge. Y'all also don't have to worry about recruiting anyone because me and Mike got that all covered. We never want to mix the two companies at all."

"Well, Chase, I made an appointment to sit down with Mr. Blackman on Tuesday."

"Okay. Don't worry about it. I will take care of Mr. Blackman."

Now, I was really thinking and wondering how much longer I could keep this information to myself. I was looking around the room and started to notice a lot of people grabbing their noses between their two fingers. They were all so free, laughing and joking, as they went back to partying, as if nothing had happened. I still hadn't seen a Wallstreet bag in here, and by the looks of things, I just may never see one either. Everyone was so careful. I went with the flow, agreeing with Chase and enjoying the night like any other night we'd come to the club. Tonight, was pimps' night, and the best dressed pimp would win a free event planned at the club. There were, at least, one-thousand club members now, so Chase and Mike were bringing in close to one hundred million a year. The club had been open for two years now. I guessed, with the sales of Wallstreet, the club membership fee, and the firm, these two were very rich men. I didn't understand, know, or realize how much power and respect these two guys had over everything they did and the people they dealt with until tonight. They were businessmen at the firm on Wall Street and businessmen at the club distributing Wallstreet. They were dangerous and not to be played with in anyway. They were always full of surprises, which led me to believe there was so much more to their lives that had yet to be discovered. I just knew, no matter what I found out, it was way too late to turn my back on Chase now. I had come too far with everything to walk away, and I was so very much in love with Chase, so walking away would never be an option. I knew, for a fact, that they did not want Jacelyn or me involved in anything. It had taken them so long to even reveal who they were to us, and by that alone, I knew they already had plans to love us and protect us by any means necessary.

Standing in front of Chase, looking at him, he was so handsome and pleasing to my eyes. He was dressed in a black tux, black shirt, and black tie that was now untied, and the top buttons of his shirt were open. At that moment, I so wished he would snap his fingers to clear the room, so it was just me and him standing in the middle of the floor, dancing. We were all now standing at the bar with drinks in our hands. I looked at Chase, grabbed his hand, and said, "Come with me."

He looked at Mike and said, "Keep an eye on things till I get back. Oh, and don't let Jacelyn out of your sight either."

Mike said, "Oh, trust me, if she has to go to the bathroom, I'm going with her."

Chase laughed and said, "Yeah, just don't go in there with her because you might not make it back out, knowing y'all two."

We all laughed. I held Chase's hand and led him to his office upstairs. He had a great view. He could see everything in the club, but they had no idea his office was even up there. The two-way glass was covered in white and gold mirror on the outside to blend in with the white padded leather walls. It looked like pretty wallpaper on the outside. We walked inside, and I went over and turned on some music. We couldn't hear what was going on in the club, unless we wanted to, and they couldn't hear us, even if I turned the speaker up to the top notch because the room was totally soundproof. I turned on some Keith Sweat and walked over to Chase, where he was looking down at the crowd. Trying to ease his mind, I started talking to him. "Chase, I know it's been crazy this past week, and I know we both could use a little distraction. Come dance with me."

We started slow-dancing in the middle of his office. His shirt was already unbuttoned, so I just unbuttoned it a little more. He kissed me like it would be our last kiss and said, "You're so sweet, Beautiful, and I can't picture my life without you. I love you more than words could ever express. Soon I'm going to make it official. You will see. I would never want to hurt you in any way or keep anything from you, so in due time, you will have everything and know everything."

I knew right then that I no longer had to piece together any puzzle, that he would eventually come clean and tell me everything. I continued to unbutton his shirt and then his pants. He was now standing in his socks and underwear. His chest was bare, but oh so buff. I ran my hands down his chest, feeling every curve and every bulge. I kissed his chest slowly all up and down. He grabbed my face and gently pressed my lips against his. I said, "Chase, you have always made love to me, and you know we've never had sex."

He said, "And like I said before, we never will. I never want to make you feel less of a woman by having sex with you. Whatever I do concerning you will always be with love, passion, respect, and consideration. I could have sex with you in the back of the limo or downstairs in the bathroom really quick, but you deserve all I can give, and that just wouldn't be my all. When I said, 'I'm going to always treat you like royalty,' I meant just that. I'm going to always give you every inch of Royal and then some. We both know it will take longer than ten minutes in the bathroom or in the back of the limo to get it all in. Once Royal gets all up in Royalty, there's no stopping him because you got that good stuff, baby. So that's why we don't have sex. Tonight, I'm about to do something I wouldn't normally do with you, and that's only because you want to. Plus, you got Royal on the rise with all this sex talk. I'm going to make love to you right here, right now until the club closes for the night. I never want you to walk out of my office in front of people with them knowing or thinking we just had sex. I have way too much respect for you."

"I don't care what people think, Chase."

"I don't either, but when it's concerning you, I do."

In that moment, all he had said made my love for him even deeper. His words confirmed that, no matter where we are, whether it be the club or the firm, he had the same level of respect for me. He unbuttoned my blouse and unzipped my skirt and tossed them on the desk. I was now standing in my black lace bra and panties from Victoria's Secret. We danced around a little more before he picked me up in his arms, wrapped my legs around him, and carried me to the sofa. Every move he made was slow and passionate. Even when he moved fast, it was still passionate. He wanted me to feel every move deep down inside, creating all pleasure with hardly no pain. Royal and Royalty basically made a movie about the differences between sex and lovemaking in the office. Each moment was long, hard, slow, and passionate. Who would want sex after all of this? I knew I didn't, and I knew I would never question it again. I also knew, if something were ever to happen in the limo, the driver would be given the day and night off.

**

After about two hours of being in the office, we finally freshened up and got dressed. We met up with Mike and Jacelyn downstairs. Chase asked Mike if everything was cool.

"Yeah, things are good. Jacelyn and I slipped out for about thirty minutes, but nobody even noticed we were gone."

Chase said, "Didn't I tell you not to go in the bathroom with her?"

"I didn't. We went to your office instead."

Chase said, "Wait. What did you say?"

Mike said, "Nah, I'm just joking. We went to my office."

149

Chase said, "Be sure, Mike, to tell the cleaning crew to hit your office first thing in the morning," and we all laughed. Chase said, "Bridgette and I just had to go over some business really quick."

Mike said, "For two hours, I'm sure y'all covered a lot of subjects and signed a few contracts, too."

Chase smiled at me and said, "Yeah, just a few."

Chase checked the bag count with Maryellen. Everything was accounted for, so we left and headed home.

Straight to the shower we went, and Royal and Royalty were back at it again. Since it was already two o'clock in the morning on a Sunday, we knew that we might as well make the best of what was left of the weekend before we had to start another crazy week. The way Royal and Royalty went at it, it was always like the first time they met, sparks flying everywhere. They both gave off so much heat, sweat, and juices that there was never a dry moment between the two. We ended up falling asleep in each other's arms while taking a break for some air.

***

Today, I planned a Sunday fun day, and I made an appointment with the interior decorator to get the new penthouse rolling. I was so ready to really get my life started with Chase, and it had to start at home. I walked into the kitchen and said, "Chase, I made an appointment with the decorator at the penthouse for around three today."

He had awakened before me, made breakfast, and went straight to work on our day off. I had to walk over and pry his laptop out of his hands. "Chase, we have to promise that our days off will be exactly that...our days off."

"Okay, my love, anything for you," and he hit me with one of the couch pillows. Playfully and while grabbing me, he said, "So whatcha wanna do until three?"

"Chase, you're so nasty."

"No, I'm not, but if you say so, it's because of you. Look how excited Royal gets being around you."

"Chase, please. Royal is not excited about me. He's excited because he's thirsty for a little milkshake from Royalty."

We played, laughed, and joked around for a while, no sex though. Then at about two, we headed out to the penthouse.

This place was beautiful, far better than when I'd first seen it. I guessed it looked better because I had so much going on and I was in love with Chase's penthouse. Now that we had a place that would be ours, I could finally see the vision Chase had when he bought it. After talking to the decorator, she understood that this was urgent and time sensitive because Chase's penthouse had already sold for $1.2 million and we had to move out soon. I wanted her to start with the walls, carpet, and furniture first. She said that would take about two weeks to complete. Then we would come back and finish the rest, but then she insisted that we choose everything today and give her thirty days. Then, at that time, we would be able to see the finished look and move right in. We all agreed to just that. She never said how much everything would cost, but there was really no set budget. When we were finally finished with her, we headed back home.

Chase said, "I won't be at the firm tomorrow. I have some business to take care of at Who's Who."

"Okay, Chase. Jacelyn and I will be just fine until you get there."

***

Monday morning, bright and early as usual, Jacelyn and I went to the firm, and the guys went to Who's Who. I had to say the firm was a bit quiet without Jeff. I was sorry he had to go, but it was for his own good and for our safety. Jacelyn and I sorted through Jeff's clients to see where he'd left off. I didn't really like dealing with other brokers' clients because they had already built a relationship and trust with them. Rest assured that Jacelyn and I were bound to build new relationships and trust with each and every one of them anyway. Once everything was sorted out, we would start making calls to them tomorrow.

Jacelyn said, "Okay. That's cool, B."

THE BACK OFFICE

Chase and Mike met up with Dr. B around eleven o'clock that morning. He knocked on Chase's office door on the first floor of the club, which was one of three. Dr. B said, "May I come in, Mr. Morgan?"

Chase said, "Only if you have my cash, and if you don't, what is your purpose for even showing up here?"

Dr. B said, "No, I have your cash. It's all accounted for. All two-hundred grand, and I added another twenty grand just to show no hard feelings and that I'm terribly sorry."

"Wait. Hold up. Mike, check him for any recording devices or wires. We have to treat him like the snake he is. You never know. He might be a dirty little rat as well."

Mike checked him and said, "He's clean."

"For your sake, Dr. B, that's a good thing. Mike, take the money to the back to be counted and bring back the twenty grand. That twenty grand is going to pay for your client's rehab bill to get him free and clean of any and all drugs. You're a doctor, so I'm sure providing for someone's health and well-being shouldn't be a problem for you."

Dr. B said, "No, it's not a problem at all. I deserve whatever happens to me."

Chase said, "You good for now, but don't ever cross me again because you won't be paying in cash, you'll be paying with your life. You'll never see the light of day again."

Dr. B said, "Can I go now, Mr. Morgan?"

"What's the rush? You leave when I say you can leave. Besides, Mike hasn't come back yet. He's making sure every bill is clean and that it's all there. That may take a while, Dr. B, so sit tight, homie, but don't get comfortable. So let me ask you this, what made you think you could sell my product?"

Dr. B said, "It was just so good, and I figured some people on the outside would love to have some. That's all."

"Well, the reason why your dumb ass pays one-hundred grand in private membership fees per year is because Wallstreet is for members only. So why in the fuck would you let or even want people outside to get it for any less than what you pay? You're just a dumb fuck that went to college to be a dumb fuck-up. I have my reasons for keeping you in the club, but you're on a very limited supply and, because of you, so is the rest of the club. As you can see, you paid a hefty fine, your membership went up, your supply is limited, and you're living on borrowed time. I hope it was all worth it. Be careful, Dr. B, be careful."

As Chase finished speaking, Mike came back in the room. He said, "The money is all clean and accounted for, and here's the twenty grand you asked for, Chase."

Chase said, "Dr. B, you're dismissed and don't forget our conversation."

"I won't, Mr. Morgan. Thank you."

MEETING ADJOURNED

"Yo, Mike, we got to go boost up security and make sure nothing gets in that's not supposed to be in and nothing gets out that's not supposed to go out. We got control of the product, but people got ways of trying to take shit out, and that's why I limited their daily supply. They're not gonna want to share if they're barely getting enough for themselves. I just know we got to get better control of things. We didn't get this far to let some dumb-ass, coke-sniffing motherfuckers bring us down. I'm never going back to the hood. I don't know about you, Mike, but I'm not. I can promise you that. Plus, we gotta talk to Bridgette and Jacelyn to put them on to everything. If something goes down, I don't want them to be blindsided or in the dark about anything. I know they are strong enough to handle things for what they really are."

Mike said, "You sure, Chase? They may want to step off."

"Trust me, Mike. They ain't going nowhere. I never said I was perfect, and I told her I wasn't, so we will just have to wait and see."

"Fine with me. I just know it has to be done real soon, Chase."

"One thing I don't want to do is lose their trust, Mike."

"All right, Chase. I hear you, man. Now let's get out of here and get back to the ladies."

***

The club was not far from the office. It was only about twenty minutes away. To see the guys walk through the door really made my day. I ran and hugged Chase and said, "I've missed you."

He said, "I missed you, too, Beautiful. Since my work is all done at Who's Who, it gave me time to come check on you. How are things going?"

"Well, Chase, everything is good. Me and Jacelyn were just sorting through Jeff's work and getting things ready to call his clients tomorrow."

Chase said, "Just track their money but don't call them just yet. I don't want to alarm anyone, especially if their money ain't right. As soon as we know the numbers are up for sure, then we can make the calls."

"Sure thing, boss. Whatever you say," I said.

Chase said, "I'm not your boss, Ms. Banks. I'm your partner. We work together. As a matter of fact, I'm going to need you and Jacelyn to run things around here at the firm for a few weeks, while me and Mike do some upgrades and clean house at the club. It won't be for long, we just need enough time to put some things in motion. I promise we will meet here every night to go over all of the things regarding the firm. I'm not just going to leave you all alone like that. Plus, I'm just a phone call away. Once things are back too normal at the club, we'll have a surprise for y'all."

"A surprise, Chase?"

While smiling at Mike, Jacelyn said, "Your surprises are always good, and ain't nothing wrong with that. I can't wait."

Mike said, "That's good, J. I'm glad you're excited. That's just how I need you to be. Oh, Chase, by the way, Jeff called. He said to tell you he's doing good, and the treatment is really helping. He said he will be done in two more weeks. He also said that the bills were very high, and he couldn't afford to stay, but since you sent him there, he had them forward the bills to you."

Chase said, "Ain't that a bitch, but it's cool. I was already prepared to take care of his bills anyway. Let's just say his treatment was self-funded and not a dime out of my pocket."

"Chase, he also wanted to know if you took care of that situation."

Chase said, "Okay, Bridgette, I get the message. I will call the facility to speak to him tomorrow. I don't want you involved in any of this. Where's the phone number?"

I gave him the number, and that conversation was over. In the back of my mind, that was another piece to this mysterious puzzle that I was patiently waiting for Chase to complete. I was not going to dwell on it, but the pieces were sure coming together on their own. One thing I could say was Wallstreet and Who's Who were both connected, which was great, because the firms seemed to be free and clear from it all.

CHAPTER 16

Promise

Chase Morgan

Everything was all set at the club. Tighter security was in place. The product had been limited, and all bags were accounted for. Jeff was out of rehab, and Dr. B sure seemed to have learned from his mistakes. Jeff was now back at the firm but on a strict watch. The girls had turned the firm into a greater success, especially with Jeff being back and levelheaded. It was now time that we took the girls somewhere and let them know what was up. Me and Mike decided to take them on a private yacht over to Atlantic City for the weekend. We bought them a few nice gifts, just to ease the topic of discussion. Me and Mike were all set to leave the club in a few to pick up the girls.

"Yo, Mike, did you have everything sent over to the yacht?"

"Yeah, man, everything is taken care of."

"I hope so since that's all you had to do all day, Mike."

"So what are you saying, Chase?"

"Nothing, Mike. It's all good."

"Nah, Chase, you trying to say I don't do nothing."

"Well, Mike, you don't, but I'm not stressing it. I was just making sure everything was straight because we break out in two hours, and we don't have time for any surprises. Now whatever else you're feeling, Mike, is on you, but just not tonight. Let it wait."

Mike said, "Whatever, man. It's cool."

***

Bridgette Banks

Chase and Mike arrived at the firm, smiling and in a very good mood. Chase greeted me with a hug and a kiss, and Jacelyn walked over and took her kisses and hugs from Mike. They had a crazy relationship, but it worked for them. Funny as it may sound, it truly worked. Chase checked on a few things and said to everyone, "It's been a great week. Thank you." He handed everyone a bonus check for one-thousand dollars each and told them to have a great weekend because he knew he was going to. We waited for everyone to leave. Then, we locked up and left as well.

There was a limo waiting when we got downstairs. No telling what was up because, even when we rode in their cars, they were full of surprises. We got in, and before we knew it, we were riding while looking out at the beautiful scenery of the ocean along the Westside Highway. We pulled into the pier and got out. There was a huge private yacht waiting for our arrival.

"Chase, you didn't?"

"Yes, I did, Beautiful."

"Chase, you're always full of surprises, but me, I'm always working so hard that I never get to surprise you."

"It's ok, Beautiful. Like I said before, I'm supposed to do this. As long as you're keeping me and Royal happy, you will always get surprises like this."

"Chase, it's not all about that."

"No, it's not, not at all. I love everything about you, keeping me and Royal happy is just a bonus, Beautiful."

"Now that sounds a lot better, Chase."

Chase laughed and, while playing around, said, "It's not what it sounds like. It's what it is. Me and Royal are getting very excited, just knowing what's about to go down on this yacht tonight."

I just laughed because I was pretty excited as well. Well, me, not Royalty. Well, not yet anyway. I yelled, "Come on, guys," to Jacelyn and Mike. "Let's get on." The two of them were always playing around.

We boarded the yacht and were greeted by the captain and eight crew members. The captain, the chef, and the crew, they were all so very nice to us. Considering the fact that this was my first time on a yacht, I didn't know what to expect, but I was super happy. They gave us fresh hot hand towels and glasses of champagne as they welcomed us aboard. The stewardess took us on a tour of the yacht. There were some spiral steps that led us up to the top deck where there was a Jacuzzi, lounge chairs, and a patio table that sat eight people. On the second level, there was an outdoor dining area. On the first level, there were four bedrooms, a living room, and a dining room area. It was beautiful. They led us into the kitchen to go over the menu with the chef. The chef said, "For dinner, I made a dish of seafood ziti with white wine, and for dessert, I made strawberry shortcake at your request."

For breakfast the next morning, the chef's suggestions were omelets, pancakes, beef sausage, turkey bacon, French toast, and fresh fruit. I said, "That's perfect, but where are the cheesy grits?"

The chef smiled and said, "What's a southern breakfast without cheesy grits? I'm sorry. I missed that one. I will be sure to whip up some grits as well for you guys."

Now that the food was set, we went up to the second deck to watch all the city lights as we departed Manhattan. Chase quickly asked the stewardess if they could set up a private lunch for the four of us and if the crew could leave the ship for a few hours once we were docked in New Jersey tomorrow. She said, "I'm sure we can arrange that with the captain. Let me go and ask him."

While we were continuing to enjoy the nice, cool breeze, looking at the New York sites, Chase held me in his arms and said, "This is all for you. I hope you enjoy it." He put his arms along both sides of me and held onto the railings. I put my arms around his neck, and we looked into each other's eyes, and that was when this magical kiss began. It was different. It felt different, and he sure felt different. He was kissing and holding me like I was going somewhere, like it would be his last kiss for a while. I guess it was just pure love.

Our kiss was quickly interrupted by the stewardess. She said, "Everything has been arranged for tomorrow."

Chase said, "Okay. Thank you," and turned around and started kissing me again. He said, "You keep kissing me like this, and we are bound to get into trouble." We had both had a few drinks and were feeling a little overheated. The stewardess informed us that dinner would be served within the hour. Chase looked at me, then smiled. He said, "An hour? That's perfect."

It gave us just enough time to shower and change, but I knew better. I knew exactly what he was smiling about. To be honest, I wished we could've just laid on the deck and made love while the stars shone down on us, but since we were not alone, we went to the room. Jacelyn and Mike were already in their room, so no worries about them. I was sure they were enjoying everything the yacht had the offer.

We entered into the paradise room, and there was champagne, white roses, and white candles all over the room. Chase hit the switch to the satellite radio and turned to an R&B station. He poured each of us a glass of champagne and started dancing with me. He was dancing up on me like he was a stripper. He was really close and was feeling my body up and down. One zip and my dress hit the floor. I was wearing a purple lace bra and panties. He said, "You have on that color that makes Royal who he is, and I'm about to show you exactly what Royal is all about." He put Royal into my hands to feel the effects of my purple underwear. I could feel him as he rose to his longest length ever. Oh, how ready was Royalty at that moment to feel every Royal inch I was holding. I hopped up into his arms and wrapped my legs around his waist, and he carried me to the bed. He laid me down very gently, then rubbed and kissed me everywhere. He played with and teased me, rubbing Royal up and down the outside of my purple panties. He kissed me some more, unfastened my bra, and slid my panties off. By this time, I was ready to explode because he was doing too much. He kissed my legs, working his way up to my thighs. Then he massaged Royalty's lips with his lips slowly up and down as my legs began to shake. As my moans got louder and my breathing got deeper, I wanted nothing more than to feel Royal inside of me, but he wouldn't stop. He kept slowly massaging until I had an orgasm. All I could say in my mind was, "Now that's love." When a guy can make you feel like that and expects nothing in return, he has some strong balls.

He finally finished, so he stopped and laid down for a second. I didn't need a second. I jumped right on top of him, trying to get a quick moment of pleasure from Royal. As I began to slide down, Chase stopped me. He said, "Dinner is waiting."

"I know but please really quick, Chase." In my mind, I was saying, Fuck a dinner.

He said, "Beautiful, nothing I do is quick, and you know that. Besides, that was all for you, and we have all night for them to meet up. Now, let's shower really quick, so we can eat." He laughed.

I hit him with the pillow and said, "You're not funny, Chase." He had never left me desiring Royal. I wanted him now more than ever, but I was guessing that was all part of his plan. We got dressed. I put on a long, flowy dress and a bra, leaving my panties off because he was going to finish what he'd started one way or another.

***

We got up to dinner on the outer deck. It was dark, but the lights from the stars and the candles lit the table. The stewardess poured us drinks and left us to eat. I was feeling so hot and bothered that I couldn't really eat or talk to Jacelyn and Mike. They were talking, but I was too focused on pleasing Royalty that I heard nothing they said. Jacelyn was the first to notice as she said, "B, did you hear me? Did you hear anything I just said?"

I tried to recover by saying, "I'm sorry. My mind wondered off."

Jacelyn laughed and said, "Where? Into space?"

Little did she know, it had wondered right under the table. I put my hand under the tablecloth in search of Royal, and I found him. To my surprise, Royal was locked, fully loaded, and ready to shoot into Royalty's target. Now my milkshake was already flowing, I mean, melting at this point, so I took Chase's hand and led him straight to Royalty. He took his feel around and smiled like it was Christmas. He slowly whispered, "Ooooh, shit," as he noticed I had no panties on and my milkshake was melting all over his hand. I smiled and winked at him. I knew exactly what I was doing.

He got up, grabbed my hand, and walked me over to the rail. He turned me, so I was facing toward the ocean. He pressed up against me and whispered, "Do you feel that? What are you doing? Why are you playing with me like this, Beautiful? You know I want you so bad, but we had to show up to dinner. It would've been rude not to after the chef went through so much trouble to prepare this meal for us."

"So, Chase, tell me, who'd you rather please? Me and Royalty or the chef?"

"You already know the answer to that question, Beautiful." He moved my hair to the side and kissed my neck. He slightly lifted my dress in the front. Nobody was able to see what he was doing because my dress was really long and flowy. I was facing forward, and Chase's tall, muscular body covered mine. He was wearing sweats and a T-shirt, so nobody could see between the sweats. He checked again to see just how much my milkshake was melting. He whispered softly, "If only we were alone on this yacht, I would bend you over this railing and put every inch of Royal right up in you."

As for me, I was thinking the same thing because I probably wanted him more than he wanted me right then. At that moment, I was ready for whatever, right then and there. I just couldn't wait any longer. It was torture. He let go of my dress, and I turned around to face him.

He smiled, tapped my nose, and said, "You're something else. I see we both had way too much to drink."

I looked back and noticed that Jacelyn and Mike had left the table. Once you leave the table, you can only go upstairs or downstairs. If they went upstairs, we would've heard them by now. Knowing that we were alone was an open invitation for me to see just what Royal was up to. I kissed Chase and reached into his sweats to bring Royal up for some air. The stewardess came up deck and said, "Can I get you anything else?"

We kept right on kissing, ignoring she was even there.

She said, "Well, okay, then. I will tell the rest of the crew not to disturb you. Enjoy the rest of your evening."

Now with nobody to interrupt us or see what we were doing, Chase picked me up and sat me on the ledge of the yacht. He stood in front of me, between my legs, and held my butt cheeks, so I didn't slip. He covered my legs and my knees with my dress and raised up the middle just enough to slide Royal right into Royalty's melting milkshake. As Royal slid in to get drowned in milkshake, Chase slowly whispered, "Oh, my God." He took a deep breath and said, "This, I promise, is not sex. I'm just continuing where we left off earlier, but trust me, it won't end out here. I just had to let him out for a few minutes." As his breathing got deeper, he said, "I just can't help myself right now, so please forgive me, even though you did this to me. I told you I would never disrespect you in anyway, so please know that I'm being a total gentleman right now."

He couldn't even talk straight after that, he just kissed me. I leaned back a little bit just to take it all in. While Royal was still getting drowned, he pulled me closer to him, as close as he could to make sure he hit the spot. He stood there, holding me tight in his arms, so that he wouldn't let me slip. He was moving slowly but forcefully, making me feel every inch. He said, "We have to stop before I bang you into the ocean." He just stood still with no movement and held me in his arms while my hair blew in the wind. He whispered, "I love you, and I will never leave you." We both took a deep breath, and that was when he went to stop Royal from drowning, but I wouldn't let him. It was too late anyway. Royal had already started adding milk of his own to Royalty's shake.

I wasn't ready to move. I wanted to hold that feeling just a little longer. He said, "See? You crazy," and laughed. He kissed me on the forehead and said, "Come on. Let's go because we will be out here all night messing with you. Besides I want this to be a special tonight, not like this. It was fine for the moment, but I can't move the way I want to move or make you feel the way I want you to feel out here."

My thoughts were, This man is amazing. He makes me feel beyond *royalty*. No matter what the missing pieces of the puzzle may reveal, it can never be bad enough for me to let him go. I will never let him go. I will never find another man who treats me the way he does. He picked me up off the ledge and helped me fix my hair and dress. "Chase, what man does these things for a woman?"

"A man that's in love with being loved, so he doesn't mind showing love to the one he loves."

"Hmmm…Chase, you're quite the poet. I'm in love with you, too. You just don't let me show it the way you do."

"Beautiful, you show it in all the ways you're supposed to." He grabbed my hand, and we went down to the main level.

Jacelyn and Mike were playing PlayStation in the living room and eating all kinds of junk food. Mike said, "Look at these two lovebirds. Y'all wanna play?"

Chase said, "Nope," and grabbed the bottle of champagne that was on ice, the container of ice cream, the strawberries they had, and the two spoons off the table. Chase said, "Sorry, but we will be taking these, and y'all have yourselves a good night now."

Jacelyn and Mike laughed as we walked to our room.

Once we got back to the room, Chase went to the bathroom, and I quickly grabbed my black lace one-piece crotch-less lingerie. He came out the bathroom, and I walked in. I quickly used the bathroom, freshened up, and put on my peaches and cream lotion. I was smelling so edible. I slipped on my lingerie, pinned up my hair, and walked out into the room. He had the room lit with candles, soft music playing, and was laying on the bed with the bucket of ice cream resting on Royal. He said, "Come get some."

I walked over, crawled on the bed, and opened the bucket of ice cream. I took a spoon of
ice cream out of the bucket, spread ice cream all over Royal, and then slowly licked it off.

"Damn, Beautiful. You're smelling good enough to eat right now."

"As always, Chase, that's the plan."

He took the spoon from my hand and said, "Lay right here. I wanna add some ice cream to Royalty's milkshake. I want to finish where I left off." He made sure to lick away every bit of ice cream until he made me shake. After that, Royal and Royalty played for a few hours until the sun came up. I was hoping that we didn't wake any of the crew with all the noise, but hey, they were probably wishing they were me, Chase, or even a fly on the wall right about now.

We didn't sleep much, but who could sleep anyway after having that much fun? We showered around nine that morning and, afterward, got dressed for breakfast. We both threw on sweat suits and slippers just to feel relaxed and comfortable after that long, hard, sleepless night we'd just had. Chase and I both put on a pair of Gucci shades to hide our eyes from anyone who looked at us. We were able to walk out to breakfast on the deck without anyone looking directly at us. When we walked up the deck, Mike smiled at us and said, "Damn! Y'all must have had a hard night."

Chase said, "Man, I was hard all night and early this morning. We had way too many drinks, and my lovely lady kept me up until the crack of dawn."

Jacelyn said, "Ooooh, do tell."

"I'm sorry, J, but good girls never kiss and tell. Plus, Chase already gave y'all way too much information."

Jacelyn said, "Well, it's not like we didn't hear y'all all night anyway."

"Stop playing, Jacelyn. Are you serious?" I asked, mortified.

"No, B. Chill. I'm just joking. These walls are pretty solid."

"It doesn't matter anyway if y'all heard us because we aim to please, and that's exactly what we were doing, aiming and pleasing each other all night and all morning. Ain't that right, baby?" Chase said playfully.

"That's right, baby," I said, and he kissed me on the cheek.

I was starving, and breakfast was looking really good. I tore up that French toast, sausages, eggs, and cheese grits. I really needed that to soak up all the liquor in my stomach from last night.

As I wolfed down my food, Mike said, "Damn! You were hungry, B."

"Well, Mike, last night, we really only ate each other, oh, and those two scoops of ice cream," I said, still slightly embarrassed.

Mike said, "Now you wanna tell it, and we really don't want to hear it seriously."

"Whatever, Mike." I rolled my eyes.

We all laughed.

After we finished up breakfast, we went to the upper deck. We put on some hip-hop and started a little party. Mike put on Jay-Z and Jermaine Dupree's "Money Ain't a Thang." Chase and Mike got up and put on a show. We laughed so hard, but they were serious. They were performing like they were superstars on top of the world. This was starting to be their anthem. Then "Big Business" with Jadakiss and Ron Isley came on. Then, "Sugar Hill" by AZ ft. Miss Jones, and the list went on. We partied and drank champagne for about two hours. Then we went inside.

As soon as our heads hit the pillow, we were out. We woke up to the stewardess saying lunch would be ready in an hour and would be served at the inside dining room table because the winds were blowing a bit too much this afternoon.

We said, "Okay, thank you."

Chase said, "Come on, Beautiful. Let's freshen up for lunch."

"But we just had breakfast, Chase."

"That was hours ago. Plus, I have something special planned. Since we will be inside, we don't even have to get all dressed up."

I threw on a cute little white dressy pants jumper with a pair of tan open-toe heels, sandals, of course. Chase put on a tan Armani sweat suit. He was looking fine. He even put on his jewels. You would've thought we were having company or going out on the town. I didn't expect anything less from him, though. If you have the cash to do it, then do it, and who's to stop you?

"Chase, you're looking so handsome. I guess you don't know how not to get all dressed up."

"It's just a sweat suit, Beautiful."

"Yeah, just a sweat suit that makes you look like you just stepped out of a *GQ* magazine."

"You're looking cute as always, Bridgette."

"Thanks, Chase. You're so sweet."

We went out to the living room area where Jacelyn and Mike were playing a game. The crew had set up the dining room so beautifully. Everything was gold and white linen, white plates, gold flatware, and the glasses were tinted gold. There were beautiful white and purple roses in the center of the table. We all knew that purple meant royalty, so this lunch had to be a special occasion. The stewardess came into the dining area and said, "Lunch will be served in ten minutes. Mr. Morgan, once we serve lunch, the crew will be leaving the yacht for a few hours. If you need anything, you can radio us."

Chase said, "Okay, cool, but we shouldn't be needing anything."

Lunch was served. It was a spread of seafood. There were lobster tails, salmon, shrimp scampi, spinach salad, baked potatoes, seafood pasta salad, and fresh rolls. There were four buckets of champagne on ice. The stewardess, the deck hands, and the captain finally left the yacht. Lunch was the bomb, especially the pasta salad. They left us lemon wipes and hot white hand towels on the table. We cleaned up and sat in the living room. After all that food, we wanted something sweet, so Chase said he would go in the kitchen to find some snacks, but first, we needed to talk.

Chase was looking so serious. It was a look I had never seen before. He said, "Look, the purpose of this trip is to let y'all both know how incredibly special you both are to Mike and me. We appreciate everything y'all have done for us. Y'all motivate us both to do better and be better at all we do."

Jacelyn and I just sat there and smiled because we definitely didn't expect a speech.

He said, "Please let me get everything out before y'all two respond. As y'all know, we all come from the hood, and we all wanted out so bad that we would do just about anything to get out the hood, off the streets, and away from the lives we were accustomed to, especially away from the drugs and the violence. We started out as stock brokers and built up so much cash and knowledge that we opened our own firm on Wall Street. The firm went through the roof, and money was flowing in like crazy, so we then opened Who's Who, the most expensive, exclusive, extravagant private members club in Manhattan. I believe we are the only private membership club like this, besides golf club memberships, but they're not even pulling in what we do. We never completely left the streets. We continued to distribute coke in the hood for about two years. What we sold was in high demand, so we decided to move it from the streets to the club and sell to the richest of the rich. We wanted to keep the money under the same roof, so everything could be monitored enough for us not to get caught. Yeah, people on the streets were heated, but we managed to put someone else in the hood on, so we could cut ties with the streets all together. We had almost five-hundred members the first year we started out, and they paid fifty-to-one-hundred grand per year in membership fees. We introduced the coke to the club one night as a test, and that test turned into millions. These people were willing to pay whatever they had for it, and we weren't about to stop supplying them. It's like this, who would go down? If we went down, the entire club and its members would go down with us. These people had too much to lose and so did we, so we knew nobody was gonna tell, and everything would be kept quiet. Since coke was now a part of the club, we had to come up with a name for it. We couldn't have people walking around the club asking for 'coke.' We all needed to speak the same language. That's when we came up with the name 'Wallstreet.' It was a great name, considering we are from Wall Street and so are a lot of members of the club. When you hear Maryellen say, 'Stocks are up on Wallstreet,' that's letting everybody know that the coke is on its way up and ready for purchase. None of the club members are clients of the firm, and everything about the firm is totally legit. The club is legit as well. It's just that we push weight through it. We have several bank accounts for the club and the firm. We'll give y'all that information when we get back home. We have safe deposit boxes all over where we keep millions of dollars in profits from Wallstreet. There's no trace of Wallstreet, except through the club members. Oh, and Jeff. Yeah, that's right. Jeff. One of the doctors from the club decided he wanted to sell Wallstreet outside of the club, and it just so happened to be to Jeff. That's why Jeff was sneaking around my office. He was looking for money to pay the doctor for Wallstreet. It don't come cheap to club members, and Dr. B definitely didn't give Jeff a break when he sold it to him either. We have this rule that, if anyone gets hooked on Wallstreet, we will help them get clean. We are not out to harm or hurt anyone, especially not one of our own. That is why Jeff was in rehab for thirty days, and as for Dr. B, well, let's just say after parting with two-hundred-twenty grand and getting his ass beat, he won't be making any new sales or thinking about selling anything for a long time. Besides, all he can think about is his next hit. We limited the supply everyone gets, so no drugs will be taken outside, beyond the club walls. They're greedy dope fiends that are hooked, and with a limited supply, trust me, they ain't trying to share it or sell it to anyone. We boosted up security at the club and at the firm, so y'all have absolutely nothing to worry about. One big part of making y'all partners was to keep y'all busy at the firm and away from the club. The only reason we bought y'all in to work at the club was to see what y'all was really all about and how y'all would act around money and fame, and it didn't change y'all, not one bit. Y'all conducted business, kept it classy and professional, and that's exactly what we wanted to see. Now I know we shouldn't be telling y'all all of this because, even though y'all from the hood, y'all cut from a different cloth. Y'all was born and raised in the church. We were, too, but we didn't stay in the church like y'all did. I'm telling y'all this because these are things y'all need to know in order for us to move forward. There will be no secrets between us. The most important part of a relationship is trust, and we need y'all to trust us and know that everything is good."

Jacelyn and I looked at each other and said "wow" at the same time.

"That's a lot of information to take in, Chase."

"Well, before y'all two say anything else, please let me finish."

They pulled out these boxes. Chase had one, and Mike had one. They both opened them and pulled out these name-plated diamond bracelets that had the word PROMISE written in script. Chase came over to me, kneeled down, and put the bracelet on my wrist. Mike did the same to Jacelyn. Chase said, "With all that I've said to you, I promise to protect you and love you beyond words. I promise to give you the world and treat you like royalty. I promise to be honest and never keep secrets from you. I promise to support your dreams and all your decisions. Lastly, I promise to sell the club. I just need a year to find the right buyer. I thought about keeping it and just stopping Wallstreet all together, but it's too late for that. We've come too far, and the club would really go down without Wallstreet, so that's out. The only reason why people pay membership fees that high is because of their access to Wallstreet. This bracelet is a promise to be and do all of those things I just said. Beautiful, I don't want to lose you. I can't do this without you. You're the best thing that's ever happened to me, and I will walk away from it all to be with you, just say the word. I just need you to know it's your call. Will you ride this out with me, or do you want to walk away from it all?"

"Chase, I have never doubted that you would be all those things and more. I trust you with my life. Before I answer your question, though, I need to tell you that I knew about Wallstreet. I knew it was a drug, and I knew it was connected to you in some way. I found the bag in your trunk the day I drove your car to get the things for the office party. I started to piece things together when we were at the club. I began to notice how people would sniff their noses with their fingers and also, when Maryellen would say 'Stocks are up on Wallstreet,' I noticed how the room would cheer like they'd just hit the lottery. I stopped piecing things together, though, because I figured, if you wanted me to know and it was something I needed to know, you would've told me. I could have very well walked away then, but I'm still here. Thank you, Chase, for telling me and trusting me enough with this information. You're a very smart man, and I know you will always choose what's right when it comes to us. There's just one thing that you have to promise me."

"What's that?"

"To love me with nothing. It's not about the money, the club, or the firm. If it was all gone today, I need you to promise me that you will still love me and show me the love you show me today, tomorrow. You've always known that I can take care of myself, Chase. I come from money, and I have my own money, so I'm not in it for things or your money, Chase. I'm here now because I love you, and I know, with everything in you, that you love me, too. If you can promise me that, Chase, then I'm down for the ride."

He said, "I promise, I swear I promise to love you at all times through richer and richer through good times and good times, till death do us part. So, does that mean you accept my promise, Beautiful?"

I jumped in his arms and said, "Yes, yes, I do."

Mike looked at Jacelyn, smiled, and said, "Yeah, exactly what he just said. No need to repeat it." Then he said, "No, for real, Jacelyn, I love you, and I would never do anything to jeopardize the love we have. Do you accept my promise?"

Jacelyn said, "Yes, crazy. Why wouldn't I accept it? I'm a ride or die chick."

Chase said, "Well, I have something else that was supposed to be part of the promise, but I decided to hold off because this something else is not about those promises; it's about a lifetime of promises. I was really planning to do this in a few months, but what the hell? No time better than the present."

He got down on one knee and held up a small box. The color of the box was robin egg blue, which is also known as Tiffany Blue. Along with the white bow that was lovingly attached to the top of the box, I knew that Chase had gone to Tiffany & Company. He opened it and said, "Beautiful, will you accept my promises for life?"

All I could do at that moment was break down and cry.

He said, "So I take that as a yes."

I covered my mouth with my hand, closed my eyes, nodded my head, and said, "Yes."

Chase put the ring on my finger and grabbed me off the couch, picked me up, and spun me around the room. He yelled, "She said 'yes.' You don't know how happy you just made me, not only are you willing to ride this out with me, but you agreed to be my wife. I told you it would happen soon enough and it's happening now. We have to celebrate."

Mike said, "We sure do." Mike then turned to my sister and said, "Jacelyn, are you down for a double wedding?"

And he pulled out his own Tiffany box and got down on one knee. Jacelyn said "yes" before he could even get another word out. We all laughed so hard. While Guy's "Let's Chill" was playing in the background, Chase shook up a bottle of Moet, popped it open, and sprayed it all over everywhere. He poured some Moet in our glasses and made a toast. He said, "First off, I told you, Beautiful, in the Bahamas, that it wasn't the first and it wouldn't be the last time you heard this song. I've never wanted to just chill with you. I've wanted to settle down since the first day I saw you. Cheers to a happy life ahead for the four of us."

We sat down and looked at our rings.

I said, "I can't wait to tell my mommy."

Chase said, "Well, she already knows."

"Chase, you tell them everything."

"No, wait. It's not like that. I had to tell her because I had to ask them if they were cool with it. I needed their blessing, Beautiful. Both her and your dad said 'yes,' so it's cool. Look on the bright side, she hasn't seen the rings, though, so you can show her that."

Jacelyn said, "Yes, now we have an event to plan."

Chase said, "I've been telling her that for a while now. She just wasn't listening to me."

I looked at him and asked, "So, Chase, this is the big event you've been telling me we would be planning soon enough?"

"Yep, it sure is."

"Chase, you knew you were going to propose to me months ago?"

"Yes, indeed."

Jacelyn said, "This is going to be the epic event of the century."

"I don't want a big wedding, Jacelyn. I want to get married on a tropical island with our immediate family and close friends."

Jacelyn said, "No, we're doing it up, and we're gonna do it at the club. The club is big with plenty of space, and it's free."

"I don't know, J. With everything going on at the club, I just don't know about that there."

"Were you not listening, B? They said they'd handle everything, so we have no worries."

"Jacelyn, please let me think about it."

"Come on, B. Let's just do it up. Besides, we only get to do this once."

I looked over at Chase and asked, "Is this okay with you?"

He said, "Only if it's okay with you."

Mike said, "Everything is cool with me. It's whatever y'all want."

"Okay, it's cool with me then, Jacelyn. I just don't want to announce it at the club just yet. Let's just keep this between the family for now."

As Mike and Chase nodded, Jacelyn said, "My thoughts exactly."

We sat on the couch, relaxing, trying to find a movie.

I said, "Chase, what's up with that snack you were going to go get us two hours ago?"

"Oh, yeah! Let me go see what I can find since we still have about two hours before the crew comes back to start dinner."

Chase and Mike went into the kitchen to whip something up while Jacelyn and I sat there and talked about everything Chase had said.

"B, why didn't you tell me you knew something about Wallstreet?"

"Because, J, you bug out over the least little thing, so it was best that I kept it to myself. Prime example, if we wasn't on this yacht right now, I'm sure over one hundred people would know about our engagement. Please don't go around telling anyone that Chase and I are engaged. Let us be the ones to spread our own news."

"Okay, B, you don't have to be all jumpy about it. We are supposed to be celebrating, and I can't wait to start planning the wedding."

"Well, J, in order for this double wedding to work, we're going to have to agree on everything, and I do mean everything, or it's going to be the tropical islands for me and Chase. I really don't care if I get married at the justice of the peace on Queens Boulevard or in Las Vegas with Elvis fake-ass Presley, just as long as I'm married."

Jacelyn laughed and said, "You're crazy, B."

"No, I'm not. I'm seriously stating the facts, J."

The guys came back with some strawberry shortcake the chef had prepared the night before, some ice cream, chips, cookies, and fresh fruit. Chase said, "This should hold us over for now."

"I hope so, Chase, because I've worked up an appetite."

We sat and watched the movie *Paid in Full* and ate junk food. Chase and I fell asleep on the couch while Jacelyn and Mike went out on the top deck in the Jacuzzi. Who knows what they were doing in there, but I, for one, didn't want to find out. The crew came back around six-thirty in the evening. We had already cleared the table and put the dishes in the kitchen. They all were so eager to find out what the special occasion was, so I lifted up my hand and showed them my ring. One of the stewardesses said, "Wow! That's huge! Congratulations!"

I said, "Thank you," and sat back down on the couch. I didn't speak on Jacelyn and Mike because that was their news to share, just as I had told Jacelyn earlier about me and Chase. The stewardess informed us that the chef would be making a special dinner.

Chase said, "Well, tell him to make it light because we had too many snacks a while ago."

She said, "Okay, I will be sure to tell him."

Chase said, "As a matter of fact, since we're still docked, can you find a pizza spot like Dominoes or something? I just want something regular."

She said, "Sure. Let me see what I can find."

We continued to lay on the couch, watching TV, waiting for her to come back. We hadn't been outside all day because we were drained from the night before. We'd only had about three hours of sleep. We were sure to be in relax mode tonight. The stewardess came back and said she'd found a Dominoes nearby, and they would deliver to the yacht. So we ordered twelve large pies, six orders of twenty buffalo wings, six orders of twenty honey BBQ wings, and bread sticks, which was enough for the crew as well. We didn't bother to ask Jacelyn and Mike what they wanted because they were in the Jacuzzi. We just got what we knew they would want.

Once the pizza came, we called them down to eat and gave the crew the rest of the night off. We already knew where the snacks were, so we really didn't need them for anything else. Mike asked, "Who's idea was this?"

Chase said, "Mine. Why?"

"Because it was a good one."

"Yeah, I know because I was getting tired of eating all that fancy food."

After we ate, Chase went into the kitchen and made us some strawberry smoothies, and then we went to bed. Mike and Jacelyn went back up on the top deck. Before Chase and I fell asleep, we talked for a bit. He asked me how I felt about everything.

"Well, to be honest, Chase, everything was pretty overwhelming. It was a lot to take in all at once, and the proposal was so unexpected."

He put my hand inside of his hand and said, "So do you like the ring?"

"Yes, Chase, I love it. I'm sure this ring could buy a house or, at least, two cars."

He said, "Yeah, you're just about right."

I kissed him and told him how much I loved him. He said, "I love you more," and moved my hair from my face to kiss me once again. He pulled me close, wrapped me in his arms, and we fell asleep.

***

The next day, we woke up to the horn of the yacht docking back in New York. We showered and got dressed pretty quickly because we were ready to finally get home. The stewardess had fresh fruit croissants and orange juice waiting in the dining room for breakfast. We sat and ate a little and then were ready to exit. Chase had an envelope with a ten-grand tip in it that he handed to the captain as he shook his hand. As the crew said "bye" and "congratulations" once again, the limo pulled up, ready to take us back home. We got back home in no time because we practically lived right down the block. After we walked into our home, we both plopped down on the couch, too exhausted to do anything.

"Chase, thank you so much for a beautiful weekend."

"You're welcome. It was my pleasure."

"I'm definitely going to plan our next outing, though. You know what, Chase? I'm going to plan it for this coming week, and I promise it's going to be lots of fun, something very unexpected and well needed for all of us. You just be ready, Chase."

He winked at me and said, "I stay ready, Beautiful."

CHAPTER 17

Surprise! Let's Roll

I t was Monday morning, and that meant back to work, as usual. Chase and Mike went to the club, and Jacelyn and I went to the firm. Things were running smooth, and I felt safe knowing the guys were checking the surveillance around the clock. Jeff being back cleared us both to focus on our new clients like Mr. Henderson. His investment had him at a huge profit gain, and it was now time to generate his monthly report, figure out what his next investment would be, and trade or sell some things, if need be. Our monthly meeting would be tomorrow morning because we closed month-end tonight. We were expecting to close this month with great numbers. One thing I could say was Chase knew his stuff when it came to teaching stock trading and investments. He taught me within about three days, and now I was a pro at it.

There was so much pressure with the wedding stuff that I just wasn't really ready to announce our engagement to the firm just yet. I was just going to wait until they noticed the ring. I was speaking to Jacelyn about it on our drive to work that morning, and she was so hyped to tell everyone. That was the difference between us. I told her that some things are just best kept untold. After the whole Jeff situation and with the club, we could have technically become targets. I was not the least bit worried about it, but it was just a thought, you know? We should, at least, wait for the engagement party, I thought.

I called Jacelyn at her desk extension. She answered, "Yo, B, what's up?"

"Jacelyn, you have got to stop calling me 'B' at work. Anyway, I want to put something together this Wednesday. I promised Chase I would plan something that he would love. I'm leaning toward bowling. It will be fun and something normal for a change. There's a bowling alley near Mommy's house, so her and Dad can come, too. We can play teams, guys against girls. With Mommy on our team, we are sure to win. I still have some shirts left from the last match. Chase has his bowling ball and shoes in the closet, and I'm quite sure Mike has the same as well."

Jacelyn said, "That's cool. We are going to have some fun, B."

We got to work planning the party and finishing up our other work. By the time we looked up, it was already two in the afternoon, so we ordered a salad from the café downstairs, and they bought it right up. Chase and Mike came around four to help us close the month out and run the reports. By the time we were done, it was eight o'clock. We had had another successful month. The day was over, so we grabbed dinner and headed home.

***

Finally, the next morning, in the large conference room, we had our monthly meeting. The firm had pulled in $1.2 million in profits. Our clients should be nothing but happy, I thought, oh, except for a few that were a bit older and never wanted to move their money around. So there was a slight drop in their investments, but that was what they got for not listening. Once the meetings were over, the day was done, so we went on to the next day, which was business as usual.

Finally, it was Wednesday morning. I asked Chase to ride with Mike today, so we didn't have too many cars to drive because it was bowling night. He asked, "Why?"

I told him we were going to see my mom to show her our rings. What I didn't tell him was we were meeting her and my dad at the bowling alley. He agreed and said, "Yeah, let's go show her, and I hope she'll have cooked a nice dinner by the time we get there."

It was another successful day at the firm. We got all the reports shipped out and started making moves on our next investments. I heard Jeff screaming as the numbers were going up on Mr. Henderson's accounts. The phones were ringing off the hook, so I was sure Jeff's excitement helped the clients that were calling in on the other phones. Sometimes, it was good to make noise, and I was so happy to see Jeff doing well. Since leaving rehab, he was more focused and into making money now. He felt like he owed Chase and Mike for helping him by saving his job and his life. I could honestly say that Chase and Mike would always come through for their employees, which were now ours, so we had to do the same. We were definitely going to make this firm number one on Wall Street.

The workday was done, so Jacelyn and I shut down everything, and the guys came to help us lock up, as promised. When we left, Chase rode with me in my car, and Jacelyn got in the car with Mike, and they followed us. Chase told me he had a surprise for me. He said he was working on it, and it would take a few weeks for him to reveal it.

"Really, Chase, what's the point in saying you have a surprise if I have to wait a few weeks to find out what it is?"

"Just don't worry. It's going to be worth the wait. You'll know soon enough."

With Jacelyn and Mike not far behind, we hit Interstate-495, heading toward my mom's house, riding and bumping in between radio stations Hot 97 and 105.1. Traffic was crazy on the 495, so it took a while for us to get there. After two hours, we finally made it to the bowling alley. Chase said, "Yo! This is your surprise outing?"

"Yup, it sure is."

He said, "This is going to be good. I hope you're ready to get beat because I'm a beast at bowling."

I laughed because I was a pro and my mom was a straight beast.

He said, "I wish you would've told me because I would've bought my own bowling shoes and my own ball. Now I have to buy a pair of new shoes from here because I'm not walking in shoes someone else walked in."

"Relax, Chase. You know I thought of everything. All of your stuff is in the trunk, and I got a bowling shirt for you, too."

With a smile, he said, "Say no more. It's on now."

The four of us went inside. My mom and dad were already there and had chosen two lanes. Chase said, "Okay. I see now. This is going to be interesting. Y'all down for a little wager?"

Mike said, "Yeah, we got to redeem ourselves from that pool game."

"So what's it going to be, Beautiful. What's the bet?"

"Well, since I picked last time, I think you should pick this time."

He said, "Okay, if we win, we get front row season tickets to the Knicks game."

"That's too easy, Chase. You know one of my clients works for the Knicks, and I get free tickets."

"Okay, a trip to Las Vegas then, where I'll get a chance to spend some of your money, win some money, and check on some of my people out that way."

I said, "Now ya talking. The loser takes the winner on an all-expenses paid trip to Las Vegas? Now that's a wager, Chase. Let's do this."

We all suited up while Jacelyn set the board up. She put their names up as losers and ours as winners. After a good laugh, I said, "J, don't do that."

Mike and Chase said, "No, leave it because she's gonna be eating those words real soon."

I laughed because I knew they would be the ones eating words. I looked over at my mom and said, "Oh, Ma, look at my ring."

After taking a good look at my ring, she happily said, "It's beautiful. Congratulations."

Chase said, "Yeah, Ma, it is but not as beautiful as she is," and he leaned over to kiss me.

"Chase, don't be trying to butter me up because you're gonna loose."

He laughed and said, "Not at all, not at all."

Mike and Jacelyn were over there, eating and drinking. My mom and my dad were up to bowl first, then Chase and I, then Mike and Jacelyn. My mom hit a strike her first roll. BAM! Then, my dad hit a strike. I yelled, "Okay, Pops, I see you."

Mike said, "My man, Mr. Bill."

We laughed. I was up next.

Chase said, "You sure you gonna make it?"

"I'm always a sure shot, baby."

I winked at him and hit a strike. BOOM!

He said, "Damn! I'm on the wrong team."

He rolled twice for a spare. He said, "All your beauty distracted me from rolling a strike."

I said, "Just be ready to pay up."

Now these two dummies are up and they're up there playing around, I thought as Mike and Jacelyn stood and prepared to bowl. I had to remind Jacelyn that there was a bet at stake, so she'd stop playing, but she kept right on playing with him and ended up rolling a spare. Luckily, Mike rolled a spare, too.

We kept going at it. Now it was the last round. We were at 286. They were at 280. It was anyone's game. Moms hit a strike. I hit a strike, and Jacelyn hit a strike. Then, my dad hit a strike. Chase hit a strike, and Mike hit a spare. And with that, the game was over, and we won. My mom, Jacelyn, and I all started dancing, doing the cabbage patch. I walked over to Chase and said, "Oh, poor baby," and kissed him. I said, "Chase, when should I start packing, or will you pack for me again? Better yet, since you're paying, why don't we just go shopping when we get there?"

Chase was disappointed, but Mike voiced it when he said, "Damn. We lost again, man. We have to stop going up against them."

"Yeah, y'all sure do. Like they say, 'if you can't beat 'em, then join 'em,' Chase," I said.

"A bet is a bet, and a promise is a promise."

"It sure is, Chase, and we are on our way to Las Vegas. Baby, fuel up the jet."

CHAPTER 18

Security Investment

I t had been a few weeks now since we'd really been out. We'd been working nonstop at the firm while the guys worked at the club. Chase told me, before we left for work that morning, we were going out to dinner that night. We'd both been taking turns cooking at home because we had been eating out just a little too much. Chase had become accustomed to this life but not me. I'd grown up in the kitchen, and there was nothing like a home-cooked meal. Please, there are just some things you will never find in the restaurant, and that's the soul, love, life, and laughter that's found in a home kitchen. I was starting to realize, though, all work and no play, was not the way to go. I was ready to play a little and have some fun, so I was excited about going out tonight. A day at the firm was filled with the excitement of signing new clients, stocks rising, and the loud noise from taking a hit. It was all crazy and overwhelming at times, but I loved it. The day had gone by fast, just as any other, and the guys came to lock up and take us out. Chase said, "Y'all ready to hit the town?"

"Yes, sir."

"Then let's go. Y'all becoming workaholics."

"I know, but you made me like this, Chase, and that's a true fact. We are all workaholics."

"Yeah, yeah, I know, but that's all about to change, Beautiful."

We headed out and ended up at this bar and lounge in New Jersey. It was cool. It was an after-work crowd. The music was bumping, and the food was great. Chase dragged me onto the dance floor for a little fun. He said, "Come on. We're not going to stop doing the things we love."

We started out dancing, and we were gonna go out dancing. I smiled and whispered, "I love you. You always know how to make me smile."

"I love you, too, Beautiful."

Very soon, there were several people on the dance floor with us, even Mike and Jacelyn. We were dancing to Next's "Too Close." The DJ had the club jumping. We danced a few more songs and were ready to go.

He drove back to Manhattan, down to the pier on the Westside Highway, and we got out. Looking at the moon and the stars both shining down on the water was a beautiful way to end the night. It was actually the first time we'd been somewhere without Jacelyn and Mike. They were good anyway; we weren't too far from home. Chase said, "Are you happy at the firm?"

"Yes, I'm happy."

"Good because what's most important to me is your happiness. I told you before I had a surprise for you. I want you to follow your dreams, not mine. To be honest, the only dreams I've ever had were to get out the hood, make lots of money, and find someone to share it with, and I've accomplish all that. So now there's nothing left for me to do but enjoy life. Now you, on the other hand, you had dreams before you met me. I have already applied and paid for your college tuition. You start law school in two weeks. One of the members at the club is a college professor, and he helped me with all the details. That's you, Beautiful. That's your dream."

"Sometimes not every dream becomes a reality. What about the firm, Chase? Who will run things there if I'm in school?"

"You will because law school is only part-time in the day, so you can leave school and go make sure everything is running smooth at the firm. You'll still have full control, but you're going to need an assistant, which I have already taken care of. He starts next week. Both you and

Jacelyn will be going since it was her dream to become a lawyer as well. Besides, this will be something that helps all of us. You can study business law and criminal justice, so if we ever have a situation where we may need an attorney, you can be just that. Just look at it as us protecting our investments."

"Chase, you're a man with many surprises, but I never thought this would be one of them. I've been thinking about law school for a while, but I left it as a thought because there was so much more going on. I never thought this would become my reality. I didn't mean to sound ungrateful by asking so many questions, it's just that the firm, you, and everything that you are has become my life, and I would never walk away from any of it."

"You're not walking away. Like I said, think of it like you're making moves to protect your investment and what we're building."

"Chase, you're not an investment to me."

"I'm not, but the firm and the club are. You've invested time and energy into both of them, and that has got to count for something, Beautiful."

"Yeah, you're right, Chase. I didn't see it that way."

He stood behind me and held me in his arms. He reassured me not to worry and that everything was going to work out just fine. He turned me around and kissed me, then whispered softly in my ear. "I wish I could make love to you right here, right now under the stars."

"Chase, were you always this romantic before you met me?"

He smiled and said, "No, not at all. It's you, you bring out the best in me. No woman has ever satisfied both me and Royal. To be honest, you're the first to satisfy me emotionally, mentally, and physically. This is why I treat you the way I do. It's because of who you are, what you mean to me, and the love you give to me."

After that lovely comment, he held me in his arms and moved me side to side as if we were dancing to music, but there wasn't any. It was just the sound of our voices and the sound of the water moving back and forth. All I could say was, "Lord, I thank you." Not everyone is blessed to find their soulmate, but he was sent just for me. He was far from perfect to the world, but he was perfect in my eyes and in my heart. It was getting late, and it was cold out, so we decided to head home.

The night wasn't over just yet. When we got home, Chase had laid out my college applications, receipts, and orientation schedule. He'd also bought me a Fendi backpack and all kinds of school supplies. He said, "I just want you to be prepared for your first day of school." He always thought of everything. I jumped in his arms and wrapped my legs around his waist to thank him. He spun me around and fell backwards, onto the bed. He said, "You know what we need?"

"What, Chase?"

"Give me a second," and he rolled me over on the bed. He turned on some lovemaking music that played throughout the entire house. He walked into the bathroom for a few minutes and came back to get me. He had lit some candles and run a bubble bath. He helped me out of my clothes and we got in.

I sat behind him with my legs wrapped around him. It was such a long day, so the bath was relaxing and so needed. I sat there and started thinking about everything that had happened over the past few months. I thought about today's events and how me becoming an attorney one day was no longer a thought; it was my reality. I thought about the reasons as to why we would need an attorney at the firm and the club. I realized that we would really need one if things went down at the club. There were a lot of snakes and jealous people in this world, so no telling what could happen or who or what we'd be up against in the days ahead. I knew one thing was for sure, and that was I was not going to dwell on what could happen, but I could damn sure be prepared to pick us up if someone tried to bring us down.

Chase called me. He said, "Hey, Beautiful, where did you just go?"

"Oh, I was just thinking."

"About what?"

"My life, Chase, for the past few months and how lucky I am to have you."

He turned around to face me and pulled me down to the other side of the tub with him. He said, "Come give me some, love."

I wrapped my arms around his neck and wrapped my legs around his waist. Then I instantly felt Royal on the rise. "I see now why you wanted me to come down here with you."

"Nah, it's not just me. We both did." He laughed.

Once he kissed me again, things got really heated. He didn't have to say another word. Royalty was ready to slide down on Royal, for him to hit home base. We were always going at it, long, hard, fast, slow, but never short. We ended up in the shower to wash down but that lasted all of five minutes before we were at it again. He picked me up out of the shower and carried me, soaking wet, to the bedroom. He laid me on the bed, then stood over me, and asked if I was ready for a royal round three. For once, I was speechless. At that moment, there was so much hanging over me. His six-foot frame and his nine inches of Royal with water rolling down his chest which all looked so sexy, so inviting, and so chocolate that I couldn't do anything but stare. I just loved me some chocolate and lots of it. After we made it through round three, Chase said, "Before round four, let me go get us something to drink."

"Chase, you know we ain't making it to work tomorrow if you're talking about a round four."

"I know we're not because you have orientation tomorrow, and I intend to get you there safely and on time."

He went to the kitchen and came back with two glasses of Kool-Aid. I laughed because this was a first. No water, no champagne, but Kool-Aid, and it was perfect. "Chase, you should have bought the whole pitcher in here."

"Yeah, you're right. Let me go back and get it."

Watching him walk away was such a sight to see. He had the nicest butt cheeks and the muscles in his legs were to die for. My man was a model, just picture perfect. I walked behind him, enjoying the view with a sheet wrapped around me. When we hit the kitchen, I had no intentions on round four starting in there, but then Chase picked me up, laid me across the counter, opened the sheet, and started to find whatever he could in the refrigerator to make me edible. He had whipped cream, grapes, ice cream, pineapples, strawberries, and chocolate syrup.

He took his time to create the perfect sundae right on my body to only lick it right off. He turned me and Royalty to face him and Royal and asked if I was ready for more. I took matters into my own hands literally because I wasn't about to be answering no damn questions the way I felt. After having dessert eaten off my body, why wouldn't I be ready? I wrapped my legs around his waist, put my arms around his neck, and Royalty had Royal front and center, locked, loaded and ready to shoot. We ended up on the floor, the couch, and then against the living room window. We knew nobody could see us, but it was just the excitement of us knowing we could see out with the feeling of the world looking in.

It was a movie in the making for sure. Round four was over, and we finally got that Kool-Aid. I felt so good and so excited at the same time. As we laid naked on the living room floor, we began to talk. "I'm about to be walking down the halls of NYU, one of the best schools in the state, thanks to you."

"No, it's not thanks to me. It's all thanks to you. You have the brains and the beauty, and I'm gonna try not to wear your beautiful brains out no more tonight because I need you to be able to focus on school in the morning and not me and Royal."

"Stop playing, Chase, because round five starts right now, and we're both about to be not worn out but knocked out."

We laughed, got up, grabbed the Kool-Aid, took a shower, and got in bed.

I didn't even remember us falling asleep, but the sleep was good. I was well rested. I woke up ready and full of excitement. I got dressed, threw on a gray sweat suit and my Nikes. I pulled my hair back in a ponytail, put my jewelry on, put on my lip gloss, and I was ready to go. It was like I was in high school again, and I was getting ready for the first day of school. Chase said, "Good morning, Beautiful. You're up early and looking cute."

"Thanks, Chase. I'm ready for my orientation."

"I'll be dressed in a few."

It was funny seeing Chase dressed down in a sweat suit since he was always in suits. He only wore sweat suits when we were out of town on vacation or something, so this was good to see. He looked so cute in sweats, a T-shirt, and Timberlands. He threw on his watch, jewelry, and a baseball cap. Come to think of it, we both looked like we were going to school. If we went to the same school and I saw Chase walking down the halls, I would definitely be late to class every day. We were both finally ready to go, so we met up downstairs with Jacelyn and Mike. We grabbed breakfast from IHOP and headed straight to the college.

***

Wow! It was so nice to see hundreds of people walking the halls from class to class. All the students met for orientation in the auditorium. They actually let the guys stay with us the entire time. We were there for a total of three hours, including the tour. They gave us our class schedules and start date. Two weeks couldn't come fast enough for me, and I was looking forward to all that law school had to offer me. Jacelyn seemed more excited than me because it was more of her dream career than mine. Finally, there was something she loved other than Mike, and I knew she would be good at it. She was a partner at the firm, but it was definitely not something that she wanted to do. We were given the gift of success, not a dream of our own success, and now that would all slowly begin to change. Orientation was done, so the four of us headed home.

I invited Jacelyn and Mike over to have some drinks and celebrate while Chase and I packed up a few things. Jacelyn danced around the house, showing us how happy she was. She hadn't been this happy since she met Mike. Well, if she was, she hadn't shown it. It always seemed like she and Mike were only happy when they were in each other's company. See me, on the other hand, I was always happy, knowing that, no matter where Chase and I may spend the day, I got to fall asleep and wake up in his arms every night and every day. That was more than enough happy for me. From school, the move, the engagement, my mom moving, the club, the firm, and Chase, it all felt so surreal, like a dream that I was going to one day wake up from, but until then, I planned to live every minute of this dream to the fullest. Eventually, everything that happened in our lives would go from dreams to nothing but reality. We could all bet our lives on that.

CHAPTER 19

Old Money $$ New Money

Out with the old and in with the new, but it was always good to keep some of the old around, especially if it was of any value or even a bit of insurance. It had now been forty days, and it was finally moving day. We packed all that we wanted and donated the rest to charity. The moving company had bubble wrapped everything and loaded it into the truck. We really didn't take much. Jacelyn and Mike were all packed up and ready to move as well. The last of the stuff was out of both apartments, and we were ready to roll. Since none of us had seen our penthouses since we'd hired the interior decorator, this would finally be a surprise for us all. We each drove our own cars over to the new house. It wasn't that far away from the old house, though; it was just a few blocks away. When we got there, we were greeted by the doorman. We introduced ourselves and let him know that the moving trucks were on the way to unload our things into both penthouses.

The wait was over, and we were finally going up to see our new homes. There was an elevator marked *Penthouse A&B*, which was a private elevator for the penthouses only. That was great because our moving in wouldn't stop the elevator access for the other tenants. This one lady came off the other elevator and looked at us crazy, maybe because we were young African-Americans moving into the penthouses. I don't know, but I immediately said hello to her before Jacelyn or Mike noticed how crazy she was looking at us. She said, "Hello! Are you guys moving in?"

I said, "Well, yes, we are."

She said, "Congratulations and welcome."

We all said "thank you" and walked onto the penthouse elevator. I'm sure when the doors closed, she asked the doorman questions that he had no idea how to answer and would never know, for that matter. I'm sure she could remember seeing the decorator bringing in all our furniture for the last month or so, and now she knew exactly who it all belonged to.

"Hey, Jacelyn. Did you see how home girl was looking at us?"

She said, "No, and I'm glad I didn't."

"I'm glad you didn't either because you would've got crazy with her."

"Jacelyn, you have to promise to be nice to everyone in the building, even home girl."

Chase said, "Mike, you, too, because the attention is definitely on us now. They're going to be searching, trying to find out how in the hell we can afford to live here, not to mention in the penthouse, but both penthouses at that."

For a minute, I had to remind Chase, Jacelyn, and Mike that it didn't matter what people thought or said about us because we earned every dime of our money. "I know Wallstreet is different, but that is a totally separate enterprise that does not, in any way at all, fund our lifestyle. With that being said, let's celebrate our success in our new penthouses."

We stepped off the elevator, walked up to our door, entered the code on the keypad, and stepped into a penthouse set for a movie or magazine. The den was all white with white carpet, a white leather sectional with gold pillows, a gold piano, and a fireplace. The living room had a red leather sofa and two lounge chairs. The sofa was huge. It was as large as a king-sized bed that was pieced together. It had to be, at least, ten feet long and ten feet wide. Three people could lay comfortably on it. There was a floor-to-ceiling waterfall against one of the walls that changed colors and had a fireplace on another wall with a sixty-five-inch screen TV above it. Next to the window set Chase's motorcycle. It was truly a showpiece. He said he didn't think he would ride it anymore, not for a while anyway, so that was the best place for it to be. It was all clean and polished like it was brand new. He had even had them drain the gas out of it. The kitchen, dining room, and living room were all connected and opened to each other. I loved it because, if we had company over or if I was in the kitchen cooking, I would still be able to talk to everyone from either room. The only thing that was separate was the den and the bedrooms. The kitchen was huge, and it was truly a chef's kitchen with all white cabinets, marble countertops with an island and golden knobs and faucets. There were four full bathrooms, one in the master, one in each guest suite, and one in the hallway. The bedrooms were amazing. The custom bed that was delivered on our first night was still there. Our decorator had furnished the bedroom nice enough to be in *Home and Gardens* magazine. The bathroom was just as big as the bedroom. The bathtub was so huge, and you know I was ready to hop in at that moment. I lived for a good bath. Everything in there was his and hers from the sinks, to the closets, to the huge wardrobe mirrors. The bedroom was cream and gold with cream-colored carpet. One of guest rooms was set up as if it were a five-star hotel with a king-size suite. Who wouldn't want to be a guest here? But knowing Chase, who could be? The other guest room was turned into a theater room with a wall-to-wall screen and surround sound.

Jacelyn and Mike's penthouse was just as nice. They both were way too excited. All Mike wanted to do was play his games on the big screen in their theater room. We all were so pleased with the final results. The decorator had really outdone herself. Both Chase and Mike wrote her final checks and added a little bonus on top. Then she was on her way. On that note, our tour of Mike and Jacelyn's house was over, and we finally went back home to take it all in. Chase laid on the oversized couch and pulled me down with him. He said, "I can't believe this is all ours, Beautiful, considering we came from the hood. We might not fit in around here right now, but we will soon enough. You know what?"

"What, Chase? I know what you could really use right now," and he walked me into our new bathroom. Since the decorator had already set the bathroom with candles and stuff, all he had to do was light them and run the water. He ran the water, threw in some soap, some bath beads, lit the candles, hit the lights, and helped me in. He said, "This one is just for you. I want you to relax." He kissed me and went in the room to hang up a picture. I laid in the tub and talked to God.

"Lord, I've always dreamed of the type of man I wanted to fall in love with. In my heart, I didn't want to judge anyone, but what woman wants a guy who's a square, or a guy that's always serious, or a guy that's cocky and stuck on himself, or a guy who knows it all, or a guy that's demanding and controlling? Who wants a guy that hasn't been through anything in life? A true man is not perfect at all. Most women want a man who's funny, not afraid to be loved and give love, a guy who's tough with people but not with her, a wise man, a smart man, a business man, a hustler, a giver, not just a receiver, a man that's not a punk and a man that will stand when he has to but knows his limits, a man that's level-headed and thinks rationally, a spontaneous man, an adventurous man, a godly and God-fearing man. Despite his flaws because we all have them. Despite his past because we all have one. I love Chase with all the God in me, with all the hood in me, and with all the love in me. I love him because he always tells me he loves me and also shows me love. I love him because he's not perfect. I love his successful side. I love his hood side, and I even love his thug side. I love his hustle and drive that allows him to survive. I love the passion and care that shines through his eyes. I love him because he makes me smile. I love him because he brings out the best in me. He prays with me and for me. He comforts me. He protects me, and he builds with me. I love him mostly because he loves me. Lord, Chase is my definition of my imperfectly perfect man that you have created just for me, and I will ride with him through eternity."

Chase came back about thirty minutes later and said, "Beautiful, who are you talking to?"

"God, Jesus, and my guardian angels. I was just thanking them for creating and sending you to me."

He held a towel open as a signal for me to get out. I stepped out, and he wrapped it around me. He kissed me and said, "You're the sweetest person I know, Bridgette, and God couldn't have blessed me with a better blessing than you. How was your bath, Beautiful?"

While he playfully hugged me from behind, we walked out of the bathroom, and he escorted me into the living room where he had hung up pictures of the two of us from every trip we'd taken. He had hung them on the living room wall, down the hall, and by the entry door. He had even hung pictures of my mom, my dad, Jacelyn, and Mike on the wall. It looked like I had stepped into an art gallery. On one entire wall, he'd hung up a full body picture about the size and length of a bedroom door of the two of us dancing at the masquerade ball. He even had a picture of us at the pool hall. Where he had gotten that from was beyond me, and who had taken these was even more of a mystery. He said, "I will never forget the first moment I held you in my arms."

While crying like a baby, I looked at each special moment. Everything he did was always so nice and so thoughtful.

He asked, "You like it?"

"Chase, I loooove it."

"I'm glad you do because it took some work putting all this together. Plus, I never want you to think I'm not the handyman type. I can hang some pictures without hiring someone to do it."

We laughed.

I went into the kitchen to get us something to drink while he went and took a shower. He decided to order a pizza which arrived minutes after his shower. He wanted to make a toast with cherry Kool-Aid. He said, "Cheers to making it from the lower south side to the upper east side and from the hood to Wall Street. We're like the Jeffersons now, and I think we're definitely gonna need a maid."

"Yeah, we can definitely use some help around here, Chase, since we're always so busy, and I have school now."

"Well, we can get to work on finding one ASAP."

After eating the pizza, we washed up and got in bed. I laid on my side. He laid right behind me with his arm around my waist. We fell asleep.

***

It's was a cold Friday morning, and we both were up bright and early, ready to start our day. We went downstairs to the gym in the building, worked out for an hour, then headed to shower and get dressed. I always looked forward to him getting suited up, so I could tie his tie as usual. As long as he was able to put on a suit, I would make sure his tie was tied. When it was time to go, Jacelyn and I headed to school, and the guys headed to the club. So much had changed in the past few months. We had started law school, and we now had so many new clients that made us lots of new money. All our old money was still rolling in from all our old clients. The club had gotten lots of new money of its own and had almost reached its maximum capacity of members. They had recently signed ten new members, so it was time for Chase and Mike to throw their Saturday welcome event. Chase and Mike wanted me and Jacelyn to host this event to welcome all of the new money coming into the club. It was a group of ten people, and they were considered to be some really high-rolling investors. They loved to throw money around. Chase said, "I don't care what money they throw around as long as they're throwing it my way, and as long as their membership is paid in full, they're all right with me. We have to watch out for some of these rich cats, though, because they try to use money as power, instead of using their knowledge as power. A smart man can outsmart a stupid rich man any day, and I'm definitely a smart man. To be honest, all they're really interested in is Wallstreet."

Everything at the club and the firm couldn't be better. We all ended our Friday night planning for Saturday's event.

***

We made it to the club Saturday afternoon, just to make sure everything was in place for the welcome event. By the looks of things, everything was on point and ready to go. The club doors would open within an hour, and since we had an hour to waste, I had Chase help me test out the music with the DJ. As we were on the dance floor, here came Jacelyn and Mike, dancing with us to the group Jodeci's record. None of us could pass up that moment of fun. While we were having so much fun, we didn't realize the hour had come and gone.

Members were starting to enter the club, and now it was time to host and mingle. People hadn't seen Jacelyn and me in a long time and always wondered where we had gone. To their surprise, we hadn't gone anywhere. Maryellen still made her intro as usual because neither Jacelyn nor I were about to take part in anything involving Wallstreet. As we were meeting and greeting, one of the new members walked up to Chase and asked him to cater a party at his mansion, serving up Wallstreet as the main course. He said, "I will pay you top dollar, Mr. Morgan. Name your price."

Chase asked, "What's your name again?"

"Edward."

"Well, Edward, it's like this. Wallstreet is only served behind these walls, and it is for members only. If you're looking for a caterer, I highly recommend Leslie's on Fifth Avenue."

Edward jokingly said, "Come on, Mr. Morgan."

The look on Chase's face could have killed the guy, but Chase kept his cool. Chase said, "Oh, and, Edward, I really suggest you get to reading your rule book. It has a lot of information in there that will thoroughly explain everything about the club to you, and if you should have any questions for me after you've fully read it, by all means, ask away, but I'm quite sure you won't. I promise you'll never ask me anything like that again after reading the first few rules and the very last one." Chase's last words to him were "Enjoy the club, Edward" as we walked away, leaving him to unclog his memories of the rules he had so quickly forgotten.

One thing I could say about Chase was that he was not to be messed with. He said what he wanted to say in a calm way, but he always said it in a way to let you know he meant what he said. I felt very sorry for the one that ever crossed him.

Shortly after the Edward situation, this lady walked up to him and said, "Well, hello, handsome. I have a question for you. Do you know when you're going to take the limits off Wallstreet?"

197

He said, "There's two things wrong with the questions you just asked me, ma'am."

She asked, "Well, what's that, handsome?"

"For starters, please address me as Mr. Morgan at all times, and two, please don't ask me questions you really don't want to know the answers to. Enjoy your evening, ma'am."

He then grabbed my hand, once again, and we walked away. I think she was so turned on by how he spoke to her with authority that she didn't even realize how bad he had shut her down and dismissed her.

I thought, The people in the club are on a roll tonight, boy.

Chase said, "All I'm concerned with tonight is all this new money floating around. I'm not at all concerned about what they want. Let's just say the old money is getting just a little too comfortable around here, but there's always a way to cut them off and make room for more new money."

Mike said, "Yeah, I hear you, Chase. I've always made it clear that they all can be handled; you just say the word."

Chase said, "I keep telling you, Mike. In this line of business, we have to be careful with the way we handle things, especially since we have an inside operation. It's not like the streets, where we can just off people and start a street war and still keep our territory. In here, the fight is a little different; we stand to lose everything we worked so hard for."

"I want to do a meet and greet twice a week, and on the other days, I just want to watch from my office. I need to see what's really going on in here from afar, to see who's who and who's doing what. We've been giving them too much access to us, and it's about time to get low again like we were before and only show up when necessary."

As Chase and Mike were having their little side conversation, Jacelyn and I were betting chips at the roulette table. Chase walked up behind me and said, "Beautiful, can you come with me please? I need to dance with you."

When the DJ saw us headed to the dance floor, he played James Brown's "Blues and Pants" at Chase's request. We stepped like Nia Long and Lorenz Tate in *Love Jones*. It was basically the hustle, but we put our own little spin on it. We danced, and we laughed. It was so much fun.

There was a crowd of people around us, watching us step. It actually wasn't the first time for some of them to see us dance, and it definitely wouldn't be the last. Chase said, "I really needed that. I needed to get my mind off these crazy-ass people in this club."

After a few dances, we took a break for some water. As we walked off the dance floor hand in hand, he said, "You always know how to boost my spirits up, Beautiful. When I'm next to you, everything goes away. I think of nothing but you. I see nothing but you, and I hear only you. You have that effect that makes me block everyone and everything out. You're my peace."

I just smiled at him as he led me back to the dance floor. I rested my head on his shoulder and started to dance another round with him to Jaheim's "Anything" as it bumped through the speakers. He softly sang some of the words to me: "You can have anything I've got. All of me right on the spot..." Then, he whispered, "I can't wait to make you Mrs. Morgan."

As the song was almost over, we saw security running past us very quickly. A fight had broken out in the casino hall, which was where we had left Jacelyn and Mike. Chase quickly grabbed my hand and dragged me to his office and said, "Wait here. Jacelyn will be here in a minute."

I just started praying because I prayed it had nothing to do with Jacelyn and Mike. Within minutes, Jacelyn was rushed in.

"Did you see what happened, Jacelyn?"

"All I heard was arguing and then a fight broke out. Next thing I know, security was dragging me in here."

"Yeah, Chase dragged me in here, too, as soon as security started running through the club."

We waited about thirty minutes before the guys came back. Mike's hand was all messed up because, when he went to break up the fight, the dude swung on him, and sorry to say, he swung right back.

Concerned, Chase asked, "Mike, you good?"

"Yeah, I'm good, man."

"Well, you and I both know you've been wanting to fight since Jeff and Dr. B, so I knew it was coming. I just didn't know when."

Mike said, "Well, I'm not the one you should be asking though."
They laughed.

Then, Mike asked, "Are you good, though, Chase?"

"Yeah, shit just got a little crazy tonight, but I'm good. Seriously though, Mike. Next time, you gotta let security handle things. That's what we pay them for. We start breaking up fights and getting caught all up in fights, that's when liabilities become a concern. It's cool though since it's over now."

Chase said, "Ladies, I'm sorry. I should've asked if y'all were okay when I first walked in here, but I know y'all are okay because y'all were dragged to safety. Girls, listen. If anything ever goes down in the club, we all will meet up right here. Just come in here and wait for us until we get here. Since the club's been open, we've never had any situations like this before, but you never know with these idiots. Now since we've boosted up security and put a limit on Wallstreet, they've started to bug the hell out in here. How I see it is, they're basically substituting Wallstreet with liquor, and that ain't good. We can't have a bunch of drunken coke heads running around in here acting a damn fool. Mike, you and I are going to arrange a club meeting with all the members. Since we have so many members, we have to set up five different meetings, starting next week. I'm going to have Maryellen set things up. They really think I'm playing with them, but they're about to see that I'm not. I'm about to go straight hood on all of them. If they don't attend the meeting, their membership is finished. Y'all two stay here while Mike and I go make sure the club's clear. Then we can go home."

Jacelyn and I started talking since we had some time on our hands.

"Things are getting crazy, J."

She said, "They sure are, B."

"It felt like we were back in the hood for a second. I know it's a club and things are bound to happen, but I just didn't think it would happen with this particular group of people. It just goes to show that the hood is everywhere, and many of these people could have come from the hood just like we did. They give no respect to the words of Rakim and Eric B's 'It ain't where you're from, it's where you're at.'"

"Jacelyn, I really think they should sell the club now and start something else up. They made one million dollars the other day just by signing those new members and the money from other members that joined the club these last few months. They even have their fair share of the firm's money."

"Well, B, it sounds like a good plan but try telling that to Chase and Mike."

"Well, Jacelyn, they promised they would get out, and we have these bracelets right here to prove that. They said give them a year, but I think now's the time before shit gets out of hand. Although I love this club, I love the four of us more, Jacelyn. Also, I know you really want to have our wedding here, Jacelyn, but if things don't get better here and fast; it's definitely not happening here."

The guys came back to get us after the club was all clear. Then we left. I asked Mike if he wanted to go to the emergency room for some x-rays. He said no because his doctor would check it out in the morning.

"Well, okay, Mike, as long as you're good. Let's get out of here then."

***

When Chase and I got home, we sat on the couch and started a deep conversation.

"Chase, I'm happy to be home with you right now. Home is the best place for us to end this crazy day."

"Yeah, being here with you, Beautiful, is the best thing that could happen to me right now. This club has been getting out of hand ever since Jeff and Dr. B, but I'm about to put a stop to it all."

"Chase, have you ever thought about just selling the club right now and getting out before next year?"

"Yeah, I think about it every day. I was gonna call one other person that I trust the most with this information, and that's my man Ice. I want to see if he's wants in. I only call Ice in emergency situations, so when he hears from me, he knows it's not a social call. He knows to be ready for whatever. Problem is, I've already come to an agreement with the suppliers of Wallstreet. I remember that night all too well. There's one thing about getting in the business, and it's as easy as someone offering you a bag of twenty-five-cent chips, but try getting out the business, and you'll pay with your life, and that's by getting killed or going to jail or paying up lots of cash. Bridgette, I know you remember the night of the meeting, too. It was that night I put on all black and went out to get those gyros. Then the next day you found that Wallstreet bag in my trunk. I had never handled Wallstreet before. I have people to do that. I was ready to back out, but they weren't having it. They handed me two large duffle bags full of Wallstreet. They had another distributor that, let's just say, he's no longer with us, and they wanted it off their hands, so they gave it to me to get rid of. That's how you were able to find that baggy. Yo, the Columbians are not to be messed with. They said that, if I didn't wait to sell the club and if I sold it now, I would have to pay them for all the product that I agreed to sell for the rest of the year, which added up to a lot…damn sure over one-hundred million. We have one-thousand members, and they each spend, at least, one thousand per night on Wallstreet, so you do the math. I wasn't about to give them all the money that I have made over the last two years to satisfy a debt. Besides, there are only a few months left to go. They said 'no takeover.' New owners, new business, so we had to finish what we started, so the thought of selling and a takeover happening is off the table for now. I'm gonna still call Ice, though, to see what he suggests and to see if he wants in when our time is up. I also wanted see if he will be my best man since Mike can't be. He's the closest person I have to a brother, even closer than Mike."

"Wow, Chase, you really have a lot on your plate with Who's Who and Wallstreet."

"Yeah, I know, but I can't let that stop me now. I have to keep pushing for these next few months. That's all. As long as I have you by my side, Beautiful, I can conquer the world. What I've begun to notice is that it's not really good to mix old money with new money. When it's all said and done, I'm going to move on to something new and even better than Who's Who. Who's to say? I may retire altogether. I have more than enough old money and new money to do so. So the sky is the limit. I'm not sure what will happen, but one thing I do know for sure, it won't happen without you, Beautiful."

CHAPTER 20

Pearls, Gold & a Little Ice

For the first time since the engagement, we met up with the wedding planner. There was just way too much going on with school, the firm, and the club to even focus on planning our own wedding. I had the wedding planner meet up with the four of us at our house. Mike and Jacelyn made it over on time and actually before the planner arrived. They were often late because Jacelyn was always taking forever to get ready. Mike always tried to hurry her along because he hated being late. I guessed her being on time that day was only because we lived right next door or it could have been all the refreshments that I'd set out for the planner. Jacelyn and Mike hadn't been in the door all of two minutes before I had to yell at them. "Can y'all please wait for our guest to arrive before y'all start eating up all the food?"

Mike, being smart as usual, said, "We are guests. We don't live here. Plus, we ain't even ate breakfast."

"Well, Mike, now who's to blame for that? You or Jacelyn?"

Of course, he said Jacelyn, and we had no choice but to laugh.

"Okay. Go ahead and eat, Mike. Help yourself to whatever is here."

He said, "Thanks, sis. Good looking 'cause I'm starving."

While the two of them ate, Chase and I sat in the living room, watching TV.

It was around two when the doorman called to let her up. She had finally arrived. Her name was Katie, and she was well known for planning celebrity weddings. I offered her some refreshments, and we got right down to business. She showed us several books which had photos of some of the previous work that she had done. They were all so amazing. I didn't really want a traditional wedding, but I knew my mom wouldn't have it any other way but in a church. I wanted to just get married at the club and then move into the next room for cocktails, then in the next room to party, and I also wanted to have the patio set up, but I knew better. I wasn't raised like that, and I knew that we had to put God first in whatever we did. We started off with God, which meant we finished with God, so a church wedding it would be. We picked my mom's church out on Long Island. We decided to charter four buses for the family that didn't want to or couldn't drive. The guest list was already at five-hundred people. I was not sure where all these people had come from, but the list kept getting longer. It was mainly Jacelyn and Mike that kept adding people. Each couple chose to use one invitation. Since it was a double wedding, the invitation would read something like this: *Please join us at the double wedding celebration of Chase Morgan and Bridgette Banks and Michael Starks and Jacelyn Banks and so forth.* We were going back-and-forth on colors and couldn't decide, so we just agreed to go with pearl white, gold, and a whole lot of ice, crystals, that is. We chose to have live entertainment, singers, comedians, dancers, and a gospel choir to sing at the wedding. Chase said he wanted an all-white Lamborghini with gold rims. He said, "But not to worry because Ice will be bringing that as a wedding gift."

Mike said, "Well, if that's the case, make it two then."

Jacelyn and I both agreed to ride in on a horse-drawn carriage, along with our dad sitting between the two of us. We picked a beautiful cake that was five tiers high. The top tier would be made out of two half-moon hearts, so we'd each have a keepsake cake. Katie had set up an appointment with the bakery, so we could go for the cake tasting. The flowers were easy since we wanted thousands of off-white roses. We wanted some of them to be dusted in gold shimmer. My bouquet would be purple roses with one white rose in the center, and Jacelyn's would be red roses with one white rose in the center. We didn't go over food because the club would be making all the food. That was if everything went according to plan. With everything we'd chosen for the wedding so far, it was gonna cost $350,000, and that was not including all the extras. I was sure it was going to be, at least, $500,000, if not more, by the time we were done, knowing Chase and Mike. We hadn't even gone dress shopping yet, but Katie set a date for us to have the full-dress experience at Kleinfeld's, which we were so excited about. The guys were gonna have their suits custom-made. Once we finished all the add-ons, Katie said, "Okay, I have enough for now, and if you guys come up with anything else, please feel free to give me a call."

Thank God everything was done. After Katie left, it was time to relax.

The guys were more excited about the wedding than we were. Chase asked Mike who was going to be his best man. Mike said his cousin Melvin. They called him Money Mel for short.

I asked, "How is that short? The 'Money' added a whole 'nother name, Mike."

We laughed.

"Where is he from?" I asked Mike.

"Atlanta. Well, New York, but he lives in Atlanta now."

"Oh, okay, he's a country boy. We're going to have to meet him before the wedding, Mike. We gotta make sure our wedding photos come out looking good."

We laughed.

"So, Chase, who's this Ice I keep hearing you mention?"

"Oh, Ice? That's my other half, my brother. We grew up together. We pushed weight together. We went to school together. We got beatings together, got girls together, made cash together, and most of all, we broke bread together."

"Wow! So y'all real, true blood brothers then? Well, Chase, you know I have to ask you as well. How does he look? Does he look anything like you?"

"Look, Beautiful, I'm not about to be telling you how no other nigga look. Plus, I can't be the judge. If it makes you happy, I'll hit him up right now."

Chase picked up his phone and dialed Ice's number.

Ring.

Ice answered and said, "Chase, what's good, bro? What's up with you? It's been a minute."

Chase said, "Yeah, bro, I know. Yo, Ice, I need you on some real shit, bro, some BI and some personal shit. The BI I don't really want to get into over the phone. Let's just say it's about the Wallstreet business. On the personal note, I'm getting married soon, and I need you to be my best man."

"Are you serious, C? You really doing it?"

"Yeah, Just, I'm serious. I've got to be serious if I'm calling you, right?"

"Say no more, C. I'm there, whatever you need."

"Good looking, bro. I really need you to come out here ASAP, so we can discuss this Wallstreet business and so the Mrs. can meet you. She's scared you might not look good in the wedding pictures."

"Yo, C, she funny. I'm a good-looking dude."

"Ice, I definitely can't be the judge of that."

"True, but say no more. I'll be there next Friday. I'll keep you posted on my flight and everything though. Yo, C, you know we gotta turn up for old times since it's been a while."

"Oh, yeah, Ice, before I forget, I'm gonna need two Lamborghinis for my wedding day. Both of them can be all-white with gold BBS rims."

"Okay, C, not a problem. That will be my wedding gift to you. I'll get them ready and fly them out some time next week."

"Ice, I'm gonna need the interior to be gold as well. As a matter of fact, tell ya boys to hit me when they're ready to customize it. By the way, the two Lambos are not his and hers. The other whip is for Mike."

"Mike? What's good with him? He good?"

"Yeah, he good. He's getting married, too."

"What? Y'all on a whole 'nother level with this marriage shit. I'm not trying to settle down now, maybe one day but not today. That corporate life done changed y'all, C."

"Nah, Ice, we still the same. We just found two ladies that accept us for who we are and what we do. I can truly say they love us, bro."

"Well, I'm nothing more than happy for y'all, and I can't wait to come meet the ladies and check you on the BI. Tell Mike I said I'll see him at the craps table. Better yet, we gonna keep it hood, C-Low at the crib. Tell 'em to be ready. Yo, C, I still can't believe this man. Congrats, man, seriously."

"Thanks, man. Hit me when you're on your way."

"I will, C. Love you, bro."

"Love you, too," Chase said before getting off the phone. After he had ended the call, he said, "Okay, ladies. See? It's all set. He said yes to being my best man. He's sending the cars. He's coming to meet y'all, and most of all, he's coming to talk some Wallstreet business. I'm just hoping he's wit' it."

Mike said, "Cool."

"Now, I have a question for you, Beautiful."

"What's that, Chase?"

"Do you mind him coming over to the house?"

"No, I don't mind, Chase. Why did we buy a house with a guest room if we can't have guests?"

"Well, I only said 'come over.' I said nothing about staying. Beautiful, that's something I have this entire week to figure out because you know we be doing some stuff in here on a regular that can't be seen or known."

Jacelyn said, "Eww! Okay."

Chase said, "Yo! Ewww is right, and we mostly do it on the countertop right where you're sitting."

We fell out laughing.

Jacelyn said, "And this is why we need to go home, Mike."

Chase said, "Jacelyn, don't act like y'all's countertops are squeaky clean."

Mike said, "Yeah, because they damn sure ain't. We even hit the guest room and the guest bathroom."

I said, "I'm just glad I'll never have to be a guest at y'all's house."

Mike said, "Well, you always have an open invitation, sis."

"No, Mike, I'm good. I'll pass. Nah, but seriously y'all we've accomplished a lot today. Mostly everything is planned. We just have to get our fashion together, taste the cake, and create the menu. Chase, why don't y'all get fitted when Ice gets here?"

"Yeah, I'll see. We may just get fitted in Vegas when we go."

"Vegas? Wow! That reminds me, Chase, of our bowling bet."

"Yeah, I know. That's why I said it. I would get to kill a few birds with one stone. We can go soon or just go for our honeymoon."

"Chase, I'm not sure if I wanna do Vegas for our honeymoon. Besides, what's romantic about Vegas?"

"Well, you just think about it then, Beautiful, because I'll go any-where you wanna go, even if it's right here on this couch."

"On that note, Jacelyn and Mike, I'm not kicking y'all out, but y'all gotta go. I need some alone time with my man. Make sure y'all take some of this food home with y'all."

Mike said, "You know we are 'cause we ain't about to be cook-ing today."

Once they left, me and Chase crawled up on the couch and talked about the wedding and Ice. "You're gonna look smooth, baby, in that Lamborghini on our wedding day. What color suit are you going to wear?"

"I don't know yet. I'm still thinking about it."

"Well, I think you should wear an all-white suit with the jacket trimmed in light gold with a gold tie and handkerchief to match."

He kissed me and said, "That sounds perfect to me. This is why I love you so much. You always think of everything, Beautiful."

"Yeah, I know. Stepping out that white and gold Lamborghini, dressed in an all-white and gold suit, you'll be turning heads for sure, looking like you just stepped off a movie set or *GQ* photo shoot. I think you should get fitted but not reveal the color until the day of the wedding."

"You know what, Beautiful? I have an idea. I just might have him change my whip to an all-white Maserati instead, just let everyone be themselves for, at least, one day."

"That sounds like a plan, Chase. I'm going to go to Kleinfeld's with Kate, Jacelyn, and my mom. I'm going to choose three of my favorite dresses and the one I absolutely love I will wear to the wedding. Not even my mom will know which one I chose until that day. It's a double wedding, but we all need to have our own special moments. I'm not sure what Ice should wear since I've never seen him before, but since he'll be standing next to you, maybe he should wear an all-white suit, or all light gold suit would look good, but I have to see him first."

"Well, Beautiful, speaking of Ice, he hasn't been home in years, and I need this to be the best homecoming a man could ask for. Plus, his birthday is next week, and it's the start of a New Year, so we gotta go out with a bang. He probably thought I forgot, too, but, how could I? We used to turn up every year for his birthday until he left. I definitely want to throw him something at the club. On Saturday, we will do our regular meet and greet, but we will hire lots of entertainment, including strippers. I'm not a fan of strippers, but Ice loves them. I can't see the reason why because it's not like you can take them home, even if you wanted to, but all men see strippers differently, so who am I to judge? I may even invite a few friends from the old neighborhood."

"Okay, well, whatever you want, I will make it happen, Chase. Just promise me that things will not get out of hand because this is a private, members-only club, and it's our place of business."

"I promise it won't, Beautiful. All I need is for you and Jacelyn to put it together for next Saturday. We need to make Ice feel welcome, especially if he's gonna take Wallstreet off our hands."

"Now that you put it that way, I will set up a private VIP section away from the members, and I'm sure with Mike, the guys, you, and all the entertainment, he will feel more than welcome."

He kissed me and said, "Thanks."

"Well, Chase, now that we're done talking, what do you want to do for the rest of the night?"

He smiled and playfully grabbed me, pulling me on top of him. He said, "Let's play some strip poker. First one with everything off must please the other one with no extras after."

"Now, that's torture, Chase. How will either of us make it through the night with no extras?"

"Willpower, baby, and self-control." He laughed and slapped me on my butt.

"Okay, Chase, we will see. Let me get the cards."

Chase got up and put on some music and made us some drinks. I went to the room to put on socks and an extra shirt since I knew Chase was a pro at poker. I went into the living room where Chase was ready and waiting. I said, "Oh, I see you're ready. Well, let the games begin."

I won the first hand, so he took off his shirt. The second hand, Chase won, so I took off one of my shirts and laughed. Chase noticed and said, "You're cheating, but I'm gonna let you slide because you're gonna lose anyway."

And that I did. I lost every hand after that. Well, it looked like Chase won the bet, and I had some pleasing to do. I didn't mind because pleasing him was what I did best. Good thing about it, he never said I had to please him and Royal. He only said 'him,' so, I thought, Let's see how long his will power and self-control holds up. I gave him a nice little lap dance to get him all worked up. I massaged and kissed him everywhere. I sprayed Cool Whip all over his body and licked it off. Then I went searching in the refrigerator and freezer for more edible items. I decided to go with the ice cream. When I closed the freezer door, he was standing there, smiling. I tried to run, but he grabbed me, picked me up, and sat me on the counter. He took the ice cream from me, opened it, and started kissing me. He was being so sneaky. He started rubbing my legs and then slowly spreading them open. When I saw he was headed straight for Royalty, I laughed so hard inside. He was talking about willpower and self-control. He was trying to seduce me and Royalty just to please Royal. It was not gonna happen because I wanted to be the winner of this self-control and willpower challenge. Even though he looked so damn good and Royal was locked, loaded, and ready to shoot, I had to maintain my self-control. It was his bet, not mine. I playfully pushed him away and hopped off the counter. I got some cleaning spray and wiped down the countertop while he stood behind me and said, "Look what you started. You feel that?"

I said, "I sure do, baby," with a big smile on my face. I pushed him back and ran toward the living room. He chased me and tackled me down, playing with and tickling me. He managed to get a good touch of Royalty, and that was when the will power went straight out the damn window. What started off as a playful card game on the couch ended with Royal and Royalty putting it down or should I say putting it "up" in a steamy, hot shower.

***

The week had gone by so fast. Ice would be in town tomorrow. All the birthday festivities were set. Stanley was set to pick Ice up from the JFK Airport by five tomorrow evening. Chase decided to let Ice stay with us for the first night since they would be up all night anyway, and then he would see about letting him stay for the remainder of his trip.

"Good morning, Chase," I cooed.

"Good morning, Beautiful. How's my lovely lady this morning?"

"I'm actually feeling really good. And I'm glad to see you're in a very good mood. You must be excited to see Ice?"

"Well, I'm not going to say all that, but it's just been a long time since I've seen him."

"Well, Chase, the wait is over. He's on the plane. Thank God, I don't have school today, but I do have to get to the firm."

"Okay, Beautiful, I'm going to drop you off and then come back home."

"Are we going out to dinner tonight?"

"No, your mom cooked up some soul food, so Mr. Bill is dropping it off for us."

"Really? That was nice of my mom. I really miss her cooking. We gotta go out to the house to visit, Chase."

"Okay, maybe next weekend, if the club don't get too crazy on Saturday."

We left home about eight in the morning and headed to the office. Chase and Mike dropped me and Jacelyn off at the office as promised. Neither Jacelyn nor I got much work done all day because we were too busy thinking about meeting Ice and all the festivities that would take place upon his arrival. Ice is JFK bound and should be ready for pick up really soon, I thought. I didn't know what to expect when I saw him, but like Chase always said, "I will see soon enough."

CHAPTER 21

Smoking Guns

Everything was all set for the night's events, well, all except the guest of honor. The flight that Ice was on had to make an emergency landing in Miami. He ended up staying the night at the airport until he was able to catch another flight. He was supposed to arrive around six in the evening and head straight to the club. The entertainment wouldn't start till around nine anyways, so the timing couldn't be better.

Last night, after dinner, we had time to check on the club, so we didn't need to arrive till around seven today.

We all decided to head to the mall since it had been a while since we'd been out shopping. Just because the entertainment and guest of honor would be a little different didn't mean we were going to be any different. Chase wore a black Armani suit with a gray shirt and black Armani shoes. I wore a strapless black Armani sequined dress that was cut a little below my knees and had a split that rose up slightly above my left knee. It was black, but the sequins looked like diamonds. I also picked up some silver Armani heels. Mike wore a black Gucci suit, a red shirt, and black Gucci shoes. Jacelyn wore an off-the-shoulder red Gucci dress with some black Gucci heels. All of us looked like we had been dipped in diamonds. Chase said, besides him and Mike, Jacelyn and I had to be the finest things in the club tonight. Finally, after picking up

215

the jewels, we were done shopping, and we went to meet the hairdresser and barber at the house.

It was around six in the evening. Just before we were headed out to the club, the phone rang. It was Ice. He said he had just landed and was going to grab his luggage. Then he was headed to the club. We kind of knew the guys would be drinking tonight, so we decided to have Stanley drive the limo for the night. Stanley arrived around six-thirty, which was perfect timing. As we were riding, Chase grabbed my hand and said, "It's been a long time since I've been out with these cats, so look out for me and make sure I don't drink too much."

I looked in his eyes and promised I would. I held his hand the rest of the ride to the club. I said a prayer that the night would go smoothly with no problems because, Lord knows, we didn't need anymore.

***

Not only did we arrive in style, but we arrived at the club to a red carpet and flashing cameras as usual. Chase and Mike went to check on the club and Wallstreet while Jacelyn and I went to host the event. This was one night I wished Wallstreet wasn't dancing around in the club, but we all knew that was just wishful thinking. At around seven-thirty, Chase and Mike walked in with an entourage. There were six guys and one girl trailing behind them. I couldn't really get a good look at everyone, but I knew the one with all the diamonds had to be Ice. Chase said he got the name Ice because he always wore nothing but diamonds, so I was certain that it was him. Who knew who the girl was on his arm? But it really didn't matter. Now that our guests had arrived, it was time for the show to begin. Chase nodded at Maryellen, and that was when she made her intro. "Good evening, ladies and gentlemen, welcome to Who's Who, where the richest players come to play. We have a very special guest in the building tonight, and it's somebody's birthday. Please make him feel welcome. Happy Birthday, Ice."

At that moment, the spotlight was shined down on him. Everyone clapped, cheered, or whistled to acknowledge his birthday. "Last but not least, ladies and gentlemen, stocks are up on Wallstreet, so enjoy your evening." The crowd cheered once again like their favorite team had just won the Super Bowl.

Chase said, "Yo, Ice, you hear that? That's nothing but cash, baby. If Wallstreet was legal, this would be the most lucrative business ever known to New York. See, Ice, I told you they go crazy for that Wallstreet, but we'll get into all of that later. Let's just enjoy the night."

Chase, Mike, and Ice started popping bottles and making noise. They started pouring some out for their fallen hood soldiers, "the dead homies."

With Jacelyn and I hosting the event, it was hard for us to steal a minute with the guys. The strippers arrived around nine and were all set to dance for the guys for two hours. I looked over at the guys and noticed that, although Ice walked in with a girl on his arm, it didn't stop him from receiving a few lap dances from the ladies. Chase and Mike stood to the side, watched, and had a few more drinks. The music was bumping, and it was the first time hip-hop was played for a straight two hours in the club. Everyone seemed to be enjoying the ladies, even a few club members.

The time had come for the ladies to exit, so Jacelyn and I went over to wrap things up. We let them know we might work with them again since they conducted themselves in such a professional manner. I thought it might be nice to have a ladies and gents' night at the club. Of course, we had to run it by Chase and Mike, but money was money, and if that was a way for the girls to make some legit tips from these thirsty-ass rich dudes in the club, by all means, I was down with helping them. The ladies left, and we finally had a few minutes to catch a break. That was when we were introduced to Ice and his girl Stacy and the five other guys. To my surprise, one of the guys was Mike's cousin Money Mel. Mike never mentioned he was coming, so it had to be last minute. It was a little dark, so I couldn't really get a good look at the guys, but I knew I would see them up close and personal come breakfast time. I could hear the guys telling Chase and Mike how fine Jacelyn and I were. Chase said, "Yeah, I know," then grabbed my hand and led me to the dance floor away from them. As we were dancing, I could tell Chase had had a lot to drink by the way he was dancing on me and grabbing my butt. Chase usually drank Moet, not hard liquor, because he was always in business mode and couldn't drink liquor like that. Royal was on the rise, and Chase was kissing me so much that Royalty's milk was shaking up, but I knew this wasn't the place or time. Plus, this wasn't Chase's normal behavior, so I took him to his office to talk and let him sober up a bit.

I made Chase use the bathroom, wash his face, and drink some water to flush out the liquor. The conversation was so needed, so I said, "Chase, remember you told me to look out for you, and I'm doing just that. Do you realize how drunk you are? Do you realize how you were feeling all over me in front of everyone?"

He said, "Yeah, I'm sorry, I can't help myself. You're looking really good tonight, especially in that dress." He picked me up, sat me on his desk, pushed up my dress, and said, "Royal wants some Royalty right now."

"Chase, wait. What are you doing? You're drunk."

"I just want a little. That's all I need you to give me, Beautiful. I need you to help me right now. Please, Beautiful, I promise it will be real quick, and then we can get back to the party."

He started kissing and feeling all over me again. In my mind, I was like, Wait. Real quick? Yeah, he's definitely drunk, but for some reason, I just couldn't resist him. He was my world, drunk or sober. He reached for Royal, and before I knew it, for the first time since we'd been together, we had sex on his desk for a quick twenty minutes. When it was over, he kissed me. Then he said, "Let's get back to our guests." He seemed temporarily satisfied, but I wasn't a bit satisfied, to say the least. I was a little uneasy about what just happened, since he always made love to me, and we never had sloppy sex, or drunken sex, for that matter. I now knew what it felt like and why he never wanted to go there with me. Maybe if he wasn't drunk, I would have enjoyed the quick twenty minutes. Once he started, I didn't stop him because I didn't at all believe him when he said "real quick," but damn, he was telling the drunken truth. Don't get me wrong now. I love me some Chase and Royal. It was just that, tonight, they both felt different. I really couldn't wait until breakfast in the morning when he was sober because he was definitely going to remember this night because it was one I wouldn't ever let him forget.

We both freshened up in Chase's private bathroom and went back down to our guests, but not before I let him know he'd had way too many drinks. I told him that that was enough for the night. He must have really noticed the disgust on my face and the tone of my voice because that was when he pulled me to the side, looked in my eyes, and said, "I'm sorry. Please forgive me, and I promise not to have any more drinks tonight."

When we got back to the VIP, we noticed that the dancers may have left the club, but the DJ still had the music bumping and the party was still jumping. Ice and Mike were rolling dice in the VIP with bottles in hand. They straight bought the hood to the club tonight with a game of cee-lo in the cut. Jacelyn walked over and took the bottle from Mike and whispered, "That's enough."

He was cool about it and said, "Okay, Miss J, whatever you say. You're the boss."

Once Ice saw Mike wasn't wit' drinking no more, he grabbed his cash off the floor. Then, he escorted his girl to the dance floor. I grabbed Jacelyn and told her to come dance with me right outside the VIP section while Chase and Mike stood back and watched. Jacelyn and I hadn't even been on the dance floor for five minutes before one of Chase's drunken friends came up dancing behind me; dancing so close, he was grinding on my butt. I turned and pushed him away, but he grabbed my arm. I said, "Get the fuck off me," and pushed him again, but he just kept grabbing my arm. Why in the hell did he wanna go and do that for? Because, after Chase saw that, he jumped over the VIP section, and Mike followed suit. This was exactly why you couldn't mix your old friends with your new friends. It was like mixing old money with new money. It just never added up correctly. There always seemed to be a dollar short somewhere, and right about now, Chase was about to be one friend shorter than what he walked up in here with.

Right when the hood was about to jump out of me, Chase pushed him and said, "Yo, Troy, what the fuck are you doing dancing and grabbing on my wife like that?"

I said, "Chase, he's drunk."

Chase snapped and said, "Please let me handle this, Bridgette. Just go over there."

Oh, shit, hearing him call me "Bridgette" let me know he was pissed. I thought, Shit is about to get real now.

Troy said, "Chase, man, you know how we do with these bitches."

Before ole boi could fully get "bitch" out of his mouth, Chase snuffed him, and from there, they just started fighting. Chase was damn sure getting the best of him. Hell, I thought he was gonna kill Troy. I had never seen this side of Chase because he always moved in a way that I didn't have to. You can take the guy out of the hood, but you damn sure can't take the hood out of the guy. Troy wasn't no little guy, but neither was Chase, and although Chase was defending my honor, I wanted the fight to be over before more damage was done. I didn't know what else to do but call out to Chase to try to get him to stop because I knew better than to go try to break it up. Things were getting worse by the minute, but since we all grew up in the hood, it wasn't anything new to me. It just was something that I hadn't witnessed in a long time and especially not involving Chase. I just started yelling, "Chase, you're gonna kill him." I was hoping my voice would snap him out of it, but it didn't stop him. I yelled, "Mike," and that was when Mike and Ice went to break it up, but neither Chase nor Troy were trying to hear that. Turning on everyone, Troy swung on both Mike and Ice. At that moment, Chase looked back at Jacelyn and me and said, "Go to the office now."

Troy and Mike were now fighting. Chase tried to break them up, but there was no stopping Mike once he got started. I wondered where the hell the security was because they never came. I didn't want to go to the office because I had promised Chase I would look out for him, and I really didn't want to leave while he was fighting, but Jacelyn grabbed my hand and started pulling me. As we turned and began to walk away, I turned to look back, and that was when Troy pulled out a gun and pointed it at Chase and said, "All this over some bitches? Chase, we go back too far for this shit."

At that point, all the guys tried to calm Troy down. One of them said, "Yo, Troy, it ain't that serious."

Troy said, "Really? It ain't that serious? For who? This shit serious than a motherfucker, and I'm about to show you just how serious it is," and he fired off a shot in the air. Then he looked over toward Jacelyn and me and said, "Chase, I hope those bitches were worth it," then pointed the gun into the crowd and opened fire.

The few hundred, nosy people that stuck around to watch the fight started screaming and running. Well, everyone except me. I was in shock. I just knew Chase was shot. I couldn't run or do anything. All I could do was fall to my knees and cry out to God. While beginning to pray, I heard more shots being fired. BOOM, BOOM, BOOM, BOOM, BOOM. Then POW, POW, POW.

"Lord, please don't let anyone be hurt. Please let Chase be okay." I managed to get under a table that was near me. I know, for a fact, that Troy had aimed that gun right at me and pulled the trigger. I was praying that he didn't see me under the table and try to come finish what he had started. It was an all-out war zone in the club, just like in the movies. It was still pretty dark in the club, so I couldn't really tell who was who. All I could manage to see were the colorful lights changing and bouncing off the back walls. The room was actually spinning. I could hear Chase calling my name and Mike calling for Jacelyn. Then they stopped. They had to have gone to the office looking for us, but we'd never made it there. The yelling and screaming around the club was loud and crazy, but I managed to hear them calling out for us again. I hadn't seen Jacelyn since the shots were fired, but I knew she couldn't be too far away from me. Maybe she was hiding, too. I tried calling her and Chase, but nothing would come out of my mouth. I guess I was still in shock. At one point, my body was really hot, but then it became cold, and I began to shake. I had no idea how my dress had gotten so wet; maybe a drink spilled on me when the crowd started running, but what I did know was that I was freezing. Things happened so fast. The last thing I remembered before Jacelyn and I started walking away was Chase and Ice trying to break up the fight between Mike and Troy. Things were starting to get blurry, but I could still hear Chase calling out for me and the sound of his voice was getting closer. I tried calling him again, but he just wasn't hearing me. I could hear him flipping tables, and I could hear glass breaking. He was yelling, "Mike, they have to be in here somewhere. They're not in none of the offices." Then he yelled, "Somebody turn the fucking lights on."

Mike yelled, "J, where did you go? Please! I have to find you."

Chase was yelling over and over, "Bridgette, where are you? Oh, my God, Beautiful, where are you? If you can hear me, please say something."

I was trying so hard to yell for him, but he still couldn't hear me. Then his voice started fading, and my vision started to fade. All of a sudden, I thought that I might have been having a panic attack because I was losing my breath. I started choking, coughing and gasping for air, then everything went black. What happened next even shocked the hell out of me.

TO BE CONTINUED...

PART 2
COMING SOON

Nobody really knows who's who until the gun smoke clears. Shots were fired, and people went crazy, screaming and yelling. Then, all of a sudden, the room went silent. Blood was shed. Cops were called. Lights were spinning, and doors were shut. Now we all have questions...Who got shot? Who's the other shooter or shooters? Who's dead? Who's alive? Who's the real Ice? Who leaves? Who stays? Who takes over? There are no questions about what, when, where, or how?

The question simply is WHO'S WHO?

Find out in the next book titled

Who's Who

coming soon

Thank you for reading **ESCAPING WALLSTREET**.
I hope you enjoyed reading this book as much as I did writing it.

Be sure to email kreativemindzpubllc@gmail.com or stop
by my website www.brittannicholson.com and leave some
comments about the first book of the series and be sure to
stop by again once you're done reading the next book.

Also follow me on Facebook and Instagram

http://www.facebook.com/iiambrittan
http://www.instagram.com/iiambrittan

If you are unable to log on to the website,
you can always mail your comments to:

P.O. Box 888
Amityville, NY 11701

Once again, I thank you for you continued support throughout my
journey as an author. Truthfully without you all this would not be
possible, so I thank you and may God continue to Bless you all.

BRITTAN NICHOLSON

UNDERNEATH THESE EYES
I AM BRITTAN

KRE-A-TIVE MINDZ PUBLISHING

ABOUT THE AUTHOR

Brittan Nicholson is the author of *Escaping Wallstreet*, which is the first of a four-part series. This is her debut novel. In it, she details the story of a young lady's rise, from living in the hood to having more money than she knows what to do with it. Much like her main character, Brittan is often described as a beauty with brains who is about her business. Brittan has used these assets to achieve many goals and to amass a resume that anyone would envy. This list of accomplishments shows that she's more than just a captivating beauty. In her writing, she invites the reader in, showing what lies beneath the eyes to her soul. She is a gifted storyteller who knows how to tell a story that simultaneously entertains and teaches. Her creativity takes her to higher heights as she brings her visions to life. Brittan brings a wealth of knowledge and experience to her writing. Her diverse background helps to inform and enhance her unique stories. She is a gifted storyteller who has already completed four novels. She also encourages, inspires, and coaches others to become writers.

Before Brittan became a writer, she worked in the medical field in its financial sector, for over twenty years. Taking a leap of faith, Brittan gave up her 9-to-5 to pursue her dreams of becoming an entrepreneur in her own right. Helping, motivating, inspiring, and encouraging people is Brittan's forte. After years of voluntary service, she became a certified life coach through the teaching and leadership of Tony Gaskins, and she is the founder of O.L.I. (Outside Looking In) Life Coaching Services. She coaches and gives solutions to many as they face life's most difficult situations, and she also specializes in helping the parents and families of the incarcerated. Because of all that she's been through and because she's come out on the other side, she has honed her writing. To maintain control of her creativity, she founded Kre-A-Tive Mindz Publishing, her very own publishing company. She is not only a writer. She is also a writing coach. She coaches others on how to bring out their own creativity from within. So that one day they to can share a piece of their soul with the world through their writing, just as she has. With dreams of becoming a screenwriter, she has begun taking courses to further her education as a writer for film and television.

Nothing is more important in life to Brittan than showing love, giving love, and being loved. Family tops the list of what is of utmost importance to her. She is an independent parent to four children. She is also a grandmother to one beautiful grandson. She has always felt that achieving her dreams was important because, in accomplishing her goals, she is an example to her children. Her unwavering belief in God has helped her through every trial and tribulation that she has ever endured. She is open about being a survivor of physical, sexual, verbal, and mental abuse and being abandoned in more ways than she can count. These experiences did not make her bitter; instead, she became more humble, compassionate, loving, forgiving, and grateful. She claims not to be a victim but a victor through it all. When asked if she would change anything about how her life unfolded, the answer is a simple no. All that she has been through has made her who she is today. She does express that, in life, the only thing she would change daily is the view in front of her. Being on a tropical island in paradise underneath the sunrise and sunset is her definition of the perfect view.

When she isn't writing and helping others, she enjoys indulging in the simple things. She loves binge watching movies and shows on Netflix. She loves sharing a good laugh and telling jokes. She loves seafood and strawberry ice cream. Her favorite meal is, hands down, shrimp and grits. She loves big cars and sneakers that keep her feet happy. She loves spending time with her family, and without a doubt, she loves traveling to destinations that will change her view and continue to broaden her mindset. Most of all, she loves God and is a living testimony of his many blessings. She currently resides in Long Island, New York.

Made in the USA
Middletown, DE
01 June 2021